BIG JOE

WYATT SHEPARD

PROLOGUE

Joseph "Big Joe" Chambers had been riding hard for the past three days. Although dust and dirt had settled into all of his nooks and crannies, making him stiff with filth and sore from long hours in the saddle, he pushed on. Sophie's letter had seemed desperate, and he knew that if anything had happened to her that he would blame himself.

"Come on, girl," he urged his mare. He knew she had almost nothing left to give, and although he was never one to overwork his animals, he couldn't let her rest until he'd gotten to Narrow Bluff and found his sister.

Her travel-worn letter had arrived three days ago. It had passed through so many hands that the directions had been almost unreadable, and it was dated from nearly eight months earlier. She had never been one to complain, so he knew how serious the situation in Narrow Bluff must be if she was begging for his help against the ever-increasing crime in the small town, which the local sheriff turned a blind eye to. He'd left for Narrow Bluff the same day he got the letter.

Now, three days later, he knew he must be nearing the

town. He had consulted the map so many times he had it memorized, and he was fairly certain he was within a few miles of where it should be. His overfull bladder urged him to take a break, but he pushed on, eager to assess the situation in the town and certain it couldn't be too much further.

His palomino's sides were heaving for air as she strained up the hill as quickly as she could, and she was flecked in sweat and foam. "I know, Goldie, I know," he murmured. "We're almost there."

Goldie crested the hill and the view opened below them. Sprawling beneath him was the ruins of a broken town. Layers of dust covered every building, most of whose windows were shattered. A shutter flapped in the dry wind, creaking on rusty hinges. Dread washed over him as he surveyed the abandoned town.

He rode Goldie cautiously down the main street, her hoofbeats clopping too loudly in the otherwise silent ruin. He stopped in front of what must have once been a saloon and slid off his mare before tying her to a hitching post. Although he had both the map and Sophie's letter memorized, he pulled them out of his saddlebag and pored over them once again. This just couldn't be Narrow Bluff. His shocked brain felt numb and uncomprehending.

Almost as if he was watching from above himself, he saw his rough finger tracing the trail from where he had begun to where he was now. Without a doubt, he was in the right place. He had to find Sophie. Maybe she was still here, hiding.

Scrabbling through the directions she had written, he lifted his gaze back to his surroundings, hunting desperately for her house. She had said it was a two-room cabin on the far western edge of town with whitewashed shutters. Not even bothering to remount his exhausted mare, he barreled down the main street, dust swirling around his boots as he ran.

He could sense that the town was deserted, but he maintained the caution ingrained in him from years as a sheriff. He swiveled his gaze from side to side as he ran, assessing his surroundings and looking for threats.

He stopped in his tracks as the buildings on the edge of town, a line of cabins similar to the one his sister had described, came into view. His focus, though, was on the blackened patch of dirt that sat in the center of the line of homes. The few half-burned pieces of wood were the only things that marked the spot as having once been a structure. Though it could've been any of them, something deep inside told him that this one had been his sister's.

Snapping out of the daze, he broke into a full-on sprint, adrenaline pumping as if there was anything he could do at this point. He muttered a silent prayer as he closed the gap, hoping with every fiber of his being that he was mistaken.

Stepping into the charred ruin, his eyes began flitting from spot to spot, searching for any sign of who had lived there. Finding nothing in the area nearest the entry, he charged to the spot with the largest amount of scorched wood remaining. A chill ran through him despite the summer heat as he searched, bending down to move the boards out of the way. A slight glimmer caught his eye just as he was about to move to check another spot, and he leaned down to get a better look. He moved the piece of wood sitting over the chunk of metal and his vision began to go dark as he reached down to pick it up. His ears ringing, he dropped to his knees.

It was a silver necklace with an ornate depiction of the

Virgin Mary. Sophie had worn it every day since their mother's death, and she never went anywhere without it. There could be no mistake. He'd come too late. He kneeled in the wreckage of the ruined house for quite some time, beseeching God with muttered prayer after muttered prayer.

He heard a few soft clops from behind him and came back to himself as Goldie's nose poked into the back of his head. His fingers formed a fist around the necklace as he stood, clutching it so hard that the metal bit into his palm. For the first time, an emotion other than shock or numbness broke through. Starting deep in the pit of his stomach, he felt a burning rage swelling. For a moment, he saw red, and he had to bite back a primal growl of fury.

Breathing deeply through his nose and forcing his jaw shut, his vision cleared, but the rage did not abate. Instead, it cooled into an inflexible ball of steel within him. Carefully, he slid the necklace into his pocket and turned to leave the cabin.

Whoever did this would pay.

Music from a piano tinkled out of the saloon's swinging doors as Big Joe slid off his horse and tied her to the hitching rail next to a tired-looking mule. He thought he must look something like the mule; he had slept fitfully for a few hours after leaving Narrow Bluff, then had spent the day in the saddle pushing on to the town of Widestone. His eyes stung with exhaustion and, at this point, he wasn't sure where his dirt and sweat encrusted pants ended and his legs began. A bath and sleep were far less important than finding some answers, though.

Mounting the steps to the saloon, he pulled off his hat and pushed through the swinging doors. The saloon was dim and smoky, and it took a moment for his eyes to adjust. A tall man with stooped shoulders stood behind the bar, wiping down the counter with an old cloth. Bartenders, he knew from experience in his own town, always had a finger on the pulse of the town. Joe headed toward him, leaning on the counter and giving the man a nod.

"What'll it be?" the man asked.

"Beer," Joe responded. "And some information."

The bartender poured him a tankard of foaming beer, and set it in front of Joe. He seemed friendly enough, but he was naturally cautious in his reply. "Depends on who's asking."

"I just came up from Narrow Bluff," Joe started, and the bartender nodded in understanding.

"Bad business, that."

"What happened there? My sister wrote to me, asking for help, but by the time I got there, it was abandoned," Joe said, before taking a quick gulp of his beer.

The bartender crossed his arms and leaned on the bar. "Bandits. Narrow Bluff had been havin' a problem with 'em for a while now. Their sheriff didn't do much to deter 'em, and the bandits knew they could pretty much have their run of the town. Things got out of hand, though, and Narrow Bluff ended up ransacked. They just tore the place apart. A bad, bad business," he repeated when he'd finished.

"Were there any survivors?" Joe asked, trying not to get too hopeful in case the answer was a flat negative.

"Well now, we had some. They straggled into Widestone with only what they'd been able to salvage and they've set up here."

Joe's hand tightened on his tankard. "Have you heard of a Sophie Chambers among the survivors?"

"I can't rightly say," the man replied. "I only moved to Widestone, myself, a few months back, to work here at my friend's saloon, and that was after Narrow Bluff was raided. If you're wantin' to find someone, I would say the sheriff is your best bet."

The tiny spark of hope Joe had felt wavered a bit, but he forged ahead. "Where can I find him?" he asked.

"His office is attached to the jail, and you can find him there most mornings around 8:00 or so. If anyone can help, he can."

Joe nodded his thanks and laid a coin on the counter to pay for his drink. It looked like he would have to wait for answers, and he chafed inside at the delay. If there was any chance his sister was still alive, he wanted to find her immediately. He didn't want to think about the other possibility.

Downing the last of his beer, Joe jammed his hat back onto his head and left the saloon, brow furrowed in thought. He walked aimlessly down the road, fiddling with the necklace in his pocket. Accusing thoughts filled his mind as the events of not just the past few days, but the past few years, crowded in.

He never should've let his sweet younger sister marry Jack. Joe supposed Jack Wells was a nice enough man, but he was a coward, and that was irredeemable in his eyes. He had no spine, and no gumption to fight—and you needed both to live out here in the West. This was harsh territory, and it was no place for a weakling. Sophie's own compassionate spirit had looked past her husband's deficiencies as a protector, and Joe wished he had put his foot down and demanded that she refuse Jack's hand in marriage.

Joe's soft spot was his sister, and now it looked like that weakness on his part may have had dire consequences for her. Could he have stopped her from being involved in the disasters of Narrow Bluff if he'd trusted his judgment and refused to let her wed Jack?

His thoughts were interrupted by something running into his legs. He instinctively grabbed the shoulder of the young boy that was now looking up at him with frightened eyes. The boy was panting, his small chest rising and falling in quick gasps.

"Please, sir," the boy begged, looking behind him.

Joe followed the boy's gaze and saw a group of older men running down the road. It looked like they had been chasing the little boy. They slowed to a walk, but didn't stop, as they saw Joe standing with the boy. Joe gently pushed the boy behind him, and the boy was only too happy to hide behind Joe's six-foot-tall frame.

Joe folded his arms, and looked at the group of men, raising one eyebrow. "Now, what could have three grown men chasing a little boy?" he asked softly.

The men looked slightly abashed, but one of them lifted his chin and said somewhat defensively, "He cheated us on a bet."

"Really." Joe said it flatly, and the man flushed.

"We was playin' cards at the saloon, and sometimes we let him sit in on a game. He's young, but he ain't too young to learn that you have to pay off your debts and play fair."

Joe looked down at the boy who was still hiding behind him. "Well?"

"I didn't cheat!" the boy insisted.

Joe turned back to the men and sighed. "How much?"

"Two dollars."

Joe dug out his wallet and counted the money before handing it to the men. He didn't say anything further to them, but he could tell that they were embarrassed. Not too embarrassed to take the money, though, and Joe couldn't fully fault them for that. Two dollars wasn't substantial, but it wasn't a tiny amount, either. The men shuffled off, and Joe turned back to face the boy.

"Let me tell you something, son," he said. "You don't want to mess with men that much bigger than you. Even if you didn't steal from them—" he paused, seeing the boy about to argue with him. "Calm down, now, I didn't say you *did* steal. But, even if you did, you shouldn't be gambling with men like that. They can take your money by force and you wouldn't be able to stop them. Wait until you're a little older."

The boy nodded, looking at the ground. "Yes, sir," he said. He rubbed his foot in the dirt, before continuing, "Thank you for paying them, sir."

"Be more careful in the future," Joe murmured.

The boy nodded again. Joe was about to continue walking when the boy's eyes lit up. "Say, do you need a place to stay? I don't have money to repay you, but I could take you to my mama's boarding house. Hers is the cleanest in town and she makes the best pie." He said the last part proudly, his chest puffing a little.

Joe considered the boy silently for a moment. He wouldn't be able to see the sheriff until the next morning, and a night of sleep and a bath were much needed. Besides, maybe the boy's mother would know something about Sophie, given that the survivors from Narrow Bluff would've needed a place to stay when they'd arrived.

"I'd appreciate that, son," Joe said. "Why don't you come with me to get Goldie and then you can show me the way to your mother's."

The boy happily agreed, trotting after Joe back toward

the saloon. His earlier shyness and chagrin had already evaporated from Joe's reprimand. He peppered Joe with questions about Goldie and where Joe had come from as they walked. Joe responded, but his mind was elsewhere as he fiddled with the necklace in his pocket. He dipped his head respectfully as a smartly dressed preacher stepped past.

If he'd known who the man really was, he'd have been more likely to greet him with a bullet than a nod.

THE BOY RACED AHEAD of Joe and Goldie to bound up the stairs of a three-story frame home. The paint was peeling, but the front porch was neatly swept and wildflowers bloomed in window boxes. Joe tied Goldie to the hitching rail, murmuring that he would procure food and a home for her soon. She whinnied softly in response as he patted her neck and looked into her intelligent eyes.

"Good girl," he said softly. "I'll be back for you soon."

"Are you comin'?" the boy called. He was standing at the door waiting for Joe.

Joe patted Goldie one last time and then followed the boy through the front door. He was greeted by the delicious aroma of cooking food, and his stomach growled in response. It had been many hours since he'd last eaten, and at this point, he would've been happy with a crust of bread, but it smelled like he was in for something much better.

They had walked into a large front room with small dining tables scattered around it, as well as a few chairs for sitting. It looked like this dining and sitting room took up most of the downstairs space, although Joe assumed there was a kitchen and living space for the boy and his mother in the back.

"There's my mama," the boy said, pointing to a woman laying two bowls of stew and a plate with thick slices of fresh bread in front of a careworn-looking couple. The woman smiled tiredly in thanks while the man reached into his pocket and carefully counted out two nickels for the meal. It was obvious they didn't have much money. The boy's mother accepted the coins after a moment of hesitation, and then briefly squeezed the man's shoulder, before turning away.

"She lets a lot of people eat free," the boy whispered to Joe, seeing his attention on the exchange. "She has to take money from folks who can pay, but she don't charge hardly nothin'. Just enough to keep makin' the food and keep runnin' the house." The boy, though so young, looked proud, and Joe sensed that he revered his mother's goodness.

Joe stood for another moment, quietly watching. The boy's mother was now laying a slice of apple pie in front of an elderly man with an unkempt beard and torn coat. She gently but firmly waved away his offer of a single dirty coin, and brushed off the man's thanks. She spoke softly to him, and Joe could just barely make out her words: "Can't have you going hungry as long as I have a home. Think nothing of it."

"Want to go to talk to Mama?" the boy asked Joe.

"Lead the way, son." Joe nodded, and followed the boy through the dining tables.

The woman looked up and caught sight of her son.

"Will! There you are! Where have you been?"

Will. So that's the boy's name, Joe thought, realizing he had never asked.

Will looked down, now, returning to the same shyness with which he had addressed Joe when Joe was lecturing him. Sensing the boy's unrest, Joe stepped in.

"Pardon me, ma'am," Joe said, taking off his hat and holding it against his chest.

The woman turned to him, and Joe saw exhaustion shining out of her green eyes, but she mustered up a smile.

"My name is Joseph Chambers, but folks call me Big Joe, or just Joe. Will, here, told me you ran a boarding house."

"Nancy Riley," she said, extending her hand to shake his. "But you can call me Nan, most everyone does. I do, indeed, run this boarding house. Were you needing a place to stay?"

"Yes, ma'am, that would be greatly appreciated. A meal would be wonderful, too. It smells right delicious."

Nan smiled, and her eyes crinkled in a way that transformed her exhausted face. For a moment, Joe was struck with how beautiful she was. Her hair, though in a neat bun, was a thick and shiny auburn, which set off her unusual green eyes. She was a little too thin, though. It seemed as if she was the one who needed a good meal, although Joe could tell she must be one who worked hard from dawn until dusk. It was no wonder she was nothing but lean muscle and bone.

Nan led Joe to an empty table, and said, "I've got a stew on tonight, and there's fresh bread I baked this morning. Of course, there's always a pot of beans simmering, if you'd rather have beans and potatoes. What would you like?"

"The stew sounds just perfect, Nan. And some of that bread, too, if you would," Joe responded. He had questions for her about his sister, but he needed to get some food into his stomach to quell the gnawing hunger, first.

Nan nodded to him, and bustled away, calling Will to go

with her. They disappeared into the kitchen, and Joe sat back in his chair. Exhaustion settled onto his bones like a heavy blanket as he waited, and he stared at the grain of the wooden table without really seeing it. His mind drifted back to the horrible scene of desolation in Narrow Bluff.

A couple of minutes later, he was startled by a soft thunk as Nan laid a bowl of steaming stew in front of him, followed by a plate of fresh bread slathered in butter. The stew was thick and loaded with chunks of meat, potatoes, and carrots. Joe looked up and smiled appreciatively. "Thank you, ma'am, this looks downright heavenly."

Nan smiled back, but it was only a slight smile. Joe paused, surprised. "Is something wrong, ma'am?"

Nan surprised Joe by pulling out the chair across from him and sitting down. "Call me Nan," she said, looking at him appraisingly.

"Sure," he responded, then waited, sensing that she had more to say.

"Joe, Will just told me a little of what happened with the men from the saloon. I don't know why you stepped in to help him, but I do thank you for your intervention. He knows better than to go into that place and to gamble. It can be tough to balance raising that boy alone and taking care of the boarding house." She shook her head wearily, and then squared her shoulders, as if realizing she was sharing too much. "I'd like to pay you back for whatever he owed those men. I don't have much, but I would be happy to give you a place to stay for the night. If you need to stay longer than a short while, I can find something for you to help with as payment for the longer stay. There's always something to be done around here, and I could surely use an extra set of strong hands around the place."

"That sounds like a plan to me, and thank you for it," Joe responded. He dug into the stew and ate a few bites without speaking. The stew, though simple, was flavorful and well made. Nan was about to rise, but Joe stopped her by continuing to speak. "I can tell Will is a good boy, even if he did get into some mischief today. I don't think he'll go making that same mistake again. You're doing a fine job by the boy."

Nan thanked him, her manner returning from one of vulnerability back to her usual brisk efficiency. She rose and pushed in her chair. "Is there anything else I can get you? A slice of pie to finish off your supper?"

"I won't say no to that, ma'am—Nan," he quickly corrected, seeing her green eyes flash in mock warning. "I do have one more question. Would you mind sitting with me for a spell?"

"Well now, I suppose it wouldn't hurt to rest my feet for a few minutes more," Nan replied, settling herself back into her chair.

"I know some of the folks who had to flee Narrow Bluff stayed with you," Joe began. Nan nodded. "My sister, Sophie Wells, is from there, and I was wondering if you'd seen her or heard of her. She's married to a Jack Wells."

Nan paused, thinking, and then shook her head regretfully. "I'm sorry, Joe, but I don't know her. That doesn't mean much, though, because there are other places she could've stayed in town. I do have other boarders from Narrow Bluff, though. Maybe some of them might know her, or, of course, you can ask the sheriff."

15

"I'll do that, thank you," Joe said. He swallowed his disappointment, but Nan seemed to sense it.

"What you need is to finish filling your belly and get a good night of sleep. I can tell you're run ragged," Nan said. "When you're finished here, you can have the room on the second floor, just to the right of the stairs."

Joe thanked her, and asked where he could take his horse for some care. "Is there a livery in town?"

"There is, but I've got a small barn in the back if you'd like to board your mount here. There's still some feed and some tools to brush your horse. It's not fancy, but it's free."

"That'll do fine, thank you, Nan," Joe said.

Nan stood, smoothing her apron over her plain dress. "Enjoy your supper, Joe. I'll be back with your pie in a minute," she said, leaving for the kitchen.

Joe turned his attention back to the good food, sopping up the last bits of stew with a hunk of the bread. He knew Nan was right, that he needed to take some time to rest, but all his thoughts ran toward the next morning and his hopes that the sheriff would have information about where to find Sophie.

3

Dawn was peeking its thin rays through the shutters of Joe's bedroom. Though it was still barely light, it was enough to rouse Joe from his fitful sleep. He had tossed and turned throughout the night, deep rest eluding him. His thoughts had circled endlessly, going through all the possibilities of what could have happened to Sophie. Images of her burning in the house fire tortured him, and he chased them away, but they were quickly followed by images of her being taken hostage by the bandits, or ravaged, or killed. Though, not one usually prone to over-anxiety or worrying about things outside of his control, Joe had been unable to control his anxiety about his sister. He felt more unrest and fear over the situation than he ever had in any of the dangers he had encountered as sheriff back home.

Joe laid awake for a long time thinking about Narrow Bluff and Sophie before he finally sat up and swung his feet over the edge of the bed with a groan, rolling his shoulders to work out some of the soreness. It didn't take him long to pull on his pants and boots. He peered into the tiny mirror on the wall above the chest of drawers. He was scruffy, not having shaved since the morning before he got Sophie's letter, but he figured it could wait a little longer. Shaving wasn't too high on his list of priorities, right now.

He buckled his gun belt around his waist, grabbed his hat from the table by the bed, and took one last look around the room. He still had Sophie's necklace in his pocket, and he added her letter, as well. Everything else could stay until he got back.

He slipped as quietly as he could down the creaking stairs into the dining hall, but he needn't have worried. There were already a handful of diners sitting hunched over plates of scrambled eggs, hash browns, and fatback bacon. Joe checked the clock on the wall by the front door and saw that he still had more than an hour before 8 o'clock, the earliest he could go find the sheriff. Might as well have some breakfast, then.

Selecting an empty table by a window at the front of the room, Joe settled himself to wait for Nan. He wasn't sure exactly how it worked at the boarding house, but just as he was wondering how to find someone to ask for his food, Nan bustled out of the kitchen. She carried a steaming pot of coffee, and she stopped at each table, refilling mugs briskly but offering smiles and questions about whether her guests needed anything. Spotting Joe, she made her way over to him.

"Morning, Joe, I hope you slept well," she said warmly.

"As well as could be expected," he replied honestly. "I didn't have much time for sleeping with all the questions about my sister's whereabouts."

Nan nodded sympathetically. "I can only imagine. I hope your search brings you news today."

"Thank you, Nan," Joe said. A little uncomfortable at his display of honesty, Joe steered the conversation away from himself. "Seems I got more sleep than you, though, if you've already cooked a morning feast."

"Mornings come early around here," Nan agreed. "I do have a girl that helps in the kitchen, but I'm up most mornings before dawn to start the baking and cooking. Now then, can I bring you a plate? There are eggs, potatoes, and bacon, as well as some fresh biscuits just came out of the oven."

"That'll be perfect," Joe said, and Nan left to get his food, returning quickly with a loaded plate and a steaming mug. She set them on the table for him, barely having time to accept his thanks before rushing off to assist more diners.

Joe dug into his food, barely tasting what he knew was a good meal, deep in thought about what he should do if the sheriff had no news of his sister. His solitude was interrupted by the sound of Will's chipper voice at his elbow.

"Morning, sir!"

Will stood next to him, his own plate of food in hand, clearly hoping to sit with the older man. Will gestured to the empty seat across from him, and Will took it eagerly, taking a voracious bite of his biscuit before his little rump had even fully settled into the chair.

"Slow down there, cowboy," Joe laughed.

Will nodded, but couldn't respond around the massive mouthful. Once he finally managed to swallow and could speak, he asked Joe, "So where are ya from, mister?"

"You can call me Joe. I'm from Colorado," he responded.

"I think I went through Colorado when I was a baby," Will said, his face lighting up at their shared connection.

"Did you live there long?" Joe asked. Talking with Will would help keep his mind busy, and he liked the spunky young boy.

"Nope. We just traveled through it. My pa heard there was gold in these parts, so he and Mama packed up and moved here to Widestone. We were one of the first families in town." He said the last part proudly, his chest puffing a little with importance.

"I didn't realize I was talking to a man of such distinction," Joe teased, and Will nodded, missing the humor. "What does your pa do?"

"Well, Pa always wanted to set up a boarding house like this one, but the town was really rough back then, and they needed a sheriff, so my pa took on the job. He was the only one in town tough enough to do it." Will's eyes shone with pride for his father, and Joe could tell how much the boy idolized him. Will's face became serious, then, and a sadness settled over him. "My pa died, though," he finished softly.

Joe knew the harsh realities of life in the West and knew this boy, though young, had seen his fair share of heartache and trouble. He also knew that to avoid talking about the hard things didn't help anyone. "What happened to him, Will?" Joe asked, quietly. He made eye contact with the boy, treating him as respectfully as he would treat a man his own age.

"There was a duel outside of the saloon, and someone shot him. My pa was the best gunman in town, though, so there's no way he could've lost. One of the men must have cheated," Will finished darkly, anger and sadness furrowing his brow, and he stabbed his hash browns with far more force than necessary.

Joe felt a twinge, thinking that maybe he shouldn't have asked for particulars about the boy's father. He should've realized that Nan was a widow the night before; she had mentioned that she was raising Will by herself.

"Well, now," Joe said finally. "You've got a good mother to look after you, and I'm sure she needs you to be the man of the family, now."

Will nodded, squaring his small shoulders. "Mama set up this boarding house after Pa died, because it's what he always wanted to do. She's been running it ever since, and she says I'm her best worker."

"I'm sure you are, son," Joe said, smiling. Joe had already been impressed with Nan—he had seen the way she cared for her boarders, even those that couldn't pay. His estimation of her rose even further. She was running a business, taking care of this scrappy young boy, and it seemed she didn't have much help beyond her young son and the one hired girl. She must carry a lot of weight on her thin shoulders. He mentally tipped his hat to her strength.

Joe and Will finished their meal, and Joe rose, seeing that it was nearly 8 o'clock.

"Will, tell your mother thank you for the food. I'll be heading out for the morning."

Will nodded, and scampered off to the kitchen, carrying their empty dishes. Joe jammed his hat onto his head and stepped out of the boarding house into the morning sun.

4

THE TOWN WAS COMING to life around him as Joe stepped off the boarding house porch. A woman with a basket of wet laundry was clipping a bedsheet to the clothesline in front of her cabin. Joe noticed several men with gold panning gear heading toward the streams at the base of the mountains where Widestone was nestled. Joe headed in the opposite direction, back toward the main street of the town. The jailhouse, with its attached sheriff's office, was only a couple of blocks from the saloon, if he remembered rightly.

Joe noted that the town looked fairly prosperous as he started down the main street. There were two mercantile and dry good stores, a livery, blacksmith, a bank, a small café, and even a schoolhouse down near the small church. Of course, there were multiple saloons and only the one church, but that didn't surprise him much. Most men out in these parts had more interest in soothing their souls with a shot of whiskey over a sermon. He wasn't opposed to a good whiskey, himself, but he generally stayed sober—the nature of the West and his position as sheriff made it advisable to stay alert and vigilant.

Joe made a beeline for the jailhouse. The front door was unlocked, so he stepped into the dim front room. A lean man with graying hair and a bushy mustache leaned back in his chair with his boots propped on the desk, reading a letter by the light from the window near him. A badge glinted on his chest, confirming to Joe that this was the sheriff. His gun belt wasn't even buckled on, but rested on the desk next to his feet.

Without looking up, the sheriff grunted, "Be with ya in a minute," and continued perusing the letter.

There were a couple of uninviting wooden chairs lined up by the front door, but Joe didn't sit. He leaned against the doorframe and waited impatiently, a little irked at the other man's dismissive behavior. The sheriff snorted rudely at something in the letter, and the sound grated on Joe's ears.

It must have startled the lone inmate, because, a moment later, a drunk-looking man in one of the two jail cells behind the sheriff's desk stumbled off his cot and began howling to be let out. The sheriff rolled his eyes and set his letter down. "Aw, shaddup, Cal. You'll get out when you're good and sober. Next time, don't take a piss on the floor of Murphy's saloon and you won't end up here."

Mumbling to himself, Cal slumped back onto his cot and was soon snoring, jaw slack. The sheriff rolled his eyes, then turned to appraise Joe. He pulled out a small sack of chewing tobacco and pulled a sizable piece out, stuffing it into his mouth. "New in these parts," he said. It wasn't a question. "Well, what can I do for ya?"

Joe didn't waste any breath, but got right to the point. "I got a letter from my sister about the bandit situation in Narrow Bluff, asking for my help. When I got there, the town

23

was ransacked and empty. I'm looking for my sister—Sophie Wells. Is she among the survivors that came over to Widestone?"

The sheriff pulled his feet off the desk but continued leaning back in his chair, crossing his arms and frowning. "Well now, I can't say I'm sure," he finally responded. He rubbed his mustache and gave Joe a surprisingly piercing stare, but he didn't elaborate further.

Joe's frustration with the callous and insolent sheriff rose. "Her husband's name is Jack Wells. Do you know him?"

"Can't say. Lots of folks came in from Narrow Bluff," he drawled.

Joe longed to land a punch right on the man's careless face. His absolute unwillingness to be of any help, especially on a matter this serious, was maddening. In his own town, he'd taken pride in his position as a public servant. Apparently, it was quite a different story with this so-called sheriff. Joe's jaw clenched, but he forced himself to speak calmly around his gritted teeth. "Do you know where I could find some information about any survivors?"

The sheriff pursed his lips and took his time responding. "Well now, you could go on over to the mayor's office by the bank. I can't promise nothin', but the mayor's office might keep a record book of who all settles in town and when folks pass away or leave. You could try there. Course, the Reverend in town has a list of those who perished in Narrow Bluff, too. I know, because he's been yappin' about some project he's workin' on to commemorate 'em." He harrumphed, showing his utter disinterest.

Joe bit off a curt word of thanks for the small bit of information and turned to leave the jailhouse. The sheriff was already settling back into his desk chair, boots rising to rest cross-legged on his desk. He reached for a tin cup of coffee sitting on the desk and took a noisy slurp. Joe was disgusted with him. A sheriff was responsible for the safety of his town, a responsibility that Joe had taken quite seriously. This man was a disgrace.

Joe had bigger things to worry about than the sheriff, though, so he turned his thoughts away as he left the jailhouse. Figuring that a preacher might be more willing to discuss members of his flock, Joe decided that his next stop would be this Reverend. He sure hoped the Reverend had answers. He was tired of getting sent from one person to another in this town. It was starting to feel like a wild goose chase.

Joe hurried down the boardwalk towards the small church. It was a plain frame building with a short spire, a cross hanging above the door of the humble structure. Here again, Joe found the door unlocked, so he let himself in, pulling his hat off his head as he stepped inside. The sheriff hadn't deserved such a courtesy, but this was a house of God.

Inside the small room, a tall man in simple brown trousers and a homespun shirt was sweeping the floor, gathering dust from beneath the benches that served as pews. He looked up as Joe entered, and smiled kindly. "Good morning. It's never too early to come and spend some time with the Lord. I was just cleaning, but I can slip out if you need a quiet place to pray."

Joe held his hat against his chest and dipped his head respectfully. "Thank you, but no. I was actually looking to speak with the Reverend." He looked at the man questioningly, and the man smiled.

"I may not look like much, but I am, indeed, the Reverend of this humble church. The name's Jesse Smith. What can I do for you?"

"Hello, Preacher, my name is Joe Chambers. I'm looking for some information."

"Good to meet you, Joe." The Reverend leaned his broom against the wall and came forward with a hand outstretched and the two men shook hands. "What information are you looking for? I'm not sure I'm the person to answer your questions, but I'll do my best."

"I've already been to the sheriff, the saloon, and Nan Riley's boarding house, so I sure hope you can help me."

Reverend Jesse indicated that Joe should sit on one of the benches, and Joe settled himself, the Reverend sitting down beside him. "That sounds pretty serious," he commented.

Joe nodded gravely. "I've just come from Narrow Bluff."

The Reverend's friendly smile tightened, and his eyes filled with pain as he nodded in understanding.

"I got a letter from my sister, telling me about what was happening there with the bandits, so I rode over straight away," Joe continued. "But I was too late. I know many of the survivors came here. Do you know of a Sophie Wells? I need to find her."

Reverend Jesse's smile had disappeared completely at the mention of Sophie's name, and he sucked in a painful breath. He shook his head and tears formed in his eyes. Swallowing, he said softly, "I know this is going to be tough to hear, but I know the list by heart, and your sister is in the arms of the Lord, now. I'm so, so sorry."

5

AT FIRST, the words simply didn't register for Joe. He had spent all night imagining the possible outcomes of where Sophie might be, and many of them had ended in her death, but he had held resolutely to the hope that the worst had not happened. Now, in one sentence, the Reverend had closed the doors to any remote possibilities that she had escaped and was safe.

Joe was not one for hysterics, but in this moment, he was grateful that he and Reverend Jesse had been sitting already, because he wasn't sure he could trust his knees not to have buckled from the shock of the news. For a few seconds, Joe was unable to speak. He felt frozen.

The shock didn't leave him paralyzed for long, though. A deep and helpless sadness and waves of regret washed over him. If only his sister's letter had never gotten delayed in the unpredictable mail service...if only he had been able to get to the town before the worst had happened...if only he had never let Sophie marry that Jack Wells and move far away from him... Joe Chambers was a man of action, and it galled him that he could not fix or change the situation. His baby sister was dead, and the finality of her loss tore at his heart.

Reverend Jesse sat quietly next to him, respecting his need for quiet and privacy in these first moments of shock. Eventually, the Reverend reached a tentative hand for Joe's shoulder, but stopped just shy of actually touching him. His hand dropped back to his lap awkwardly. When Joe finally lifted his head and was able to focus his eyes on the man's face, he saw that Reverend Jesse looked almost physically ill.

Normally, Joe would have asked if the Reverend was well, but right now, Joe had no patience or softness for anyone else's pain. Even now, minutes after hearing the truth of his sister's death, Joe felt the sadness inside him solidifying into a burning anger. Rage turned his vision red for a moment, as a tide of fury coursed through his veins. Fury that he knew, instinctively, could only be quenched by obtaining vengeance for Sophie. The tenderness of his new grief was swallowed up in the white-hot desire to avenge her—he would grieve fully for Sophie when the men responsible were deep in the ground.

"The bandits who killed her," Joe bit out, his voice hoarse. "I need to know anything else you can tell me about them."

Reverend Jesse swallowed uncomfortably, and his pained eyes cowed before the grim determination burning in Joe's own. Seemingly unable to sit still, the Reverend rose and paced away from Joe, finally resting his arms on the pulpit with his head hung. Joe rose, too, and was just about to ask the question again when the Reverend finally turned back around to face him.

His eyes were bleak as he began speaking. "The bandits

that destroyed Narrow Bluff are still hanging around the area. They've sunk their claws into Widestone, as well as some others. I know the town looks peaceful, but there's danger lurking beneath. A lot of people in town are paying them off, just to ensure that their businesses won't be targeted and to keep their families safe from violence, though many of them can barely afford it."

Joe's anger rose. These filthy parasites went from town to town leeching the life out of the residents, looting and extorting and killing, and no one could stop them. "What's the sheriff doing about all of this? Hasn't he raised a force of men to fight back?"

Reverend Jesse shook his head, and his face hardened into lines of anger. "Most people in town think that Sheriff Pennington is on their payroll. If they aren't greasing his fist to look the other way, or using him as a pawn, then he's choosing to turn a blind eye to it all. Either way, he's not lifting a finger to protect the town. The turncoat bastard."

The Reverend spit out the last words with pure hatred, and his hands were clenched by his side. Joe didn't even notice the fact that Reverend Jesse had used language that was much stronger than a preacher would usually use. All he felt was deeper disgust and rage against Sheriff Pennington, who this morning he had merely disliked, but now felt absolute hatred toward. It was men like that who allowed atrocities like Narrow Bluff and his sister's death to occur.

Joe needed more practical information about how he could begin to take on this group of thugs. "What else can you tell me about the bandits? Do you know their leader, or where they hide out?"

The Reverend hesitated, silent for a moment. Finally, he asked, "Are you planning to go after them?"

"I won't rest until each and every man responsible for my sister's death is boots to the sky and six feet under," Joe promised harshly.

Reverend Jesse's face blanched, but he didn't admonish Joe to love his enemy or practice forgiveness. "All I can give you is a list of names. I was working on a project to commemorate the victims from Narrow Bluff, so I have all the names of both the dead and the newcomers to Widestone."

"It's a start," Joe said.

Reverend Jesse walked into a room off the back of the main room of the chapel, presumably into his living quarters or office. A few moments later, he returned with a couple of sheets of paper, which he extended to Joe.

"I need to get ready for the day's service, but come back to me if you need anything at all. My door is always open, and I want to help in any way I can. So many have been hurt by these men, and they need to be stopped."

Joe took the list and thanked the Reverend. "Seems we're going to have to take care of this problem ourselves. I appreciate your time today, and I'll be in touch if I have any more questions." Joe nodded once at the Reverend, then turned on his heel to leave the church.

He jammed his hat back onto his head as he stepped out into the morning sun, folding the list to tuck it into his pocket. His thoughts were racing about what steps he could now take to hunt the bandits. He would need to gather more information, and it looked like his best bet, now, was to find some of the Narrow Bluff survivors now living in Widestone to ask them about what had happened to their town. He needed to know how the town had gone from being ravaged, to becoming a full-blown massacre. Although he knew the topic would be harrowing and that the ensuing conversations would be difficult, they needed to happen. He didn't like to reopen old wounds, but it was the only way to find out anything more about how to track down the culprits.

He turned his steps back to Nan Riley's boarding house. If anyone could help him find the survivors on the Reverend's list, she would be the one. He didn't know Nan all that well, yet, but he sensed that she was someone in town that he could trust and rely on for help in his quest. The Reverend, too. At least everyone wasn't as yellow-bellied as their good-for-nothing sheriff.

He had a lot of work ahead of him. These bandits were dangerous and capable of great evil and destruction. He knew when it came down to it, it was likely that it would be just him against however many men were in the nefarious group. He wasn't afraid, though. He'd faced danger many times in the line of duty as a sheriff, but even if he hadn't, he knew that there was nothing he wouldn't do to try and right the many wrongs that had been done by the bandits.

He reached into his pocket, past the list, and felt for his sister's necklace. He held it tightly, the small piece of silver biting into his hand, and he vowed internally to his sister that he wouldn't let her death remain unresolved. He could see her sweet face in his mind's eye, and he sensed that, if she could, she would beg him to go back home and not put himself into danger. She'd been a firm believer in God, and he knew she was with the angels now. Most likely, she would've gently touched his arm and reminded him that vengeance was in God's hands.

Well, he didn't know about that. One thing he did know for sure in all of the unknowns—he would make sure that whoever killed his sister paid with their life. God might command forgiveness, but Joe knew that there was something else the Good Book said, too...

"An eye for an eye."

Seemed to him he'd better follow that scripture, first.

6

"Hɪʏᴀ, Jᴏᴇ!"

Will's boisterous shout brought Joe out of his dark thoughts. He smiled up at the boy, who was shelling peas on the front steps of Nan's boarding house. Judging from the scattered empty pea pods, it looked as though Will was trying to enliven the chore by tossing the pod shells at unsuspecting birds and other small critters. In spite of himself, Joe chuckled a little.

"Good of you to help your mother, squirt," Joe said, ruffling the boy's hair.

"Will, have you finished those peas yet?" Nan's voice carried out onto the porch, and she appeared at the screen door a moment later, wisps of her auburn hair escaping her bun and a smudge of flour on her cheek. Seeing Joe, she stepped out onto the front porch. "Excuse my appearance, Joe. I'm making biscuits to go with lunch."

Joe waved away her comment, privately thinking that she looked downright beautiful. The happier thoughts ushered in by Will and Nan evaporated quickly, though, as the cloud of his

3

sister's death and the weight of the work he had ahead of him settled once more around his shoulders like a cold, wet cloak.

"Joe, what's troubling you?" Nan asked, sensing the shift in his mood. "Did you learn anything from Sheriff Pennington?"

Joe nearly snorted, but checked himself just in time, settling on shaking his head with contempt. "He was about as helpful as trying to bail out a sinking ship with a bucket full of holes." Joe shook his head again, before continuing. "He did point me to the Reverend, who was able to tell me what happened to my sister..." He trailed off, looking away. He scrutinized the nearby Rocky Mountains, focusing on them until he felt in control enough to tell Nan the rest. Now was not the time for sadness, and, quite frankly, he didn't want to get swallowed up in it while he had so much work to do.

When he looked back, Nan was looking at him with mingled compassion and horror, and Joe figured she already knew what he was about to say next. Meeting her gaze, he nodded slightly. "She didn't make it. The bandits made sure of that," he finished shortly, bitterness heavy in his voice.

"I'm so sorry, Joe," Nan whispered. "That's just awful..."

While Joe appreciated Nan's concern, he didn't want to linger on the painful subject any longer. He pushed past the moment, not letting her offer any more condolences. "Nan, the Reverend gave me a list of survivors from Narrow Bluff, and I'm looking to speak to any I can find. Do you know any off the top of your head?"

Nan nodded, but she studied him quietly. Finally, she said, "Are you aiming to go after the bandits?"

Joe tightened his lips. "I'm going to do what I have to do.

Someone needs to take a stand and get justice for all the people that have been hurt, and it looks like your sheriff isn't willing to do the job."

"I'm not blaming you, Joe," Nan said with quiet strength. She met his gaze with eyes that, although tinged with worry, were clear and brave. "It's what I would do in your shoes. It's selfish and dishonest men like that who stole my husband and are trying to bring down this town. I'll do anything I can to help you."

"Thank you, Nan," he said, sincerely grateful for her support.

"I have a few boarders here from Narrow Bluff," Nan said. "I think your best bet would be to talk with Paul O'Malley—he should be here any minute, now, for lunch. Why don't you come in and sit down to wait?"

Joe followed Nan into the dining hall and sat down at what was becoming his usual table by the front window. He placed his hat on the table beside him, shaking his head when Nan offered to get him some lunch. "Just send him my way when you see him," was all he said, before Nan nodded and left him.

Joe didn't have long to wait before Nan returned carrying a tray with a pitcher of water and two glasses. She was followed by the older man with the unkempt beard Joe had seen eating at the dining hall for free the night before.

"Joe, this is Paul O'Malley. Paul, this is Joe Chambers," Nan said.

Joe rose and the two men shook hands before sitting down across from each other. Nan set the tray down, then slipped quietly away, leaving the men to themselves.

"Mr. O'Malley, I need to know anything you can tell me about what happened in Narrow Bluff," Joe said.

"Call me Paul," the man said, and Joe nodded, encouraging him to continue. "Narrow Bluff was a good place—don't get me wrong, we was rough around the edges, but aside from a few bar fights and disputes over who could pan for gold on what land, we all got along pretty good. Most of us were folks just workin' hard tryin' to make a living, and some of us were succeedin', too. Our town was growin', some of us were findin' a good amount of gold dust and some nuggets... Well, not me so much, but some of the younger folks who was more spry than me."

Paul paused, pouring himself a glass of water and taking a long drink. When he finished, he wiped his mouth with his sleeve and continued. "Anyhow, our little town was growin' and we even got us a schoolhouse and a pretty young teacher, too. Guess word started gettin' around, and it caught the attention of them bandits. They started makin' themselves known around town—tryin' to bully the shop owners into payin' em for their so-called protection, and threatenin' the mayor. Folks started feelin' skittish. Lots more folks started stayin' in at night, because they didn't want to risk gettin' shook down or shot. It just kept gettin' worse and worse. Finally, when they thought they couldn't get much more by shakin' the shop owners down, the bastards came after us normal folks. They started to ransack our homes, and anyone that tried to stand up to 'em, ended up shot. They burned homes down to the ground, just to prove they could. They didn't care if they killed women or children, neither. Some of 'em did unspeakable things to any of the women they caught. Anyone that could get out, got out, I'll tell ya that."

Joe felt sick to his stomach hearing Paul's words. So much of this could have been prevented, and he didn't want to think about whether the bandits had raped and tortured Sophie before killing her.

"I'm workin' and savin' up money to get clear of this town," Paul was continuing. "Widestone ain't far from Narrow Bluff, and them bandits are still out there. I see the signs—it's all startin' again. The unrest, the sheriff ain't doin' a thing, and I heard Carl at the livery sayin' he was gonna have to pay up if he didn't want his business attacked. Storm's comin' to Widestone, and folks need to leave, if they can. If I was you, I'd make tracks outta here just as quick as I could."

Paul's expression was dark as he finished, but it was weary, too. "I don't have much else I can tell ya," he said.

"It's been helpful, Paul," Joe said by way of thanks. "I won't take up any more of your time."

Paul nodded to him in parting before rising slowly and shuffling out of the dining hall.

Joe considered what Paul had told him. He hadn't gleaned any information about the names or hideout of the bandits, but he figured there were others in town feeling the effects of the bandits. The sheriff would be no help to him, especially since it was more than possible that he was in cahoots with the bandits, but Joe figured he should try talking to the mayor about the situation.

Exhaustion buzzed in his head, which he now realized was aching. He had barely slept in four days, now, and he needed to rest if he was going to be at his sharpest to hunt the bandits. He decided he would get some sleep before heading to the saloon to dig up some more information. Lips got looser and information tended to flow freely when drink was involved.

He dragged himself up the stairs to his bedroom, where he kicked off his boots and unbuckled his gun belt. With a groan, he lowered himself onto the narrow bed and lay down without bothering to undress further. The afternoon sun was bright out, and he realized he had forgotten to close the shutters. Well, the shutters would have to stay open, then. Bone-deep weariness clawed at his eyelids, and he shut them against the sun. Before even a full minute had passed, he had dropped into a hard sleep.

7

It was dark out when Joe awoke. He sat up stiffly, yawning and stretching. Though he knew he would need at least a few nights of solid sleep to feel fully recharged, he felt a good deal better after his afternoon sleep than he had in days. His stomach growled thunderously, reminding him that he hadn't eaten since breakfast that morning.

Pulling his boots on, he wondered if the dining hall was still serving supper. He hoped so; not only was he hungry, but he knew he wouldn't keep a clear head if he had anything to drink on an empty stomach. Standing, he cinched on his gun belt and raked his hands through his hair in lieu of a proper brushing. A quick check reassured him that the list of names and Sophie's necklace and letter were still in his pocket, so he grabbed his hat and left the room, locking the door behind him.

The dining hall was quiet at the bottom of the stairs, and Joe saw that it was empty except for Nan and a teenage girl, who he assumed was her kitchen help. They were wiping down the tables and putting dirty plates into a crate to carry back for washing. Nan looked up as she heard his footsteps.

"I wondered where you had got to," she remarked. "Hold on, I made you a sandwich out of the leftover pot roast, in case you were hungry." She hurried off to the kitchen and came back with a thick sandwich wrapped in wax paper.

Joe thanked her. "I'll be back later. Thanks for the food, Nan." He turned to leave, and then remembered something. "Make a list of things that need fixing or chores you need done," he said to her. "I don't want to wear out my welcome."

Nan smiled warmly. "I'll hold you to that. There's a door on the third floor with a broken hinge that's got your name on it."

Joe tipped his head. "I'll see to it in the morning. Night, Nan."

"Joe?" Nan called after him softly.

Joe turned back to see her clutching her dish rag, her thin shoulders tight with anxiety, now. "Just...be careful."

Joe nodded, touched at her concern. "I always am," he said, then strode out the front door, unwrapping the sandwich as he descended the steps of the boarding house. Nan's pot roast and fried onion sandwich on homemade bread tasted like heaven, and he wolfed the sandwich down before he got to the saloon.

Just like the night before, piano music warbled out of the saloon, which was lit up, unlike the rest of the darkened street. Guffaws and cheers erupted from one of the poker tables as Joe pushed open the swinging front doors. It seemed someone had just won a hand, much to his opponent's chagrin.

Joe surveyed the rest of the room. A man with a tobacco-stained shirt was following a heavily rouged woman in a garish dress up to the second floor. Joe could guess where they were headed. A couple of brooding men nursed drinks at a table in the corner, and a rowdy group of young men swayed drunkenly around the old piano, crooning loudly. At the bar, Joe was surprised to see the preacher.

Reverend Jesse was sitting on a stool drinking a pint of ale. He looked up as Joe approached and took the stool next to his.

"Evening, Joe," he said. "Let me treat you to a beer. It's the least I can do after the day you've had."

Joe didn't protest, although he could have paid for the drink himself. "Thank you kindly, Preacher."

The bartender slid a tankard of beer to Joe, who nodded his thanks and took a deep drink.

"Sometimes I need a drink to help take the edge off," Reverend Jesse commented into the silence.

"I wasn't judging," Joe said. "We all do what we have to."

"Like you going after the bandits," the Reverend said softly, and Joe nodded once in acknowledgment. "I admit I'm worried for you, but your plan has been on my mind all day. Things are getting pretty bad here in Widestone. I think none of us want to admit what's happening, but if something doesn't change soon, it'll be another Narrow Bluff. The future is becoming more and more uncertain, and tensions are rising beneath the surface."

The Reverend was speaking quietly, clearly trying to keep their conversation private. "I've seen too much heartache, and the good people of this town don't deserve this. The people of Narrow Bluff certainly didn't..." He trailed off, before taking a distracted sip of his beer, lost in thought.

Joe sensed the deep compassion in Reverend Jesse, and knew that he had an ally in the man. The Reverend was clearly worried about more than just the spiritual welfare of his flock, but the very real dangers facing the entire town. "I aim to do what I can to put a stop to all this," Joe said, though he knew he had said as much to the Reverend earlier that day.

"I meant what I said earlier," Reverend Jesse said, abruptly. "When I said I wanted to help you in any way I could, I meant it. I can't watch the bandits take over Widestone and destroy the lives and work of these good people. It's wrong. I won't go through it again."

Joe was struck by the word "again". When had the Reverend gone through this before? "Were you in Narrow Bluff, too?" Joe asked.

"Not exactly," the Reverend said vaguely. Before Joe could ask further questions about what he meant, Reverend Jesse set down his tankard and turned to face Joe more fully. "I do know some things about the gang of bandits. Their leader's name is Earl Gallagher."

Joe leaned forward intently. Now, he was getting some real information. "Do you know anything else about him?" he asked urgently, though he kept his voice soft so no one would overhear.

Reverend Jesse nodded. "He's got more than one hideout in the Rockies for him and his thugs, and that's part of what makes him so slippery. He causes trouble and then holes up in one of his hiding places, and they're well protected."

"Do you know what he looks like?" Joe asked. He knew it

was probably a long shot, but a description would be crucial to finding the man.

The Reverend nodded slowly. "He's a middling height, a few inches shy of six feet. Brown eyes. He's lean, too. I would guess he's in his mid-forties, what with his hair starting to gray at the edges. He's a nasty son of a gun. He's more slippery than a snake, and far less trustworthy. He doesn't have a problem taking hostages—sometimes he even seems to enjoy watching the fear in their eyes when he takes them, and when he...disposes of them. He's not someone to cross. There's a reason everyone is afraid to stand up to him."

Joe had hoped for more information, but he hadn't expected such precise details, and he wondered how the preacher had come by such an intimate knowledge of the dangerous man. "Your information is more helpful than you know, but how in the world did you come by it?"

Reverend Jesse turned back to his drink, taking a long drink before shrugging and answering, somewhat shortly, "I've just talked to a lot of the survivors."

Joe accepted his answer, and took another sip of his drink. The Reverend pushed his own tankard back and stood. "I better not have any more to drink. Have to set a good example and whatnot. Have a good night, Joe," he said, tipping his head and heading for the door.

Joe watched him go and then surveyed the room again. Since he was here, he might as well glean what other information he could to help him take down Earl Gallagher. Deciding on the two brooding men in the corner, Joe stood and was about to walk toward them when he noticed a man dressed in all dark colors heading for the door just a few seconds after Reverend Jesse. Joe felt an odd prickle run down his spine. The man's beer was sitting on the table half full, and he'd left abruptly for what seemed like no reason. Joe's gut told him something was off about the man, and he'd learned through years of being a lawman to trust his gut.

Setting down his tankard on the bar, Joe slipped out of the building, keeping to the shadows. Perhaps the man had overheard his conversation with the Reverend, which could be dangerous, since Reverend Jesse had shared a lot of damning and specific information about the bandit leader. Joe figured he'd better head in the direction of the church, just in case.

Joe slid quietly around the corner of the bank that marked the edge of the main road and the start of the perpendicular street that led to the church. Straining, he thought he saw moving shadows in a darker corner of the street. Creeping closer, he saw the darkly dressed man confronting Reverend Jesse.

The man suddenly grabbed the Reverend by his shirtfront and slammed him against the wall, before punching him hard in the gut. Reverend Jesse doubled over, gasping. The man grabbed the Reverend's shirtfront and hauled him up roughly, slamming him up against the wall again. Joe was close enough now to hear the man's voice, soft but harsh with anger.

"If you're just gonna go singin' anyway, then what's the point of keepin' you around?" he snarled.

Joe reached silently for his pistol, but hesitated. He didn't want to risk hitting the preacher.

The man shoved Reverend Jesse to the ground, and began walking away. "We won't be so forgiving next time,

Smith," he spat over his shoulder, before disappearing into the dark.

Joe waited silently until he was sure the man was truly gone, before letting go of his pistol and hurrying over to the Reverend. Reverend Jesse was curled on the ground, unmoving. He hunched more tightly at the sound of Joe's running footsteps, clearly expecting to be kicked again or worse.

"Reverend, it's me," Joe said, reaching down to help him up.

The Reverend lifted his head, and relief flooded his face. He reached up for Joe's proffered hand, wincing in pain as Joe helped him to his feet. He dusted himself off gingerly. "Thanks, Joe," he said, shaken.

"Reverend, what was that all about?" Joe asked him. It seemed that the bandits had already sent someone after the preacher and were threatening him for talking, although that didn't explain why Reverend Jesse knew so much about the bandits in the first place. Or why they had known his name or mentioned that they were "keeping him around" as the man had put it.

"Not out here," the Reverend said tensely. "We can talk inside."

Joe followed the preacher the rest of the way down the dark street to the church building. Instead of going through the front doors, Reverend Jesse led him around to the back, where he pulled a key out of his pocket and unlocked the door. He stepped inside, pausing to fumble with a small lamp, which he eventually found the matches for and lit.

The low light illuminated the Reverend's small living space. The single room held a small cookstove and table for cooking, eating, and working, as well as a bed and a small chest of drawers with a basin and pitcher for washing up on top. The Reverend closed the door behind Joe and secured the latch, before stepping to the table and sitting down heavily.

"Can I get you anything before we talk?" Joe asked him.

Reverend Jesse shook his head and sighed. "Have a seat, Joe."

Joe sat across from the preacher and waited in tense anticipation for answers to the swirling questions in his mind. Reverend Jesse reached out and laid his hand on a well-worn Bible resting in front of him on the table. He closed his eyes and seemed to be drawing strength for a moment. Finally, he opened them and looked straight at Joe.

"I used to be part of Earl Gallagher's gang. I was part of what happened at Narrow Bluff."

8

BEFORE JOE HAD a chance to react, Reverend Jesse rushed on, "I can't bring myself to keep lying. I'll never forgive myself for what I've done, and I will spend the rest of my life trying to atone for my sins."

Joe barely heard the rest of the Reverend's explanation. He stood up so fast that his chair clattered to the floor, and he whipped out his pistol to train it on Reverend Jesse's face. The preacher didn't move or plead further for himself, he simply sat very still, as though resigned to his fate. Joe felt his chest heaving with his quick and angry breathing, and a rushing sound seemed to fill his ears. Nearly blinded by the red haze of rage, Joe cocked the hammer of the gun, his finger moving slowly to the trigger.

"Pa?" A soft and plaintive voice broke through Joe's haze. He blinked twice, returning to the situation, and his vision cleared. A little boy with messy dark brown hair was holding the hand of his tiny sister, who couldn't have been more than three. The children stared at the two men with wide eyes, the

47

girl was sucking fearfully on her little thumb. Though still shaking with fury, Joe carefully lowered his gun.

"It's all right," Reverend Jesse spoke to the children reassuringly, trying to muster up a smile. "What's wrong, Isaac? Did you have a bad dream again?"

Isaac shook his head slowly, before finally finding his voice. "Ruthie's hungry again," he said timidly. He still eyed Joe with fear, but he seemed to be too afraid to ask Joe who he was or what his intentions were.

Reverend Jesse looked to Joe for approval, and Joe gave him a curt nod. The preacher stood cautiously and, once seeing Joe truly wouldn't make a move, he went to the small cupboard by his cookstove and pulled a hunk of bread out of the breadbox and poured the children a small tin cup of milk.

"Go on back to bed, now," he told them, kissing the tops of their heads quickly, and patting Isaac's shoulder reassuringly when the little boy hesitated. "Everything is fine. Mr. Chambers and I are just talking."

Ruthie was already munching on her hunk of bread, but Isaac carefully carried the cup of milk back into the closet-like bedroom they shared and quietly shut the door, but not before sending Reverend Jesse one more frightened look. Once satisfied that the children were safely tucked away, the Reverend turned back to face Joe, but he didn't speak.

"Didn't know you had kids," Joe grunted, after staring at the preacher in silence for a time.

Reverend Jesse shook his head. "Not exactly. They aren't mine...or at least, they weren't." He looked down and swallowed hard. "They lost their parents in Narrow Bluff, so I took them in. Sort of a penance for my part in what happened to their town. "

Joe's brow furrowed in anger once again, and he scoffed. "Like that'll undo everything you've caused. You're the reason they don't have parents, and now you're trying to play house with them?" He spat the last sentence out.

Reverend Jesse flinched. "I know there's nothing I can ever do to make up for what I've taken away," he said quietly, and tears shone in his eyes. "But I have to do what I can. I'm sickened by the things I've done, and I've turned my soul over to God. I would die to protect those children, and I will spend the rest of my life in the service of others."

Joe didn't soften at the preacher's heartfelt confession. "Give me one good reason why I shouldn't kill you right now where you stand," he said, in a dangerously soft voice.

"I know that I am not worthy to live, and it would be just and fair for you to take my life," he responded, meeting Joe's eyes. "But those children don't deserve to lose their second father so soon after losing their home and their parents." He hesitated, then gave a bitter laugh that sounded almost like a sob. "If you didn't want to kill me before, you surely will after I tell you the rest of my story."

Joe stared at him, feeling deepening horror settling into his stomach. Somehow, he already knew that it would be about Sophie.

"I saw what happened to your sister and it's been eating me up inside. She and her husband resisted the gang more than most, and they tried to put together a resistance. Earl actually took a liking to her. I think he admired her spunk and courage. Still, he wasn't going to let her get away with that kind of defiance. He burned their house down as an example to everyone else of what would happen if anyone tried to cross him. I tried to stop it from happening, but Earl and the other gang leaders wouldn't listen. I watched as your sister and her husband burned alive in their own home." He paused here, horror at the memory written all over his face. "That was the final straw. I knew I couldn't stay any longer. Sophie Wells is burned on my memory and what happened to her is the reason I left."

Joe had already known some of these details, but hearing them afresh made him nearly sick to his stomach. "You let her burn," he said in hollow disbelief.

"I couldn't stop them," the preacher started to defend himself, but then stopped. "You're right...and I will carry her death with me for as long as I live."

"Which may not be for much longer," Joe warned. "Even if I don't shoot you tonight—and I'm still sorely tempted— Earl and his men know where you are. Why haven't they killed you?"

"I've only been allowed to stay alive because I told a handful of people that, in the event of my death, they should reveal all of the information I had on the bandits to the mayor. Those few people haven't told anyone yet, because they're too afraid that the mayor won't be able to stop the bandits and that it would be worse for them if Earl knew they had spilled the beans. They swore solemnly to do so in the event of my death, but nothing short of that could convince them to say anything."

"Why doesn't Earl just have Sheriff Pennington arrest you? He's in their pocket and he'll do whatever they say. They could have you take the fall for everything," Joe said.

"I'm sure they've thought about it," Reverend Jesse said. "But I think they know I would have spilled the beans on them in that case, as well. I'd have nothing to lose. I haven't made the information publicly known, though, because I'd lose any leverage I have over their gang, and they would have no reason not to kill me. I know they have various members of the gang keep an eye on me. They're always watching, making sure that I'm not going to compromise them."

"So, you're just trying to save your own hide, then, is that it?" Joe growled.

"I would deserve to die, and I know it," the Reverend said. "But I have Isaac and Ruthie to think about now, and I won't put them through losing me on top of everything else. Trust me, it is a far greater penance to stay alive with the knowledge of what I've done than it would be to die now."

Joe still itched to take the man down and make him pay, but he knew deep in the core of his being that the preacher was right. The man had done unspeakable things, but he wanted to see justice for the victims and was the only father those two children had now. Whatever Reverend Jesse had done, the children didn't deserve to suffer further.

"Joe, I've told you all that I can about Earl and his men. I can't help you any further, because I can't risk the children. Tonight has shown me just how ready Earl's men are to take me down if I cross any more lines, so this is where I'm going to have to step back."

Joe still felt rage coursing through his veins, and he had the strongest urge to break anything within reach, to utterly ransack the preacher's home, and to beat the man, himself, senseless. He gritted his teeth and stared at the Reverend for a long, taut moment before sheathing his pistol and walking out of the door without a backward glance. He didn't even bother to close the door behind him.

Part of Joe's anger, he knew, came from the fact that he

accepted that Reverend Jesse didn't deserve to die. He sensed that the man's repentance was genuine and that the man was already doing good works to try and repair the losses he had created. Knowing that he couldn't fully hate the man fanned the flames of his rage, like a breath of air over hot coals.

He couldn't exact vengeance for Sophie's death on Reverend Jesse, but he wasn't yet ready to forgive the man, either. He didn't know if he ever would be able to do that. What he could, and would, do was take the information from the preacher and use it to take down Earl Gallagher and his gang of thugs. There was nothing to redeem those men, and they would pay. Justice would be had for not just Sophie, but all of Narrow Bluff.

Though Joe's mind was full of these thoughts, he kept a wary eye out and a hand on the butt of his pistol as he walked back to the boarding house. Earl's men had seen Reverend Jesse talking to him, and they had heard at least some of the conversation. It was very likely that they might, even now, be keeping an eye on him.

None of the shadows on the walk back morphed into the shapes of men with guns ready to shoot him, though he'd scanned them carefully. A few minutes later, he was mounting the steps of Nan's boarding house, but he didn't release his touch on his gun until he was safely locked in his bedroom at the top of the stairs.

As he prepared for bed, bits of the Reverend's confession circled in his mind, along with mental images of Sophie's house burning to the ground as she screamed in pain and horror. Slipping his hand into his pocket, he grasped his sister's necklace tightly. He held it as he laid down, unwilling to part with this token that now represented his purpose moving forward.

Nothing would stop him on his quest for vengeance—he was more committed now than ever.

9

THE SUN PEEKING through the slats of the shutters told Joe it was a suitable hour for rising, but he had been awake since before dawn after a fitful sleep. Even before he had fully awoken, he had felt anger and tension coursing through his body. His teeth ached, and he realized when he had awoken that he must have spent a large portion of the night gritting his teeth and clenching his jaw. His dreams had been haunting and bizarre; flames encasing his sister's home, a tall and evil-looking man shooting several rounds into the air before galloping off with a yip, the Reverend's voice echoing his confession over and over...

Grimly, he rolled to sit up on the edge of his narrow bed. Resting his elbows on his knees, he ran his fingers through his hair and let his arms support his head for a moment. He stared at the floor with an unfocused gaze, gathering strength for the next steps he would need to take today. He knew he would need to gather more information about where Earl might specifically be hiding out, or which people in town were working for him.

As he sat staring at the floor, he noticed a slip of folded paper resting on the floor just inside his door. Had the bandits left him a warning message? If so, they knew not just where he was staying, but even his exact room in Nan's boarding house. Joe pushed himself off the bed and apprehensively picked up the note.

Unfolding it carefully, he was surprised to read: "I'm sympathetic to your cause. Go to the last door on the right of this hallway and knock twice. I'll be waiting."

If the note was to be believed, there was someone who had heard he was sniffing for answers and wanted to help him. He assumed the note was from someone else staying at the boarding house, or they wouldn't have asked to meet him in one of the locked bedrooms. He would be on his guard, but then, he always was.

Joe stuffed his boots on and cinched on his belt, checking to see that his pistol was fully loaded before re-holstering it. Just like the day before, he didn't bother to shave, although he did splash cold water from the wash basin on his face and brushed his teeth with his tooth powder before exiting the room and locking it behind him.

Trodding quietly down the hallway, Joe rapped twice on the specified door and waited cautiously, scanning the hallway and listening hard for sounds. It took a few seconds before the door swung open a crack, through which a blue eye peeked out cautiously. Seeing that Joe stood outside of the door, the door fully opened to reveal a man in his mid-fifties with a gaunt and weather-beaten face. Joe recognized him from the dining hall at mealtimes.

"Come in," the man said tersely. He beckoned Joe inside quickly before poking his head out into the hall to make sure that Joe hadn't been followed. Satisfied that no one was lurking, he closed the door and locked it before turning to face Joe.

"Have a seat," he said, gesturing to the sole wooden chair in the room.

Joe sat and the man sat facing him on the edge of the bed.

"My name is Archie, and I already know you're Joe Chambers."

Joe nodded, waiting for Archie to continue.

"I'm from Narrow Bluff, but ya probably already guessed that. My condolences about your sister," he said gruffly.

"Did you know her?" Joe asked, resting his hands on his knees. He strove to look calm, but he was tense. He didn't know how many more times he could bear to relive the story of Sophie's death.

Archie nodded. "Not so well as her husband, Jack, though."

Joe snorted. "Then, I'm sure you knew what a yellow-belly he was," he said bitterly.

Archie looked surprised at Joe's words and his vehemence, but he shook his head and said, "Jack was a brave man. He was among the few who would fight back against the bandits, and he sealed his fate trying to defend Sophie. In the end, it didn't do no good, of course. But he and Sophie were the ones tryin' hardest to resist. They was tryin' to get folks to fight back and defend Narrow Bluff. They didn't deserve what happened to 'em." He paused. "None of us did."

Joe sat in silence, taking in this new piece of information. He knew from what Reverend Jesse had said last night that his sister and brother-in-law had fought back, but he hadn't realized that they were the main ringleaders. If they had kept their heads down, would they still be alive? Why couldn't his sister have seen that it was a lost cause and let the bandits take the town?

Because she's a Chambers at heart, he thought with pride-tinged sorrow. *And it looks like, in the end, Jack was a better man than I ever gave him credit for.*

"I was too harsh about Jack," Joe said finally. "It looks like, in the end, he found his courage."

Archie nodded solemnly. "He weren't weak, though, he told me once over a beer that he knew some people thought that about him."

Joe knew all too well that he was among those people who had underestimated Jack Wells. Maybe if he hadn't been so overprotective of his sister and blind to Jack's good qualities...maybe they would have been friends. Maybe then, Sophie and Jack would never have left Colorado. He and Archie sat in contemplative silence for a few moments as they each privately pondered those they had lost.

Something struck Joe, and he cleared his throat. "Archie, how did you know who I was?" He hoped that word of his identity and his plans hadn't spread like wildfire through the town. That would make his daunting task only that much more dangerous and difficult.

"You bear more than a passin' resemblance to yer sister, Joe. I was struck by it the first evenin' you walked into the boardin' house. I suspected from then, so I made sure to listen to you speak. You talk like yer sister—sorta refined. Like you'd been educated. Once I heard ya talk, I was pretty sure, but I was positive once I asked Nan about you."

Joe nodded at Archie's answer. His and Sophie's mother

had always read aloud to them and saw to it that they read any classic literature she could get her hands on. She wanted her children educated. "What did Nan say about me?" he asked.

"Not too much, she ain't one to gossip. She did tell me you'd been down to Narrow Bluff, and that confirmed it for me. Folks don't go down to Narrow Bluff anymore, not without a good reason, and I figured you must be lookin' for Sophie."

Joe accepted Archie's answer without comment. The man's reasoning made sense, especially since he had been at least somewhat close with Jack and Sophie. He wasn't upset with Nan for letting it slip about his visit to Narrow Bluff, but he did feel pricklings of worry. It seemed that word was getting around—if Archie recognized him and put two and two together, who else might have done the same? And that wasn't even taking into account what had happened the night before when one of Earl's men had overheard part of his conversation with Reverend Jesse. He would need to be more careful in the future.

"What did you do back in Narrow Bluff? Before everything happened?" Joe asked.

Archie shook his head wearily. "I ran a stable in town. I had saved for years workin' as a ranch hand until I had enough money of my own to set up shop. I owned that stable free and clear, didn't owe the bank nothin'. It was my pride, and I was well-known in town for keepin' the best horses in town. When the bandits started makin' trouble, I did what they demanded. I paid my dues for their so-called protection, but it weren't enough for 'em. They got greedy and they stole all my horses. I didn't want to let 'em go, but I was afraid they'd shoot me if I tried to fight. I lost everythin'—my whole life's work, gone just like that."

His hands were clenched as he remembered, and his eyes burned with anger. "I came over to Widestone just like most of the others that got out in time, and I found a job sweepin' the saloon. It don't pay much, and it sure ain't like runnin' my own business and takin' care of my horses." He paused. "Nan has been good enough to give me a room, though. I pay what I can, but I know she's takin' a loss by lettin' me stay here so cheap. She's a good woman."

Joe nodded in agreement. He was realizing more and more what a pillar Nan was in taking care of the less fortunate in the community, even though she wasn't well-to-do, herself, and was a widow running a business, to boot. He silently promised himself that he would take down Earl and his bandits, not just for Sophie, but for Nan, and Archie, and Paul, and everyone else who had lost so much at the hands of those villains.

Archie continued. "Those bandits have taken too much from me, and they're startin' again here in Widestone. I won't stand for it, not again. I want to offer my help to you. Any way I can be of service in your plans to move against the bandits, I'll do whatever ya ask." His voice was determined and his chin was held high and strong.

Joe thanked him, grateful for the man's showing of courage and support. "Thank you, Archie. We're going to need to find more allies if we're going to have a real shot at taking the gang down, though."

"I think I can help you there. I have a few folks in mind that might be willin' to join. Meet me tomorrow night back here in this room, and I'll have 'em rounded up and waiting."

Joe and Archie stood and shook on it, while Joe thanked him again. "I'm heading down for some breakfast. You coming?"

Archie shook his head, explaining that he had already eaten, and he didn't want to risk the two of them being seen together yet. Joe nodded, agreeing with the man's wisdom in being cautious, then turned to leave the room. He peeked out of the door and scanned the hallway to make sure it was empty before stepping out.

"Don't forget about tomorrow night," Archie said before Joe closed the door.

Joe nodded. "Until tomorrow night."

10

THE FOLLOWING EVENING, Joe walked wearily up the boarding house steps. After his meeting with Archie the previous morning, he had spent the rest of the day seeking out survivors from Narrow Bluff, and then he had done the same all of the current morning and afternoon. For all the hours he had put in, he had gleaned next to nothing, and he was feeling frustrated as he opened the door to walk inside. He hoped the meeting scheduled for tonight with Archie and whatever allies he had gathered would prove more fruitful than the last two days had.

The dining hall was largely empty, the supper rush over, leaving only a few stragglers finishing their meals. Joe noticed Nan sitting at one of the tables with a few of the stragglers, Archie among them. Nan looked absolutely exhausted, her beautiful green eyes heavy and shadowed with purple. He wondered when she had last had a day to rest. Probably not since before her husband had passed away. He barely knew her, but he knew exhaustion and the feeling of carrying the world on his shoulders all too well, and he silently hoped she would be able to find someone to help her.

Archie took his leave when Joe approached the table and sat down in the empty chair next to Nan, likely not wanting to be seen in Joe's company. He gave a subtle nod to Joe in silent acknowledgement of their meeting later that night when their eyes met, but otherwise gave no indication of knowing Joe at all. Saying a general farewell, he left the dining hall and went upstairs.

"I saw a porcupine at the stream today," Will was telling his mother excitedly. "Some of the other boys were trying to throw rocks at it, but I tried to get 'em to stop. Billy didn't like that, and we scuffled a little, *but* you're not mad at me, are you, Mama? I know you always say that God wants us to watch out for those who can't take care of themselves." He said the last part with serious determination, and Nan couldn't help but smile ruefully.

"I don't like that you got in a fistfight with Billy, but you're right—I'm glad you stood up for one of God's creatures. Your father would be very proud of you for protecting one who couldn't protect itself," she said to him, smoothing his untidy hair back from his forehead.

Will nodded, satisfied and pleased, but he didn't respond, as he had just taken an enormous bite and his mouth was now full of mashed potatoes. Even with a full mouthful, he scooped another large bite with his fork and opened his stuffed mouth, trying to jam even more of the fluffy potatoes inside.

"Slow down, Will!" Nan laughed. "Joe's going to think you've been raised by wolves."

"I can't blame him, Nan," Joe said, even letting out a

small chuckle. "I've tasted your cooking, so I know just how tempting it is to shovel it down without regard for table manners. Speaking of—you wouldn't happen to have any food leftover, would you? I'm right famished, and I think I could just about eat a horse." He winked at Will as he said the last part, and Will laughed, a small bit of mashed potatoes falling out of his mouth and onto the table. Nan shook her head in loving exasperation and wiped it up with her napkin.

"Of course, let me get some for you, Joe," Nan said. She placed both hands on the table, ready to push herself up to stand and go get him some supper, but he stopped her with a quick touch of his hand on her arm. It'd been just the barest brush, but his fingers tingled a little where he'd touched her.

"I can get it; you just stay right there. I'll be back in a jiffy. Thanks, Nan," he said. He got up and walked into the kitchen, which he had never seen before. It wasn't hard to find a clean plate and cutlery. Nan kept a clean and organized kitchen, despite the volume of food she had to prepare and clean up daily. A few covered dishes sat on the back of the stove, where they were being kept warm. Lifting the lid off of one of the pots, steam from mashed potatoes greeted him. He helped himself to a large portion of mashed potatoes and placed a generous slab of roast beef from the covered casserole dish beside it, before ladling gravy over both of them. It smelled heavenly, and his stomach rumbled in anticipation.

He carried his full plate back to the table in the dining hall and settled himself again next to Nan. The other stragglers had left while he was serving up his food, so it was just him, Nan, and Will. He dug into the food and sighed contentedly, the need to appease his hunger momentarily distracting him from his apprehensive thoughts about the meeting scheduled for later that evening. Nan's question as he started in on his second bite brought it all back, though.

"Have you had any luck finding out more about the bandits?" Nan asked him. She watched him with interest and concern.

Joe took another bite to buy himself a moment of time. He liked Nan, and he was fairly certain he could trust her, but there was also the possibility that she was involved with them by paying a protection tax, or if they had threatened her. Nan was a good woman, but there was no saying what she might do to protect her son and her business. Besides, he didn't want to risk putting her and Will in danger. He knew all too well from what he'd learned from the Narrow Bluff survivors, and what had happened to Reverend Jesse, just how deeply the bandits had sunk their claws into the town.

"Not much, no," he lied. It was partially true, anyway— he didn't know exactly where the hideouts were. He quickly shifted the subject. "Did your girl go home for the day already?"

Nan stared hard at Joe for a moment, but she let his reticence pass by without comment. "I let Melanie go home a little early today. We didn't bake bread this morning, so there was less washing up than usual, and there aren't too many dishes left. Will can help me and it won't take too much time between the two of us."

Will started to sigh in dejection, but he caught his mother's warning glance and took a bite of roast beef instead. Nan smiled. "That's my good boy. Will's very helpful around here. I don't know what I'd do without him." She squeezed his arm affectionately and Will smiled back.

"Maybe there's a cookie for after washing up?" he asked with an impish twinkle in his eye and a cajoling smile.

Nan laughed. "There just might be, if you wash the dishes without complaining," she said.

"Yes, ma'am," Will said, with much more enthusiasm. "I'm finished now, so I'll get started."

"Thank you, Will," Nan called after him.

"Speaking of help, I've been here for a few days now and it's more than long enough to have repaid the debt your son incurred. I mended that door hinge for you the other day, but that didn't take but five minutes. I don't want to take advantage of your generosity, so I'd be pleased if you'd put me to work. How can I help?"

Nan smiled, but waved his comment away with her hand. "You came to Widestone with an important purpose, and that's what you need to focus on."

"I can spare some time to help you, Nan. You carry more than one person should," he said softly.

Nan relented, and blew out a breath. "I won't lie and say that it's not tiring work, but I'm grateful to have this place and my boy. I'll let you know if there's anything I need you to do, but for the most part, you won't need to worry about doing anything. Unless you bake bread?" She said the last part with a slightly teasing smile.

"Ah, that, I'm afraid, I do not," he said, smiling back ruefully. "But if you need anything fixed or something heavy moved, I'm your man."

"I thought it was too much to hope for," she said in mock despair, raising her hand dramatically to her forehead, and Joe laughed.

Joe found that, despite all of the stress and the bitter

heaviness that had weighed on him since he received his sister's letter, that he was truly enjoying this conversation with Nan. Glancing at the clock, he was shocked to discover that it was almost time for the meeting. The minutes had sped by in her company.

Quickly eating the last few bites on his plate, Joe made his apologies and said he had to get going. "Thank you for the supper, Nan. As always, it was delicious," he said hurriedly, standing up.

Nan stared at him a little strangely, clearly surprised at his swift departure and the abrupt end to their conversation. She waved him away when he reached for his empty plate. "I'll get that, don't you worry about it."

Joe thanked her again, before bidding her goodnight. She returned the words of farewell, but he could feel her eyes on his back as he walked out of the dining hall and headed up the stairs. He reminded himself, once again, that he had done the right thing about keeping her in the dark regarding the new information he had learned. His thoughts turned toward the upcoming meeting. He was unsure of exactly what to expect. While he didn't expect that Archie would have brought in anyone that was looking for trouble, he readjusted his gun on his hip just to make sure it was where it belonged, just in case he needed to draw it quickly.

He rapped twice on Archie's door, and it swung open immediately, revealing three figures crammed inside Archie's small room. Joe stepped in and Archie closed the door and locked it quickly behind him. With the four of them in the tiny space, there was barely room to move around. Joe took in the strangers—a tall woman with beautiful flowing black hair and a determined look in her striking hazel eyes, and a sturdy, broad-shouldered man of middling height.

The strong man stepped forward slightly and reached out to shake Joe's hand. His expression was firm as he gripped Joe's. "It's good to meet you, Chambers." His voice was deep and serious, matching the solemn expression on his face. "You can call me Louis. I used to be the blacksmith over in Narrow Bluff."

Joe nodded at him and looked over as the woman stepped forward and offered her hand with a confident smile. "Nellie," she said.

Joe shook her hand, as well, not bothering to introduce himself. It was clear that Archie had already told them both about him. Introductions completed, Archie indicated that everyone should sit. Nellie took the sole chair before anyone even had to offer it, leaving only the bed. Archie and Joe sat side by side, Louis opting to stand, leaning against the wall.

"So, let's get started," Archie said, clapping his hands on his knees.

"We're going to need more allies if we're going to face the bandits directly," Joe said, and the others nodded in agreement.

"I reckon there'll be more folks who'll want to join us," Archie said. "Especially folks from Narrow Bluff. We all lost too much to those thugs."

Louis nodded darkly. "That's the truth," he said. "We've gotta keep this pretty quiet, though. We can't just go travelin' around as a group, tryin' to recruit members."

"We'll keep our group secret, for now," Joe agreed. "You all know who would be best to ask far better than I would. I think in order to make this work, the three of you will have to invite others that you trust to join."

"Louis and Nellie is good people," Archie said. "I trust 'em and they've got good judgment. We'll do our best not to tip off the enemy while we're inquirin' about." Nellie tipped her head in acknowledgement, and Louis nodded in agreement.

"We need more strength, but we're going to have to keep the number of people in our group low. We'll need to be real conservative about who we let in, at first. We don't want to blow this thing before it starts," Joe warned.

"Slow 'n steady is best," Archie agreed. "We don't wanna jump the gun."

"As we're buildin' the group, we can keep meetin' every couple days, but I reckon we should pretend not to know each other when we're in public," Nellie suggested.

"That's for the best," Joe said, seconding Nellie.

"If we do get a strong enough presence," Louis said, "we might have a chance of winnin' over some of the major players—some of the richer folks, the sheriff, maybe even the mayor."

"Course, we don't know if we can trust the mayor, and we're pretty sure the sheriff is workin' for 'em," Nellie commented darkly.

"Nellie's right," Archie said. "I don't trust Sheriff Pennington further than I can kick him. I don't know about the mayor, and I reckon we better not go for him, even if we do get enough folks to join up."

Louis shook his head, and opened his mouth to disagree, but Archie overrode him. "We'll put that issue on the back burner for now. It'll keep. We've gotta get more folks into our circle, first. We've got a different issue we gotta take care of tonight—who's the leader gonna be."

"Archie, I think it ought to be you," Joe said. "You found Nellie and Louis already, and you organized this meeting."

All three were shaking their heads as Joe spoke, and Nellie spoke up first. "Joe, the three of us already discussed it, and we think it outta be you. We looked into your past—some folks from Narrow Bluff, who knew Sophie well, had heard about you. We know that you were a sheriff and that you kept your town safe. We've all talked about it, and we want it to be you."

Louis and Archie nodded. It appeared they had unanimously made this decision already. Joe took in a breath and held it for a moment, resigned. He didn't like being put into the position of deciding the fate of those who would join, and it seemed no matter where he went, he was always forced into the position of authority. Well, it looked like he didn't have much of a choice.

"Well, then, it seems like it's already decided," Joe said at last. "I'll do my best not to let you down, you have my word."

"We trust you, Chambers," Louis said simply.

"Thank you," Joe said, touched and feeling anew the weight of responsibility at Louis's expression of confidence. "First thing we need to do is find a different place to meet. This room isn't big enough for any new members, and besides, it'll look strange if people see us leaving together."

"I think I can help ya there," Archie piped up. "I been savin' every penny I could from my job sweepin' at the saloon so I could buy a big empty barn near the blacksmith's. I want to turn it into a stable, but I ain't started work on it yet. It's big enough, and we could keep a lookout when we have meetings."

"Good plan, Archie," Joe said. "Let's all meet at the barn in two days, after nightfall, say around, 9 o'clock. We'll discuss any developments and meet any new recruits."

The group agreed to the plan and then parted ways, each leaving individually so as not to attract suspicion, and checking the hallway carefully to make sure no one was watching. Joe left last, nodding once to Archie in farewell. Things had changed a lot in the past few days and they were starting to put together the beginnings of a plan.

11

EARL GALLAGHER SURVEYED the edges of his camp, making sure that there were men stationed on watch duty. Satisfied, he spat into the rocks at his feet and hitched his pants up, thumbs in belt loops. This camp was one of his favorite hideouts—it was a two days' ride from Widestone, and nestled in a grove of trees in the small valley between two mountains. The valley was tiny, hemmed in by the bases of the mountains, which provided excellent cover, along with the trees. A small stream flowed nearby, providing plenty of clean water. It was the perfect place to hole up when he and the gang weren't working. *Not that I mind the work,* he thought, and chuckled softly to himself.

Raucous laughter from his men spilled over from the campfire about fifty feet from Earl, pulling him back to the present. Time to put his feet up, and maybe get a cup of coffee. Nights in the desert were cold, and it was high time he got to kick back by the fire.

"Didn't she put up a fight?" Randy, one of his gang, was asking another member.

"Only at first," Bart chortled in response, his tobacco stained teeth glinting yellow in the firelight. "But she figured out pretty quick who was in charge—best time she ever had in her life, I'd say. Her husband ain't gonna be able to satisfy her no more, now that she's had the best. If you ask me," he said thoughtfully, his words slurring, "I earned that money I took from her house. Payment for servicin' her. Mind you, she didn't have much, so maybe I should go back and tell her she owes me some more."

His words were met with guffaws and catcalls from the other men. "Aw, now, she can't be satisfied with what *you* could give her, Bart," Lenny called out from across the fire. "I don't think you've ever had a woman without payin' her or takin' her, if you know what I mean. Don't say much about your abilities, that's all I'm sayin'."

Bart's face darkened at the insult, and he stumbled to his feet, his bottle swinging wildly, sloshing whiskey onto the ground. Some landed on the fire, causing the flames to flare dangerously.

"Hey, hey, relax, Bart!" Randy yelled, yanking Bart back down by the back of his britches. "Lenny's just joshin' ya, no need to get all worked up."

Lenny smirked malevolently, and spit a stream of tobacco juice right next to Bart's feet, just barely missing the man's tattered boots. Bart was outraged, and tried to struggle to his feet again. Earl stepped into the firelight before things got out of hand, bored with their antics.

"Now, now, boys," he said, his voice dangerously calm.

Bart instantly quieted down and Lenny looked away. The circle around the fire became awkwardly quiet, leaving only the sound of the logs snapping and popping as they burned. Taking his time, Earl selected a tin cup from the jumble of dishes on the ground near the fire. It was the least dirty of the lot, wiping it down with his silk handkerchief. He didn't cotton much to niceties of clothing, but he liked to keep a few elegancies around him, just to remind his men that he was the boss. *And a boss,* he thought to himself, *should look like a boss.* Pouring himself a cup of hot coffee from the kettle hanging over the fire, he took a loud sip, jarring in the uneasy quiet, before walking over to stand in front of Lenny.

"Beat it, Lenny," he said carelessly.

Lenny blushed deeply at the careless insult, but he knew better than to argue back with the boss. Scowling, he stood up, relinquishing his log to Earl, and muttered something about needing to go clean his gun. Earl ignored his mortified retreat, and settled himself comfortably, sipping his coffee.

He hadn't been relaxing long before he heard loud hoofbeats echoing across the rocks. Instantly, he was on high alert, whipping his gun out of its leather holster. The rest of the men around the fire did the same. Why hadn't the sentries alerted him? Earl would deal with their shoddy work later.

A dappled grey horse thundered into the firelight and skidded to a halt, a man in dark clothing sliding off. Earl was relieved to discover the man was Jimmy Ross, one of his gang that he'd left stationed in Widestone.

"I have news from town," Jimmy said to Earl, breathing hard, his clothes dusty from hard trail riding. "Jesse was runnin' his mouth to some newcomer at the saloon two nights ago. I came right away."

Earl re-holstered his gun and narrowed his eyes. "Is he

now? We can't have that..." He paused, stroking his chin, and Jimmy continued on, eager to spill the rest to his boss.

"I talked to the sheriff, and he said the newcomer is that pig Sophie's brother. You know, the one that tried to build a resistance in Narrow Bluff?"

"Oh, I remember her very well," Earl said silkily. That Sophie had spunk, but she'd been a thorn in his side, stirring up trouble and wasting his time. "So, her brother's come sniffing around, then?" Earl mused. That would never do; he had Widestone where he wanted it, and if this brother of Sophie's was anything like *she* had been...well, that might throw a wrench into his smoothly running operation.

"What'd you do with 'em, Jimmy?" he asked.

"I threatened Jesse, and I think it scared him pretty good. He don't want no trouble," Jimmy promised. "I made sure of that."

"And the newcomer?" Earl asked impatiently.

Jimmy's eyes widened, realizing belatedly that he'd made a mistake. "Well, I wanted to check in with you, first, boss, and see what you wanted," he stammered, trying to cover for his mistake.

With no warning, Earl backhanded Jimmy hard across the face, dropping Jimmy like a rock. A large red welt in the imprint of Earl's hand, including his signet ring, stood out on Jimmy's cheek. For a moment, Jimmy was too stunned to move, but he staggered back to his feet, eyes on the ground in mortification. Bart and Randy sat quietly, not wanting to say or do anything that would risk their boss's wrath. They'd been on the receiving end of his temper themselves, and they knew better than to attract his attention when he was angry.

Earl settled himself back onto his log and took a casual sip of his coffee. The men waited in silence for him to speak. "Go get my horse ready, Jimmy," he said, not bothering to look at the man. "You're riding back to town in an hour, and I'm coming with you. We have some serious business to take care of." He'd pick a few others to join them and leave Nick and Edwin to keep the rest of the boys in line.

Silently, Jimmy took the reins of his horse and began walking to where the gang kept the other horses tied up. Bart and Randy followed without a word, and Earl knew that their willingness to help Jimmy feed the horses, pack saddlebags, and make other preparations had more to do with their desire to avoid his volatile mood than anything. He didn't care; the silence helped him think.

"If you want something done right, you have to do it yourself." He rolled his eyes, slurping the last of his coffee. And he meant to go take care of this business the right way.

So, Jesse's flapping his mouth to Sophie's brother, is he?

Jesse was a liability, but he hadn't been a problem until now. Earl had considered himself magnanimous for letting Jesse leave the gang since he'd "found God"—Earl snorted at the thought—but it seemed Jesse wasn't repaying his kindness properly.

Looks like he'd have to ride to Widestone and quash this insurrection before it began. He wasn't going to wait for Jesse to bring trouble to him. He would bring the trouble to Jesse and remind him who the boss was. And Jesse sure wouldn't be ready for the trouble he, Earl Gallagher, could bring.

12

A SICKENING SQUELCH brought Joe back to the present, and he looked down. Horse dung. A string of profanities flew from his mouth, which he only bit back when he saw a mother on the other side of the street covering her child's ears and shooting him a disapproving look. Joe tipped his hat to her in apology and tightened his lips.

Grimacing, he scraped his soiled boot against the edge of the boardwalk, getting as much of the muck off as he could. He'd been so lost in thought that he hadn't even seen the foul pile right in the middle of his path. The ridiculousness of the situation struck him, and he found himself chuckling in weary resignation. Why not add this to the list of frustrations he'd been dealing with?

Shaking his head, he continued on toward Nan's boarding house, although, this time, he kept a sharp eye out for any other such mishaps. The past day and a half had been discouraging. He had spent the time since his meeting with Archie's group yesterday evening looking to speak with any more survivors from Narrow Bluff, but it had been unfruitful.

The meeting had been helpful, as putting together a group to face off against the bandits was a big step in the right direction, but he acknowledged bitterly that he was largely useless at this step in the process. He didn't know people in the town well enough to know who was trustworthy, and he didn't want to tip off the bandits that they were organizing.

He trudged wearily up the boarding house steps, grateful to, at last, be shaded from the afternoon sun. Through the screen door, he could see Nan sweeping the floor of the dining hall, pausing to wipe off a trickle of sweat from her glistening brow. He scraped his boots against the rug at the front door and checked the bottoms of his shoes. It wouldn't do to add to her burdens by tracking in evidence of his unsightly accident.

Satisfied that his boots were as clean as he could get them, he pushed open the door. Aside from the quiet chinking of checker pieces from the two older men playing quietly in the corner, the room was still, the only other sound the rhythmic sweeping from Nan's broom. Joe nodded to Nan, ready to head up to his room, but she hurried toward him and touched his sleeve.

"There's someone who'd like to speak with you," she said quietly, making sure the men playing checkers couldn't overhear.

Joe was startled, and he hesitated warily, wondering who would go through Nan to speak with him, and if that person was affiliated with the bandits. She must have sensed his discomfort, because she whispered quietly that it wasn't anyone dangerous, and beckoned him to follow her. She led him to a back room he'd never seen before, close by the kitchen. It was clearly her room for keeping track of records and payments; a large desk covered in neat stacks of papers and an open ledger crowded the surface. Joe was struck, yet again, by how much work she shouldered alone.

"Wait here," she told Joe quietly, then opened a door at the other end of the room that led to a back hallway. She poked her head out and whispered, clearly inviting someone to enter. A man in a dark leather vest and a black cowboy hat stepped into the room. He had a serious face with a strong jawline, and his eyes were grave. He stepped toward Joe and reached out to shake his hand.

"Milton Byers," he said, his voice deep and with a gravity that matched his expression. "And I know you're Big Joe Chambers," he continued. "I've heard of your work as sheriff in Shady Mesa."

Joe shook his hand, but didn't speak, waiting to hear more before letting his guard down. The man had clearly done some research on his background.

Nan took this opportunity to excuse herself. "I don't want anyone to come looking for me or get suspicious, so I'm going back out to the dining hall to keep cleaning," she said, slipping past the two men and shutting the door behind her.

Joe eyed Milton, who had now settled himself into the chair behind Nan's desk and was gesturing Joe to sit, as well. Joe did so, but not before casually readjusting his gun belt as a silent warning to the other man. Milton caught the hint.

"I take your meaning, Joe, but I'm on your side," he assured him. Joe continued to watch him warily. Milton sighed. "Let me explain more," he continued. "I was a deputy under Nan's husband, before he died. I'm now a deputy under Sheriff Pennington."

"I see," Joe said noncommittally. Learning that the man

worked for Sheriff Pennington did nothing to assuage Joe's worries.

"The sheriff," Milton said, staring at Joe hard in the eyes, "is not a man to be trusted."

Joe already knew this, but he was shocked to hear the deputy saying so. His eyebrows lifted in surprise, in spite of the careful control he'd been keeping over his features. Milton nodded gravely.

"It looks like you already guessed that," he said.

"We didn't exactly hit it off," Joe acknowledged. "What I've learned since I met him has supported my first impression of him." He sat back in his chair, eyeing Milton thoughtfully. "If you don't trust him, why do you work for him?"

"I need to keep an eye on him," Milton said. "Nan's husband was a good man, and a solid sheriff. I've long suspected that he was killed by the bandits so they could replace him with someone easier to control. Keeping my post as deputy lets me stay close to Sheriff Pennington and learn as much as I can about the bandits. I've been building up information quietly for some time."

Joe took this in. Milton's suspicions about the death of Nan's husband certainly coincided with what he had learned from Nan and Will. "So, the good sheriff is in league with the bandits, then," he said, looking to Milton for a firm confirmation.

Milton nodded. "He's one of the main reasons the bandits have been able to get so much power here in Widestone. He's not in their gang, to my knowledge, but he sure does pave the way for them. He looks the other way when they threaten folks into paying for 'protection', and if the gang needs something...well, he'll do whatever he can to help them."

"Are they paying him off?" Joe asked. "Why else would he just sit back and let them take over the town?"

"I wouldn't be surprised," Milton responded. "But he's a coward, more than anything. If he ever had an impulse to stand for justice, it's long gone. I think he's given up hope that they can be stopped and so he just turns a blind eye to it all, afraid that they'll make him pay for it if he doesn't. And they know that—it's why they pulled strings to get him made the sheriff in the first place." He shook his head in disgust, brows pulling together as he scowled.

Joe leaned forward and threaded his fingers together, resting his elbows on his knees. "Wouldn't that mean the mayor is in league with the bandits, too? He's the one who appoints the law enforcement."

"As far as I know, the mayor's clean," Milton replied. "I think they had already picked Pennington out as a replacement, and they got him to present himself to the mayor as a candidate to be the next sheriff. The mayor asked me if I wanted the position, since I had been a deputy for a year or so, but..." He paused, and he looked solemn. "Well, I suspected foul play was involved in the last sheriff's death and it seemed foolish to put myself in the same position. So, I've stayed on as a deputy and done what I could to investigate. I just can't help but wonder if things would've been different if I'd stepped up and taken the job." He dropped his eyes, and it was clear to Joe that the man still felt shame about his decision.

Joe wasn't one to show too much emotion, but he felt for the man. He knew all too well what it was to torture oneself with regrets about the past, wondering over and over about whether different choices would've led to better outcomes. He'd spent enough sleepless nights wondering how things could've been different for Sophie if he'd made different choices. Joe let Milton sit in silence for a moment, and then said matter-of-factly, so as not to embarrass the man, "We've all got our regrets, but it won't change the past. You're doing what you can now, and that's what matters."

Milton cleared his throat, obviously ready for the emotional moment to pass. He rolled his neck and shoulders a bit, as if clearing off the last few minutes, then looked back at Joe. "Sheriff Pennington is looking for information about you," he said. "Ever since you visited earlier this week, he's been scrambling, trying to figure out what you're up to. He doesn't trust you, and he's worried you're going to make trouble—especially once he found out that you're a sheriff in your own town. And you know Sheriff Pennington doesn't want trouble, he just wants to stay out of any mess, and he thinks you might come and disrupt the peace." Milton snorted. "Well, *his* peace, anyway. Lord knows this town hasn't been truly peaceful in years."

"Has he found anything else on me, besides the fact that I'm a lawman?" Joe asked. It would be important to keep tabs on the gang's lackey.

"Well, since you were asking about Sophie, he knows now that she was your sister and the circumstances of her death. I was sorry to learn about that, Joe," he said, nodding his head once as a sign of respect to Joe. "I think he suspects, more than anything, that you're going to cause trouble, but I don't think he has hard evidence."

Joe was grateful to hear that. He knew it would be hard to

keep things quiet, and he had already shown his cards, somewhat, just by asking after his sister, but that couldn't be helped. At least the sheriff didn't have hard evidence of the steps he was taking with Archie and the others.

"Since the sheriff was so interested in you, I looked into you, too," Milton said. "I suspect that you're looking to overthrow Pennington and stop the bandits. I want to join you." He looked at Joe hard in the eyes, waiting for confirmation. Joe met his gaze, but didn't confirm or deny it. He liked Milton, but he wasn't sure if the man was actually trustworthy.

"How do I know you're telling the truth?" Joe asked him, watching Milton carefully.

Milton shrugged. "I can't prove anything to you, Joe. Nan can vouch for me, and I can tell you myself that I want to help you. These evil men are destroying the good people of this town, and it's wrong. I want to return justice to Widestone, and I want scum like Pennington and the bandits gone for good." He was talking faster now, his eyes blazing with the conviction of his words. "We can't have another Narrow Bluff. Someone has to stand up for this town, and I want to be part of the movement."

Joe wanted to believe the man. They needed every good person they could get to join the resistance, but he wouldn't risk the group without more proof. He decided he would ask the others at their barn meeting that night before going any further with Milton.

"Can you come back in a few days to talk?" he asked.

Milton nodded. "I can do that."

The two men stood, and Milton moved to leave. "Wait a bit before you leave, so no one sees that we've been talking together. We don't want to raise any suspicions." When Joe nodded, Milton ducked out of the room, closing the door behind him.

Joe sat back in his chair, pondering the new revelations from Milton. After a few minutes of silent thought, Nan poked her head into the room. Seeing that Joe was still there, she entered and shut the door behind her.

"What did you two decide to do?" she asked him breathlessly. "If you're going to do something, I want to help in any way I can." She seemed to suspect that Milton had come to make a plan to move against the bandits.

Joe still wouldn't risk her safety or place his full trust in her. Not yet. "There's nothing concrete in place, yet, to be honest. I'm not even sure what I plan to do." He hated lying to her, but he had to.

She frowned, her excitement ebbing away at his dismissive words, and Joe knew she didn't believe his words. Still, she nodded reluctantly, eyes trained on him as he turned to leave the room.

13

THE STREET APPEARED DESERTED, but Joe stayed hidden in an alleyway, surveying for any signs of movement that might betray watchful eyes. There wasn't much light on the street with the church, apart from lamplight filtering through the cracks in shutters from a few homes. The main source of light was the full moon, casting long and distorted shadows.

Satisfied, at last, that no one was watching, Joe sidled carefully toward Archie's barn, hugging the edges of buildings so as not to leave himself out in the open. This was, after all, the street where Reverend Jesse had been attacked, and Joe had no doubt that the preacher was still under some kind of surveillance by the bandits. He didn't love that the barn was so close to the church, but it was safer than meeting at the boarding house, and there really wasn't anywhere else in town they could meet without attracting notice and suspicion.

Joe slid to the back door of the barn, facing away from the street and into the dark openness beyond. He rapped softly four times, the signal they'd chosen before. The door opened a crack to reveal Louis, who silently beckoned him to enter. Joe slipped through the narrow opening and found Archie and Nellie in a sheltered corner of the barn, with two other people Joe didn't know. They were sitting around a small lantern, kept burning low so as not to be seen from the street, and the minimal light cast most of their faces into shadow. Joe was disappointed to see that there were only two new faces at the meeting, but he was still grateful to have them. If Nellie, Archie, and Louis trusted these folks, they were a pretty reliable bet.

"I'm standing guard tonight," Louis said softly to Joe, who nodded before making his way quietly to the group.

Archie and Nellie greeted him quietly, and Nellie asked if he had been seen.

"I was careful," Joe said, assuring them.

"Joe, meet the two newest members of our group," Archie said, gesturing toward the new recruits. "Mack and Jeanette Brown."

Joe reached to shake hands with the couple. "We're glad to have you."

"We're ready to do all we can," Mack said, and his wife held his hand in solidarity. "Earl's gang destroyed our business in Narrow Bluff. We baked bread back there, and we've been able to start over here. We can't lose it all again."

"They done well, too," Archie said. "We all lost somethin' in Narrow Bluff, but some folks are more lucky 'n others." He clapped Mack on the shoulder. "Mack and Jeanette, here, have built a right successful business here in Widestone." Although his fortunes had not been lucky like the Browns, Archie sounded proud of his friends.

Jeanette's eyes were sober as she spoke up. "We know

we've been lucky in a way most haven't. We've been able to build up something of a nest egg, and we're ready to give funds to the cause."

"That's right," Mack agreed. "We're here to back up this operation with our resources and our support."

"That's mighty fine of you," Joe said with sincere gratitude. "Not many would be so willing to sacrifice, especially after rebuilding what was lost."

Mack squeezed Jeanette's hand, and Joe could see her eyes shining with tears, reflecting the lamp's glow. Her back remained straight and poised, though, and not a single tear spilled over. Neither of them spoke, and Joe knew they were likely embarrassed at his simple thanks.

"I have some news," Joe said. "Deputy Milton Byers came to see me at Nan's."

"Interestin'..." Archie said, rubbing his stubbled chin in thought. "What'd he say?"

"He asked Nan to arrange a meeting with me, so she set it up so we could talk in her office without anyone seeing. He said Sheriff Pennington has been trying to learn more about me, and Milton put two and two together and guessed that I might be trying to put together a force to stand up to the bandits."

Nellie's eyes widened. "If it's that obvious to him, I wonder how many other folks've guessed." Her face was taut with anxiety.

Joe shrugged, tightening his lips and shaking his head. "Earl's gang might already suspect, seeing as how one of them attacked Reverend Jesse after he gave me some information. And it's not like I haven't been asking Narrow Bluff survivors if they know anything. I've tried to keep it on the down low, but word gets around."

"More 'n likely the bandits have their suspicions," Archie agreed. "But I doubt they'll do anything just yet. They don't know you've got a group with ya, and they mightn't think one person sniffin' around is too much of a threat."

"Let's hope so," Joe said. "Anyhow, there was more that Milton said. He confirmed our belief that Sheriff Pennington is under the control of the bandits, so we should see him as a threat. He doesn't believe the mayor is in on anything, but that doesn't mean we should let our guard down."

"Milton could be a good source of information," Mack commented. "He works closely with the sheriff, and that could help us."

"Or he could be a rat tryin' to get close to us so he can feed information to Pennington and back to the bandits," Nellie said darkly.

"Nellie's right," Archie said. "None of us have spent time with Milton. I sometimes see 'im at the saloon knockin' back a pint in the evenin', but he leaves early and he don't talk much."

"He seems like a good person," Jeanette offered, "although I've really only spoken to him a few times when he comes to buy bread."

"It might be too risky to trust him just yet," Joe concluded. "He seemed sincere about wanting to help, but if none of you are sure he can be trusted, then it's not a risk we can take. Are we in agreement, then?"

The group nodded as Joe looked from face to face. "Now, then," he continued, "let's—" He paused, listening hard. Something had rustled by the side of the barn, on the other side that Louis wasn't guarding. Joe motioned the others to stay silent, before creeping silently toward the door, sliding his pistol out of its holster.

Louis had heard the sound, too, because he was also inching toward the sound. He and Joe made eye contact and signaled to each other. Joe indicated that Louis should cover him while he stepped out into the open, ready to confront whoever was trying to sneak up on them. Louis lifted his own gun, and Joe slid the door open an inch, peering outside. There was a dark shape crouched small in the shadows.

"Don't move another inch," Joe said, his voice low and menacing.

"It's just me," a tiny and frightened voice called.

"Will?" Joe asked in disbelief, lowering his gun and pushing the door open.

Will unfurled himself from the ground, trembling and eyes wide. Seeing Joe re-holster his weapon, the boy relaxed a bit, even venturing a shaky smile. "I'm glad you didn't shoot me, Joe," he said.

"I very well almost did," Joe said, yanking the boy into the barn and closing the door behind them. He checked covertly to make sure that the others had hidden. Thankfully, they'd had the presence of mind to hide themselves.

"Just what in the blue blazes were you thinking, creeping around at night all alone?"

Will hung his head and scuffed his toe in the dirt, scattering straw on the barn floor, similar to the hangdog stance he'd taken when Joe had lectured him about not gambling.

"Will," Joe said sternly. "Look at me." When the boy had done so, he continued. "It's dangerous to be out alone at night, and if your mother knew, she would be worried sick. Not to mention, the trouble you could get in if the wrong people saw you."

Will nodded contritely, but then his little shoulders tightened and he threw his head back with a touch of defiance. "I want to help you get those jerks!" he said loudly. Joe quickly shushed him with a hand clamped over the boy's mouth. He checked where Louis was, once again, standing guard, to make sure no one outside had heard.

"What are you talking about, son?" he asked, gently removing his hand once he was sure Will would talk quietly.

"I know you've been looking for the men who hurt your sister," Will said. "People think 'cause I'm a kid that I don't know nothing. But I do! I know the bad men killed my pa, and I know they killed your sister, too. I heard you tell my mama when she thought I had gone upstairs." Will looked a little ashamed, here, for admitting to eavesdropping, but he didn't apologize. "I saw how you stood up to those men who were chasing me, so I know you're not going to let the bad people keep hurting everyone. I want to help you!"

Joe admired Will's instinct to stand up to the bandits and seek for justice, but there was no way he was going to let the boy put himself in danger. "I hear you, son," he said, "but you can't."

Will started to protest, but Joe quelled it with a stern look. "The best thing you can do to help is to take care of your mother and not go getting into trouble," he said firmly. "Your mother already lost her husband. She can't lose you, too."

Will hung his head again. "I just wanted to help," he said in a small voice.

"Some jobs are just for grownups," Joe replied, not

unkindly. He was calming down, now that his heartbeat was returning to normal, but he still wasn't happy with Will for doing something so foolish, even if the boy had good intentions. "I need to take you home now," he said.

Will followed Joe reluctantly out of the barn door, aware that no amount of cajoling or argument would change Joe's mind. They had only taken a few steps when Louis suddenly charged across the barn, his face as white as a sheet.

"Get back in the barn!" he hissed sharply, beckoning them to come quickly. "Bring the kid."

Without pausing to ask why, Joe and Will hurried back inside. They had barely gotten back into the shelter before they heard the clomping of horse hooves coming into earshot. Joe pushed Will behind himself and pressed his eye to a small crack in the barn door. Five or six horses were riding into the town, and they were coming in fast.

"The bandits?" Joe whispered to Louis, his voice barely louder than a breath.

Louis nodded, his face blanching in terror. "Earl," he choked out.

Joe cursed silently to himself. It must've been because of the man who had overheard him and the preacher talking in the saloon. He'd known there would be repercussions, but he'd never expected it to happen so fast.

14

Joe was able to count five horses as they thundered past the barn a moment later. He wasn't sure where they were heading, but at least they didn't realize that they were riding right past him. The hoofbeats faded into the distance, but it wasn't until a full minute had passed that Joe finally relaxed. Releasing his pent-up breath slowly, he slid his pistol back into its holster. Beside him, Louis was doing the same.

Joe turned to check on Will. The boy was shaking, his eyes enormous. "You alright, son?" Joe asked him.

"Yes, sir," he said, nodding sharply. Joe could tell Will was trying very hard to put on a brave front.

"Louis, I need to go talk with the others. Are you okay to keep standing watch? The others will fill you in on everything we decide."

Louis nodded to Joe's question and returned to his station, his posture taut with alertness.

"Come on, son," Joe said to Will, gesturing with his head to follow, having given up on trying to hide them from Will.

Things were too urgent for that now and they had decisions to make.

The two waded into the corner of the barn where the group had been before. It was hard to see in the darkness of the interior; someone must have had the presence of mind to extinguish the lamp when they'd heard the rustling Will had made outside the door.

"Archie? Nellie?" Joe called softly.

The sound of rustling straw and a few quiet groans from old joints unbending from awkward hiding positions were all that was heard for a moment, and then the quick scraping of a match. A small flame flared, revealing Archie's face as he re-lit the lamp, keeping the flame small.

"I'm too old to be folded up like that," he muttered. "My bones ain't so young as they once was." He shook his head ruefully, but quickly sobered up and returned to the matter at hand. "What did y'all see?" he asked Joe.

Joe looked from Archie to the others, who had made their way back to the lamp Archie had lit. Jeanette had straw sticking out of her hair and was brushing it off of her clothes —Joe figured she must have tried to hide directly inside a pile of straw.

"Five horses. Louis confirmed that they're from Earl's gang."

Archie cursed softly. "I thought we'd have more time."

"D'ya think they caught wind of what we're doin'?" Nellie asked anxiously.

"I don't see how they could," Joe said, slowly. "It's possible someone may have tipped them off if they overheard any of us talking about meeting up, but I think this has more to do with what happened when Reverend Jesse and I talked in the saloon."

"We've all been real careful," Mack affirmed, and Jeanette nodded.

"We have a pretty good handle on town gossip in our bakery," she said, "and we hadn't heard anything until Nellie approached us about joining. I don't think most folks are aware that a resistance is building."

"It's looking like that's how things are going to have to stay for now, then," Joe said. "I don't think we have time to try to add more members, not with Earl's gang right here in town. Who knows what they're planning to do? We're going to have to take action immediately."

Joe scanned the faces in the circle. They looked tense, but resolute. "I know we hadn't planned on things happening so soon," he continued. "This moves up our timeline by a lot, and we hadn't even put an actual plan into place, but they've brought the fight to our door, and we can't just hang around like sitting ducks, waiting for them to make the first move."

"So, you reckon we outta mount an attack on him?" Archie asked. "There's already more of 'em than us, so what can we do?"

Nellie's eyes were narrowed, her brow creased in deep thought. "Joe's right. If we don't make the first move, there's no tellin' where or how they might attack. A lot of innocent people could get hurt if there was a shootout in the middle of town—we can't have another Narrow Bluff."

The mention of Narrow Bluff sent a shiver through Jeanette, and she nestled herself tightly to her husband's side. "We can't ever have that again," she agreed softly. "It was so wrong. So tragic."

"Now, I'm not tryin' to say I don't agree with everyone, but even if we know we gotta take the gang out, that still don't solve how we're actually aimin' to do it," Archie butted in. "We need somethin' more solid."

"We need to find out where they're staying," Joe said firmly. "We can't plan an attack without that information, and knowing their location will help us know how to move forward. One thing is for sure—I can't be the one snooping around and figuring out where they are. They're most certainly here to find me, so I can't be putting myself into the open until we're ready to take them down."

Mack nodded. "You'd best stay hidden for now, Joe. Jeanette and I have a lot of business contacts in town because of our work. We can probably do some digging without causing any talk."

"Good," Joe replied. "We'll wait for your information, then. That means we'll need to meet back here again very soon, sometime tomorrow. We can't risk being seen coming into this barn, because it's supposed to be empty, so everyone keep a sharp eye out to make sure you're not being followed or watched."

The group agreed solemnly.

"Once we know where they are, I suppose our best shot is gonna be to try and take Earl out. Whether we capture him or kill him—and mind, my vote is to kill him—the gang won't be as dangerous without Earl to lead 'em," Archie said.

"Maybe if we can take care of him, there won't be so much bloodshed," Jeanette interjected. "It could keep a lot more people safe if there isn't a full battle."

"That's the hope, Jeanette," Joe agreed. "Too many have suffered already."

Joe suddenly remembered that Will was still with him. He turned and looked down to see that the boy had sat down on the ground with his back propped against a hay bale while the group was talking. Even with the excitement of sneaking around and seeing the bandits ride by, it was very late and Will's eyelids were drooping, though he was trying to stay alert and listen to the grownups' conversation.

"We need to get Will back to the boarding house," Joe said, looking back at the group. "I can take him back. Nan would be worried sick if she knew he had snuck out, and it's my fault for him following me."

"No," Nellie said almost immediately. "I know you mean well, but the bandits have come lookin' for you. It won't take 'em long to figure out where you're stayin', which means, Nan's place isn't safe for you anymore. And if you go back, you're just gonna put them all in danger. One of us will make sure he gets home safe."

"Nellie's right," Archie spoke up. "I don't think anyone has seen us together, Joe, and I'm stayin' on at the boardin' house, too. I can get Will home in one piece. I don't stand out much, and even if someone was to see me, and the bandits found out, well...I reckon they won't remember me from Narrow Bluff. They won't see an ol' saloon sweep like me as a threat."

Joe wanted to argue with them, and he didn't want to let Will out of his sight until he knew that he and his mother were safe. The group was right, though. His presence was too dangerous, and he would only be placing them in harm's way, even if he was as careful as possible getting Will back to the house. He wished his conversation with Reverend Jesse had never been overheard, but wishing didn't change the situation, now.

He nodded slowly. "Alright. Archie, you'll take Will back to Nan's, and I'll stay here for tonight." It felt somehow wrong to sit in hiding while the bandits roamed free, but he was determined not to let his pride compromise the safety of the others. "Mack and Jeanette, we'll wait to hear what you find out tomorrow. Nellie, be safe getting home tonight. Can you fill Louis in on what we've decided before you leave?"

Nellie nodded, and the group dispersed, leaving Archie, Will and Joe.

Joe bent down and crouched by Will, whose head was now lolling on his shoulder. He'd drifted off, but his eyelids snapped open as Joe touched his shoulder softly.

"I'm awake," he mumbled, rubbing his eyes.

"I know, son." Joe smiled wearily at him. "It's time for you to go on home. Archie's going to take you and make sure you get back safe."

"Aren't you coming, Joe?" Will asked, looking uncertain.

"I can't." Joe shook his head. "It's not safe right now. Will, what I'm about to say is very serious. I'm going to need you to be real grown up for me right now. Can you do that?"

Will sat up straight, his small face grave. "Yes, sir."

Joe's heart squeezed the tiniest bit at the young boy's readiness and bravery. "Will, you can't tell anyone what you saw and heard tonight. Not even your mother. If anyone hears, a lot of people could get hurt. Do you understand?"

Will nodded gravely. "I won't say a word. I swear, Joe." He raised his small hand to shake Joe's, and Joe wondered if that was something his father had taught him.

"Good boy," he said. "I'm counting on you."

Joe helped Will to stand, and said goodbye. Archie extinguished the dim lamp, signaling the end of the meeting. For just a moment, Will hesitated, and then he quickly gave Joe a shy hug.

"You're gonna get the bad guys," Will said quietly into Joe's shirt, before letting go. "Don't get hurt. Promise?" He ducked his head, a little embarrassed at his display of affection.

"I'll do my best," Joe promised, touched by Will's gesture.

Will nodded, and turned, hurrying to follow Archie to the barn door.

Joe watched as the old man and the little boy disappeared into the night, leaving him alone in the darkness.

15

The slight creaking of the barn door awoke Joe with a start, and he shot into a sitting position, heart racing. He blew out a sigh of relief as he saw Louis slipping into the barn and quietly closing the door behind him. With a quiet groan, Joe fell back onto the pile of hay he'd used as a makeshift bed.

He had spent most of the night considering plans to take out Earl, depending on a variety of scenarios that could possibly occur. His racing thoughts, plus the chilliness of the barn, meant that he didn't drop off to sleep until nearly dawn. His body was stiff from sleeping on the lumpy hay, reminding him that he wasn't quite as young as he used to be, when he could pretty near sleep on a cactus and wake up bright-eyed and bushy-tailed. Joe heaved himself back up to a sitting position and brushed off clinging bits of straw and dust as Louis approached him.

Louis was carrying a tin bucket, which he handed to Joe. "Brought you some food. It ain't much, but I figured you'd be just about starvin' by now."

Joe thanked him and looked inside the bucket. There was

a canteen, which he hoped was full of water—his tongue felt dry and sticky when he ran it over his teeth. Which reminded him that he wished he could brush them, but his things were back at the boarding house and niceties like that would have to wait. Pulling the canteen from the bucket, he uncorked and took a long swig. The icy water banished any of his lingering sleepiness and he could feel its cold trail as it snaked down his throat and to his stomach.

After he'd swallowed nearly half the contents of the canteen, he turned his attention back to the other contents in the bucket. A small bundle wrapped in a cloth napkin turned out to be an apple, a couple of boiled eggs, and a hunk of bread. The meal was small, but Joe was ravenous, and he tore into it.

The two men didn't speak as Joe began wolfing down the food. Louis didn't seem to be bothered by Joe's lack of manners, and Joe was, quite frankly, too hungry to care about eating with grace. Besides, they had far more important matters to discuss. After Joe had eaten enough to take the edge off his hunger, he slowed down his pace and asked a question around a mouthful of bread.

"Did Will and Archie make it home alright?"

Louis nodded. "I didn't go to the boarding house, but I saw Archie this morning on the street. We didn't talk, but he caught my eye and nodded. He was letting me know it had all gone off without a hitch."

"That's a relief," Joe said when he had managed to swallow his current bite. "Will's a good boy, so I think we can trust him not to talk about anything he saw or heard last night. Hopefully, Nan didn't notice he wasn't in bed."

"Archie'll tell us later today if she mentions anything.

Anyway, we'll cross that bridge if we come to it. As for right now, we need to find you another place to stay tonight. It's not safe for you to stay too long in one place. We can figure it out with the others when we meet here later today."

Joe washed the last bite of egg down with another long draw from the canteen, emptying it. "Sounds like a plan. I just hope everyone can get here without arousing suspicion— this meeting is happening in broad daylight, and we know the bandits are around. I trust everyone to use good sense in sneaking to the barn, but it's definitely riskier than a meeting after dark. It's a risk we have to take, though. No time left to waste."

Louis nodded seriously. "I can't believe it's actually happening," he said quietly, lost in thought.

"Taking care of Earl?" Joe asked.

"Yeah. I've wanted to get rid of these bastards for years, but I was just one person and I couldn't do it alone."

"You're not alone anymore," Joe said with quiet conviction. "Earl's grip on this town is about to end."

Louis's mouth tightened and his face darkened. "He's taken too much from me. From everyone," he added hastily, as Joe looked at him intently. Louis didn't elaborate on what Earl had done to him, and Joe didn't press him about it.

"Look, Joe, we all know we're risking our lives to fight this gang, but you should know that Earl is an incredible shot. He's known for it, and it's part of the reason no one wants to stand up to him. I've heard he can shoot a hole straight through the middle of an ace card from a hundred yards. His lieutenants are more than capable, too."

Joe took in this new information. He wasn't too surprised,

but the news that there was even more stacked against the group was disheartening.

"How many are in Earl's gang?" Joe asked.

"I don't know an exact number, but I'd say at least twenty-five men."

"We saw five ride in last night," Joe said, rubbing his chin in thought. "Maybe it's a good sign that he didn't bring in his whole posse with him. Might mean he's not so worried about the situation—it's likely he doesn't know that I have allies. We could use that to our advantage."

"It's not much, but it's an edge they don't know about. We might be able to catch them off guard," Louis agreed.

Just then, the door at the back of the barn opened, causing Joe and Louis to grab their pistols and watch the door in alarm. Mack and Jeanette hurried into the barn, and the two men released their pistols, sighing in unified relief. The couple looked around the barn and made their way over to Joe and Louis as they caught sight of them.

"We've got news," Mack spilled out hurriedly before he'd even gotten to the men.

Joe and Louis rose to their feet, waiting keenly for the promised information.

"We've figured out where Earl and his boys are holed up," Mack said. "They're staying at Todd Osborne's farm, just outside of town."

Louis nodded, clearly recognizing Todd's name. "How'd you find out?" he asked.

"We were very careful," Jeanette assured him. "We know most of the families in town, so we already had a good idea of what places had the space to house them, and we knew a few of the places they'd stayed in the past. We had it narrowed down to a couple of places."

The back door of the barn opened again, and this time Archie and Nellie stepped in. Joe silently cursed himself for not having set up a watch, and asked Nellie if she would be willing to serve as the guard for the meeting. She acquiesced and took up her station.

"Mack was just telling us that Earl and his gang are shacking up at Todd Osborne's place," Louis told Archie.

Archie took this in. "Makes sense. Todd's got space and it ain't but a few minutes' ride to the town. I reckon it's about half a mile. Mack, how'd you and Jeanette figure it out?"

"Todd was one of the people we thought might let him stay, so we checked how many horses he had stabled when we were making our early morning rounds. We drop off bread to some of the farms a couple of times a week," Jeanette explained.

"We're at his farm often enough, so we know how many horses he usually has. When we saw a lot more than usual... well, that tipped us off. We didn't actually see Earl and his boys, but we know they've got to be there," Mack said.

"Good work," Joe said eagerly, intrigued by the news. "I'm glad you two were able to get us this information without casting up suspicion." He began pacing, the wheels in his head turning quickly. "Do you know where they might be staying on Todd's land?"

"Todd's got a good number of outbuildings on his property, and there's a bunkhouse that's only in use when he hires on extra hands to help with his harvest. I'd be willing to bet he's got them holed up in there," Mack replied.

The speed of Joe's pacing increased as he took in this

information, and a bold idea began forming in his mind. It was risky, but it just might work.

He stopped pacing and faced the group. "I might have a plan," he said.

All eyes were fastened on him, and the only things that could be heard for a moment were the sounds of the town life floating in from the road.

"We're well past the point of being justified to shoot Earl and his men. They've killed, looted, blackmailed, stolen, and more. Most folks around here either lived through the terrible things they've done, or they've heard about it."

Archie snorted. "There ain't no love lost on Earl and his boys, that's a fact." He spit contemptuously off to the side and then folded his arms, settling back in to listen.

"Now, from what you've told me," Joe continued, "Todd Osborne's farm is at least half a mile from Widestone, which means there shouldn't be any bystanders if things get messy. And they almost certainly will get messy."

Silence settled on to the group as Joe's words hung in the air. He looked at them in the eye, one by one.

"I'll understand if any of you want to leave."

No one moved, and after waiting a moment, Joe nodded firmly and continued laying out his plan.

"Based on the group we saw ride in last night, we know that there are at least four bandits, plus Earl. We don't know if he has any of his goons planted in town, but we should probably assume that he does. It's going to be a fight. How many of you are willing and able to use a gun?"

Louis immediately stepped forward. "I'm a fair shot, and I'm not afraid to fight," he said, his voice dark and his eyes flashing. He was taut with decision, and Joe thought again of what Louis had said earlier—and what he had failed to say. Louis most certainly had an underlying personal motive for wanting to take the bandits down, and it was something more than just losing his business.

Archie had stepped forward, as well. "Me too, Joe."

Mack and Jeanette hadn't moved, and when Joe looked at Mack, he regretfully shook his head. "I wish I could help in that way, but I've never been a fighting man, or even a hunting man. I bake bread," he finished simply, lifting his shoulders in a small shrug.

"Don't worry about it, Mack," Joe said. "You and Jeanette have already given us a huge step up with Earl's location."

Stepping away from the group, Joe hurried to Nellie and asked her about her skill with a gun.

"I couldn't hit the long side of a barn from ten feet," she said, curving the side of her mouth in self-deprecation. She shook her head. "I'm sorry, Joe, it's just not a skill I would've had much use for in the Sporting House."

Joe felt his eyebrows raise at the new information, but he stayed silent. Nellie had been a prostitute back in Narrow Bluff? He supposed it matched up with some things about her general demeanor. This wasn't the time to get caught up on such minor details, though, so he nodded, "It's fine, Nellie, I just had to ask." He turned and went back to the rest of the group.

"Well, then. It's me, Louis, and Archie, which means, we're outnumbered." He paused, and the image of Sophie rose in his mind. He clenched his fist. Even if it meant certain death, he would not rest until he had gone after Earl and gotten his revenge, but he knew that the rest of the group might not be willing.

"I know I said it before, but I'll ask one last time: does anyone want to back out, now? This is going to be dangerous, and death is a very real possibility."

He hadn't even finished his sentence before Louis spoke up, saying, "I said I was in, and I meant it. I don't care what it costs." Archie nodded in agreement. His nod was shaky, but he didn't say anything.

Joe clapped his hands together once, briskly. "Let's set to work, then. We'll need to scout out the farm and get the lay of the land. We'll set up an ambush for a time when the bandits are likely to be leaving the farm. If we have cover, we can try to take Earl out, first, and that might discourage the rest of them from trying to fight us. If we're lucky, there may not be any more bloodshed."

"I never was one for takin' a shot from a hidin' place," Archie said. "It's the coward's way, but in this case, I'd say it's downright justified. Earl's a monster. He destroyed Narrow Bluff, and he didn't care who he killed in the process—he even killed the young'uns if they got in his way." He scowled darkly, his mouth twisting in rage. "He's got what's comin' to him."

"He's taken something from everyone here," Joe said quietly, and he knew everyone in the group was thinking about the things—and people—they had lost to Earl Gallagher and his thugs.

"One last thing, before we split up," Joe said. "I need a good description of Earl. We all need to know what he looks like, so whoever has an open shot can take it."

Jeanette spoke up. "I'll never forget what that...that *snake*...looks like." She shuddered. "Earl's a little shorter than you, Joe. Maybe an inch or two under six feet. He's got dark hair, and it's going gray around the edges. And his eyes." She paused again, taking a deep breath. "I'll never forget those eyes. They're brown, but that's not the first thing that comes to mind when I think of them. What I remember most is how cold they were."

Mack put his arm around Jeanette and pulled her close. He continued speaking when she stopped. "He's got a lean build. What sets him apart is his swagger. You'll be able to tell just by the way he rides."

Joe took this in and built a mental picture of Earl in his mind, memorizing the details so he wouldn't forget. He took a deep breath and looked at the faces staring back at him.

"Well, then. It looks like we've got a plan."

16

It FELT strange not to ride Goldie to Todd's farm, but the group had discussed whether or not to take horses to the ambush, at length. Archie had been for it, saying that horses gave them more speed if they needed to get out quickly, but Louis and Joe argued that they'd be able to hide themselves on the property better without horses to give them away. The farm was only a half mile away, an easy walking distance. If they really needed to get back to town quickly, they'd commandeer a few of Todd's horses. Reluctantly, Archie had finally agreed.

The three were now making their way to the farm. Though it wasn't far, it was taking longer than normal because they were trying to stick to any cover they could to stay out of sight as much as possible. They ducked into gullies, made their way through brush and groves of trees, and kept a sharp eye out for anyone passing by. So far, only one wagon had rolled by, and they'd been able to hide before it passed them.

The men remained largely silent, each lost in his own

thoughts, mentally preparing for the coming battle. Joe went through the location of his ammo and his two guns, just as he had at least fifty times already on their journey. He had his pistol on his gun belt, loaded and ready, as well as a rifle slung across his back. Archie and Louis were toting their weapons, as well.

Joe thought about the rest of the group waiting back in the town. He knew they hated just waiting, stuck back in Widestone, but there was really no other choice. If they came along without weapons and no way to help fight, they would be a liability. Joe couldn't be distracted trying to protect them, and fight Earl and his men, too.

"Todd's farm is just up ahead," Archie said quietly. "We're about to go into the valley, and you'll see it as we come over this hill."

"We need to find a good place to stake out," Joe said. "Our best bet is to wait for Earl and his men to come out of the bunkhouse and take them out from our hiding place. I don't think there's anything we can do to lure them out without putting them on their guard, so we might be in for a wait."

The men scanned the area, looking for the best places to hide. There was a stream cutting through the small valley, and in some places rocks and boulders were jumbled. Joe made note of the boulder clumps as a possible location for stake out. The stream made it slightly less ideal, as he didn't want to get caught in gunfire while trying to ford the stream or, God forbid, slip on the muddy banks.

Louis spotted a grove of trees a little ways from the bunkhouse where the men could each find cover and settle in. It was more of an unruly line of trees than an actual grove, and Joe guessed that Todd had left them as something of a windbreak. He noted that the ground was brushy beneath the trees, which would make for better camouflage.

"We'd better spread out," Archie said. "We'll have more angles to take Earl out if we ain't all in the same place."

Louis nodded. "I don't want that snake to have a single chance to get away. One of our bullets will find him," he vowed.

Joe looked at Louis and Archie, and he knew the determination in their faces matched the steel he felt in his own soul. They didn't wish each other luck or say goodbyes— to do so would seem final, like they weren't going to make it out alive. Instead, they simply nodded to each other, and wordlessly split up.

The three men made their way to their individual hiding spots carefully, spreading out from each other. Joe chose a spot in the line of trees and brush, settling down onto his belly. The brush rubbed and poked through his shirt uncomfortably. It made him itch all over, but he ignored it. This was the best hiding spot for now, as he had an unobstructed view of the bunkhouse, which meant a good angle for training his sights on Earl. He could no longer see Archie and Louis, but he knew they were close by and watching vigilantly.

The minutes ticked by slowly. Joe shifted ever so slightly, trying to find a more comfortable way to lie in the prickly brush, but it was no use. Time crawled by, and Joe's worried impatience mounted. He had assumed that Earl and his men wouldn't stay put in the bunkhouse after riding all the way out to find him. They had gotten in late the night before, and maybe they slept in late. He wouldn't be surprised if they kept lazy morning hours, seeing as how they made their living by leeching on the honest labor of others.

As the minutes continued to limp by, doubts crept in. Maybe the information from Mack and Jeanette wasn't correct, or maybe the bandits had arisen early and were already in town. He should've come up with a better plan, one that didn't rely so much on luck.

He cursed himself silently. How much longer should they wait before calling it quits and regrouping with Louis and Archie to come up with another strategy? More than an hour had passed already. Joe glared at the bunkhouse, as if he could force Earl to open the door and come out into the open from sheer willpower alone. Of course, nothing happened.

It was time to find Archie and Louis and make a new plan. He was just about to carefully push himself back to his feet when he heard the two men yelling frantically. Instantly, he was on high alert, and his brain worked swiftly to make sense of the two men's desperate shouts. The words clicked into place—the bandits were apparently heading *to* the farm, instead of away from it.

Joe whipped around, pulling his rifle off of his back and cocking it in one practiced movement. He turned just in time to see a man drawing on him, and he hurled himself out of the way in the nick of time. A bullet whizzed past his head and buried itself in the dirt right where he had been only milliseconds before. Dust sprayed from the impact, coating Joe's face and obscuring his vision for a moment.

Joe swore and squeezed off a shot in the direction of his shooter, then scrambled to put himself on the other side of the trees, boots catching in the brush as he tore through to the other side of the tree line. Their element of surprise had been completely neutralized, and they were the ones who had been caught unawares. Joe's heart felt the adrenaline coursing through his veins, and he fought to use it to sharpen his skills rather than letting it unravel him. He had learned that over years as a lawman, but he'd never been in a shootout so outnumbered.

Breathing hard, Joe kept his back to the tree behind him, and took a careful glance to the side to count the bandits. There were at least eight, which was far more than they had been expecting. He swore bitterly once again.

Shots rang around him. It was a full-on firefight now. Careful not to lose the cover of his tree, Joe aimed at one of the bandits and fired off a round. The bullet hit the man square in the chest, and the impact sent him flying backwards to land on the ground. A bandit near the fallen man started firing shots in Joe's direction, and he knew it wouldn't be long before they got close enough to hit more than the tree he was hiding behind.

Joe had no idea where Archie and Louis had fled for cover; everything was a mass of confusion in the barrage of bullets and gun smoke. Joe had one more round in his rifle chamber, and he knew he couldn't waste it. He needed to pick off another of the men before he had to find new cover to hopefully regain some of the lost element of surprise.

Assessing the situation in tiny spurts so as not to leave his head in the open, he whipped off a shot at another bandit, but he wasn't sure if he had hit his target. He desperately wanted to take Earl down, but he couldn't tell where the gang leader was in the haze of smoke and chaos. He needed to find a new spot without being seen so he could take in more of the situation.

Glancing around desperately, he spotted the grouping of boulders near the stream. He would have to run in the open for a moment, but he just might be able to make it without being seen in the confusion. He paused to reload his now-empty rifle. He wasn't sure anyone would be close enough for his pistol, so he'd better be ready. Just as he was hurriedly reloading the chamber, a bandit came around the edge of the trees, mere yards from him.

He leered at Joe, revealing crooked yellow teeth. He grinned gleefully at Joe's unprepared state. "Time to say yer goodbyes, boy," he said, cocking his gun and preparing to shoot Joe between the eyes.

Joe spun, dropping his rifle and reaching for his pistol, though he already knew he'd be too late. Time seemed to slow down as the regret hit him. This was it, he'd never have a chance to avenge his beloved sister. In fact, he hadn't even made a dent in their forces.

Before his gun could clear the holster, a loud gunshot rang through the air.

Joe blinked twice, confused by the scene in front of him.

The bandit was crumpled on the ground, a massive hole in the side of his head, blood seeping into the dirt below him. His glassy eyes stared unblinkingly ahead of him, forever blind.

Joe couldn't move for a moment, and he stood, stunned. How was he not dead? Archie and Louis were nowhere near, so who had saved his life? His mind, moving sluggishly from the shock of nearly dying and then being rapidly rescued, struggled to make sense of the situation.

A moment later, someone stepped into his field of vision, and Joe snapped back to reality. He reached for his pistol, scrambling to pull it from its holster, but he didn't bring it to bear on the man, as his face registered in Joe's mind. It was Milton Byers.

The deputy met Joe's eyes and he dipped his head wordlessly in acknowledgment of Joe's silent gratitude, before taking his position and lifting his gun to shoot at the rest of the bandits.

17

COMING BACK TO HIMSELF, Joe wedged his rifle into his shoulder and took aim at one of the bandits. Most of them had taken cover, as had this particular one, but he was taking cover in the direction of where Louis and Archie must be, and his left side was exposed to Joe. Joe felt more assured with Milton beside him, and the desperation he'd been feeling ebbed enough for him to tap into the sharp shooting skills he possessed.

Squeezing one eye shut, he trained his sights on the man's exposed side and fired. His aim was true, and the bullet sliced into the man's chest, right at the heart. The man died instantly, falling backward and lying still.

"Nice shot," Milton said, already reloading his own weapon and scanning the open area for another target.

The scene was still covered in smoke and raining bullets, but Joe could sense that the advantage was shifting from the bandits, back to him and his men. Joe quickly tallied how many bandits had fallen. At least four of the original eight were now dead, which cut Earl's team in half. Still, he wasn't sure if Louis and Archie were still alive, but he hoped against hope that they were.

Milton was a crack shot, and his weapon gave a loud report as he shot off another round. A bandit that had been running for cover now lay sprawled in the dust, half of his head blown off. Chunks of gray brain matter and sprays of blood coated the ground around him. The sight was grisly, and Joe's stomach lurched in spite of himself.

He looked at Milton, who glanced over at him, mouth tight.

"Have you seen Earl?" Milton asked him.

Joe shook his head. "I've killed at least two men, but I don't think either of them was Earl. Course, there's a lot of confusion, so it's possible, but I don't think so."

Milton nodded, scowling. "I wouldn't put it past him to put his men ahead of him in the fighting and save his own skin." He cocked his gun again, lifting it to his shoulder and surveying the scene once more. It had grown quieter, with only an occasional shot whizzing through the air. The lessening of the shooting was unnerving and a little eerie.

"Come on, boys!" someone shouted. "Let's get outta here!"

"Earl," Milton said.

"He's still alive," Joe said, his mouth twisting in anger and frustration.

He and Milton trained their guns at the ready, waiting for any bandits that might come out into the open, but they were fleeing quickly away from Joe and his men. Joe and Milton took shots after the men, but in the few moments the men were out in the open, they were already at a hefty distance. Joe and Milton had good aim, but even their shooting wasn't enough to tackle the guns' inability to fire accurately at such a long range.

Joe cursed bitterly, squeezing off another round at the fleeing back he thought might belong to Earl. The shot hit a tree and splintered the bark, showering bits of wood. It was nowhere near hitting the bandit. Joe lowered his rifle and had to force himself not to hurl it to the ground in frustration. He clenched his fists, biting back a volley of angry words.

It galled him that Earl was getting away. No, more than galled him. Fury and rage coursed through him, and he saw red for a moment. He sucked in a deep breath through his gritted teeth, and forced himself to unclench his muscles. He needed to clear his mind. Earl might have gotten away, but he had lost a good four or five of his men, and that was something. Now, he knew that Joe wasn't a force to be trifled with.

Of course, Joe was well aware that it wasn't just his own efforts that had sent the bandits into a retreat. He turned to Milton and looked at him appraisingly. "Milton, I misjudged you," he said, reaching out to shake the other man's hand. "You saved my life, and you're a damn good shot. Suppose I should've trusted my gut about you."

Milton shook his hand firmly. "No harm done. Glad I got here in time to be of service."

Joe hadn't had time to wonder how the lawman had appeared at the scene just in the nick of time, and he opened his mouth to ask how he'd known the battle was going down, but he was interrupted by the sound of a voice calling his name.

"Joe? Joe!"

It was Archie's voice. Joe turned, searching for him, and

soon he saw the other man through the trees. He and Milton headed towards him, and broke into a run as they saw that he was clutching his shoulder. His shirt was bathed in blood, and more blood bubbled up through his clenched fingers.

"Archie!" Joe yelled, reaching him.

He and Milton lowered Archie's trembling body to the ground. Archie's eyes were already glazing over from the pain, and Joe worried he might go unconscious.

"Stay with us, Archie," he said, fighting to keep his voice firm and calm. He needed to assess the situation and see how bad the wound was. "Archie, I need to look at it closer."

Gently, he shifted Archie so that he could see his back. There was a much smaller hole on the back of Archie's shoulder. It was bleeding, as well, but not as profusely as the gaping wound on the front. The hole was a relief to Joe. It meant that the bullet had gone straight through. Still painful, but at least Archie wouldn't have to endure the agony of having the bullet dug out of his flesh.

"We need to get his shoulder bound up and try to stop the bleeding," Joe said, already taking off his own shirt.

He ripped the shirt in half. The shirt was covered in dirt and sweat, but there was nothing clean that he could use. It would have to do until things cooled down enough that they could safely get Archie to a doctor. He took half of the shirt and ripped it into two pieces. Wadding up some of the ripped shirt, he pried Archie's fingers loose from their death grip on the front of the shoulder and immediately packed the front of the wound with the shirt, holding it firmly in place to help staunch the heavy flow of blood.

"Take the other small piece and pack the wound on the

back of his shoulder," he told Milton, who sprang into action, obeying Joe's directions.

"Hang on, Archie," Joe said, trying to keep the man conscious and calm.

Holding the cloth in place with one hand, Joe took the last piece of torn shirt he had and began wrapping it carefully around Archie's shoulder. He circled it above the shoulder and looped it below the armpit, wrapping it tightly until there was no fabric left, then tied it off. Archie winced, but he didn't cry out.

"Sorry, Archie," Joe said as he finished. "I have to keep it tight so it will stop bleeding."

Archie began to nod to show his understanding, but stopped from the pain and merely rasped, "Don't worry 'bout me, Joe."

"What happened? Did you see who got you?" Milton asked him.

Archie closed his eyes for a moment, breathing shallowly through the pain. "It was Earl."

18

THE MOST URGENT thing to do, Joe surmised, was to get Archie back to town and get his wound cleaned and rebandaged with clean linen. Archie's face was pale beneath his usual tan, and his teeth were chattering a bit despite the heat and the sweat glistening on his forehead.

"I can walk," Archie said, gritting his teeth against the pain. "It ain't that bad."

"Hush up, Archie," Joe replied, firm but kind. "That's never going to work. Someone needs to stay here with Archie while someone else runs back to town. Mack and Jeanette have a wagon, and that'll be the easiest way to get Archie back to the barn."

"I can do it," Louis volunteered. "I'll be back soon with help." He barely waited for Milton and Joe to agree to the plan before he was sprinting, at a remarkable speed for someone of his stature, the half mile back to Widestone.

"Let's hope Earl's gang doesn't come back for a second round," Milton said quietly to Joe, his eyes sweeping the area for signs of danger.

Joe agreed grimly. "If he comes back now, there's a bullet with his name on it," he growled, then sighed. "You're right, though. We're in no position to fight right now."

The men remained largely quiet while they waited for help to roll in, both on high alert for any sign of Earl and his men. Joe kept a sharp eye on Archie's condition, as well. Archie was resting with his eyes closed, his brow furrowed, but he didn't say anything. Joe noted with relief that his color was improving with the opportunity for rest and now that the bleeding had been staunched. Archie was no longer so pale, and he was breathing a bit easier.

After about half an hour, Milton's spine jerked straight, his full body at attention as he listened. "I think I hear wagon wheels," he said to Joe. "I've got a hand on my gun, but I'd bet it's Mack."

Joe could hear the wheels now, too. He shaded his eyes and watched as the wagon appeared over the hilltop and started into the valley. A man and woman sat at the front of the wagon, with a man standing in the bed behind them, waving his hat.

"That's Louis waving," he said.

A minute later, the wagon rolled up beside them and Mack pulled the horses to a stop. Louis was already jumping off the wagon, and Jeanette was looking at Archie with worried concern.

"How's he doing?" she called to Joe.

"Better than he was at first," Joe replied. "We'll know more when we get to the barn. We need to hurry."

He, Milton, and Louis gathered around Archie, ready to lift him as gently as they could into the wagon bed. Joe supported Archie's upper back, careful not to pull on the injured shoulder. Milton and Louis each lifted one of Archie's legs. Together, the three men hefted Archie onto a blanket Jeanette had waiting at the edge of the wagon bed. Once Archie was settled on the blanket, the men hopped into the bed and pulled the blanket so that Archie was safely in the bed and near the driver's bench. Through all of the shifting, Archie clenched his teeth, only emitting one quiet groan, but otherwise biting back his screams.

The ride back to Widestone was short, but it must have seemed an eternity for Archie. Joe saw how every jolt over a rock or uneven rut in the road jostled the wounded man and sent pain shooting through his frame. Finally, they rolled into the edge of town by the church and headed for the barn. It was a quieter edge of town, and there weren't too many people about, which was a relief, as there was no hiding the group of people hauling a bandaged man into an abandoned barn.

"I brought supplies," Jeanette said, bustling in after the men with her arms full. "I've got alcohol to clean the wound, and clean fabric we can use for bandages. I'm going to need some of you to help hold him down while I clean his shoulder."

Louis nodded, eyes grim. "It's gonna hurt like the dickens, but it's gotta happen." He and Joe settled by Archie, ready to brace the man, while Milton went to the door to stand guard.

Jeanette took a small piece of clean cloth and poured alcohol on it, talking soothingly to Archie as she worked. "Archie, I know you wouldn't believe it, but I've done this before. Mack cut his leg with an ax while chopping logs years ago, and I was the only one on the homestead to tend to him."

She unwrapped his shoulder and gently lifted the packed cloth on the front of his shoulder, then gently began to mop up the dried blood caked around the bullet hole.

Archie hissed through his teeth as the alcohol-soaked rag came into contact with the jagged edges of the hole in his shoulder, but he didn't scream. That didn't occur until Jeanette had to pour some of the alcohol directly into the wound; then, the screams were as a wild man, and he thrashed violently. Joe and Louis had to hold him down with all their strength to keep Archie from further tearing his wound.

"Shh, shh," Jeanette hushed him gently, her eyes now glistening with tears. "I'm almost finished. It will be over soon." Her practiced fingers worked more quickly, cleaning the rest of the old blood. She folded a length of clean cloth and packed it gently against the now-clean wound. It was no longer bleeding as much, and she looked at Archie, trying to smile. "It's not as bad as we thought, at first, Archie. It's not bleeding too bad anymore."

Archie couldn't reply at the moment, but he was much calmer now that the cleaning was over and the burning had subsided. He was able to lie quietly while Jeanette finished packing both sides of the wound and rewrapped his shoulder in clean bandages. Mack lifted his head so that Archie could gulp down a shot of whiskey for the pain. The liquor helped Archie to relax a bit, and he was no longer breathing in ragged gasps.

"I know that wasn't pretty," Jeanette said to Joe quietly as she began cleaning up her supplies, "but I think it should heal up fine. I don't think we need to send for a surgeon."

"You're a good lady, Jeanette," Joe replied with gratitude.

"You and Mack likely saved Archie's life by bringing him back to town and getting him cleaned up."

Jeanette shrugged off his praise. "Anything we can do to be of help. Archie just needs some rest, now. I'll take these things home and get rid of them," she said, referring to the bloodstained cloths, "and bring him back some food."

Joe thanked her, and she nodded once. She and Mack loaded up the wagon and left, Milton closing the door behind them. He headed over to Joe and Louis, who had settled themselves onto the ground next to Archie and was watching over the man. Archie's eyes were closed, and Joe suspected the man would slip into an exhausted sleep soon.

"I don't think anyone saw us," Milton said to Joe as he neared. "No one seemed to notice all the movement by the barn."

"Good," Joe said. "Milton, something has been on my mind now that I've had a moment to breathe. How did you find out about the shootout?"

"That was a stroke of luck, as it turns out. Earl and his men had been at the sheriff's office this morning, so I learned that Earl had been keeping their horses at Todd's farm but they hadn't actually slept there. I think they were aiming to trick you, in case you'd found out they were in Widestone."

Joe groaned as he heard Earl's wily plan. If the men he'd brought with him had shot a little more accurately, or if Milton had never shown up, things could easily have gone a lot worse for their resistance. "So, he was a step ahead from the beginning."

"When Earl and his men left Pennington this morning, I thought I'd better follow them to see where they were heading. Of course, I didn't know about the ambush. I kept my distance, but I trailed them to Todd's farm."

"Good thing, too," Joe said. "Your good instincts saved my life."

Milton shrugged. "Right place, right time. I did what had to be done."

Joe didn't offer any further thanks, not because it wasn't felt, but because he could sense that Milton wouldn't want the praise. The man was clearly built for seeking justice, and, in his mind, he had done what any right-minded person would have done.

"We need to make a plan for fighting Earl." Joe started as the barn door opened, and Nan stormed in.

Joe, Milton, and Louis scrambled to their feet, surprised at her entrance. Her face was a mask of anger, and Joe's stomach sank.

"Looks like I should've kept an eye on the door," Milton muttered to Joe. "I'll just head back to guard it again."

Joe nodded wordlessly and braced himself for Nan's impending outburst.

"Joseph. Chambers." Her voice was nearly shaking with rage. "Who the *hell* do you think you are?!"

"Whoa," Joe said, holding up his hands, trying to stem the tide of her fury. "Nan, what's going on?"

"As if you don't know! Will told me everything—"

Joe groaned, rubbing a hand across his face, but Nan barreled on.

"Yes, he did, and he was right to tell me! I'm his mother! He couldn't very well keep it a secret—word is spreading all over town about the shootout on Todd's farm this morning!"

"Nan, I can explain," Joe said hurriedly. "Take a breath, now."

Her eyes bulged and she opened her mouth to continue her tirade. Joe raised his hands again in surrender and apologized before she could begin, knowing instantly he had said the wrong thing.

"I'm sorry. Let me try again—I can explain what happened," he said, as calmly as he could. He looked to Louis and over at Milton, who both nodded.

"Best to tell her," Louis said.

Joe took a deep breath and began. "Some of us have formed a group to take Earl and his gang out. We've been meeting to plan and to add members. Will followed me here one night and overheard our plans. Nan, I promise, I would never knowingly put him into danger. That's why I wasn't the one who took him home that night, and why I haven't been back to your place since."

Nan's chest was still rising and falling rapidly, but now her eyes widened in surprise. "Joe, that's not why I'm so angry. I know you'd never put Will in danger, and I know it's not your fault that he overheard."

Joe was taken aback. "Then..."

"I'm angry because you didn't tell me about any of this. You've trusted all of these other people, but not me!"

"Nan, I didn't want to put you in danger. I care about you and Will, and you've already been through so much. You have a business and you have a child. You're all he has left. I couldn't risk that," he said quietly.

"That wasn't your choice to make!" she said, her voice quiet, but also taut with intensity. "My husband died trying to protect this town, and I want these bandits gone as much as everyone else. We've all lost something, and it's dangerous for all of us."

"You're right. We have all lost something," Joe said, but he didn't apologize. He still felt that if he had to go back, he would do the same thing. He never wanted Nan to be placed in harm's way.

"You should have added me to the group," she continued. "Why is it the right thing for you to do, and not for me? You think I should be less involved because of Will, but that's exactly why I *should* be involved—if we don't stand up to the bullies, then what kind of world are we leaving behind? Will needs to see that good people will always fight back."

Nan folded her arms around her thin body, her fist clenched. Her chin was raised and defiant, her green eyes flashing with determination. "Don't you *ever* think about trying to leave me out of this again. I'm here to fight, and you can't stop me."

19

EARL SWORE BITTERLY and fluently to himself. He'd been doing so in regular intervals for the past hour, as wave after wave of anger washed over him. He'd been made to look a fool, and Earl Gallagher was never the fool. He'd had Joe and his ramshackle group outnumbered by a good amount, and yet, somehow, they'd still lost the fight. They'd had to run away licking their wounds, like a whining dog kicked by an angry master. The mental image filled him with mortified, impotent rage, and he swore again.

Larry, who had been walking beside him, lagged a little at the fresh spew of vitriol from Earl's lips. He had been in Earl's gang long enough to know that Earl, always volatile, was at his worst in moments like these. Larry clearly hoped to avoid having that rage turned against him by hanging back and taking up as little of Earl's attention as possible, but his strategy backfired.

Earl turned on him. "Why're you hangin' back like a yella-bellied coward? What, you scared or somethin'?"

Larry shook his head and hurried to walk at Earl's side once more. He knew it was useless to try and defend himself. Earl continued muttering his furious diatribe to himself.

"We shoulda had 'em cornered. They were *ours* for the takin' and what happened? They sent us runnin' for the hills!" He finished with a string of such salty language that even Larry was amazed that Earl could string so many profanities together and in such an imaginative way. Larry didn't say anything, aside from nodding and agreeing with everything Earl said.

In this way, they eventually arrived at Sheriff Pennington's office. Earl slammed the door open, and it hit the inner wall with a crash. Sheriff Pennington, who had been lounging at his desk with his boots up, jumped in surprise, his boots scrambling off the desk as he stood, looking at Earl fearfully. Larry closed the door behind Earl and leaned against it with folded arms, staring Sheriff Pennington down hard.

Earl's chest was rising and falling with his furious breathing. "Pennington, you fool!" he screamed. "I warned you!"

"Earl, what're you talkin' about?" The sheriff's eyes were wide with fear, and his hands were raised, almost a gesture of surrender.

"Your deputy," Earl bit out, grinding his teeth.

"Milton?" Sheriff Pennington seemed to be having a difficult time keeping up.

Earl strode around the desk, grabbing the sheriff's shirtfront in his fists, giving a good shake, before pushing the man down into his chair. He shoved his face right into the other man's and spoke now with dangerous quiet. "Of *course*

I'm talkin' about Milton, you idiot. I warned you about him. Told you he was too straitlaced. Told you he'd cause trouble with his old-fashioned ideas about *justice*." He spat out the last word with dripping sarcasm.

"Milton's a good deputy," the sheriff sputtered. "I only kept him on 'cause he does most of the work and takes care of everythin' for me."

"Your laziness cost me!" Earl shouted now, flecks of saliva landing on Sheriff Pennington's face. He was too petrified to wipe them off, and the spit slid down his cheek, untouched.

"That goody-two-shoes killed two of my men!" Earl continued. "We had Joe 'n his boys good and licked, and Milton got in the way!"

"What're you talkin' about, Earl?" the sheriff asked. Confusion mingled heavily with his fear.

"Course you wouldn't know," Earl mocked him. "You're always shootin' the breeze in here! Mind you, that's the way we want it, most of the time, but today you made a big mistake, boy."

Sheriff Pennington flushed scarlet at the insults, but he didn't stand up for himself, and Earl continued his explanation.

"We went back to Todd's farm this morning for our horses, and we found Joe 'n some of his boys waitin' to trap us in an ambush. We caught 'em by surprise, and had 'em real scared—outnumbered eight to three. We shoulda won, but Milton came in and turned the tide. Which means, you're to blame!"

"What can I do?" the sheriff asked fearfully. "I'm sorry about yer men, Earl, but I couldn't have known—"

Earl cut him off. "Shut up!" he growled, and the sheriff stopped speaking.

Earl now stepped back, inhaling deeply and closing his eyes. A disquieting calm seemed to settle over him, and the sheriff shivered as Earl smiled dangerously.

Opening his eyes, Earl spoke with calm deliberation. "You're gonna put bounties out for Joe Chambers and your deputy, Milton. There were other men, but I don't know who they are. More's the pity."

The sheriff looked like he was going to protest, and Earl speared him with a glare. "And you'll put those bounties out. Do you know why?"

Slowly, Sheriff Pennington shook his head. His knuckles were white from clenching the arms of his chair.

"Well," Earl said in a silken voice, laden with relish at his own words. "If you don't do as I say, you might just go home to find somethin' you wouldn't like much." He paused, here, and slowly pulled a knife from its sheath on his belt, never breaking eye contact with the sheriff. Gently, almost lovingly, he stroked the edge of the knife. "I wouldn't want anything to happen to those kiddies you got at home. Little Tommy has to be ten by now, don't he? And your little girl is almost seven, now, isn't she?"

The sheriff was shaking now, eyes bulging in terror at the threat. He swallowed hard.

"Ah, what was her name?" Earl mused theatrically, clearly enjoying himself, now. "Lily, was it?" He didn't wait for the sheriff to answer. "She's growin' into a pretty little thing, ain't she?" He smiled lasciviously, and the sheriff looked like he was going to be sick.

130

"Now then. What were you sayin' about those bounties?" Earl asked.

Sheriff Pennington opened his mouth to speak, but at first, nothing came out. He tried once again, and this time, had more success, although his voice was strangled. "I'll get those made right away, sir."

Earl's face split into a grin, and he walked around the desk to clap the sheriff on the shoulder. The sheriff jumped at the touch, but he sat stiffly under Earl's grasp, too afraid to move. "Good boy," Earl smiled cruelly. "I knew you'd see reason."

Giving the sheriff one last shake, Earl let go and headed for the door. He paused, turning back one last time. "Oh, and Sheriff? Try not to mess this up, will ya?"

Sheriff Pennington sat frozen, and Earl smirked. Larry guffawed, clearly trying to garner Earl's approval.

"Shut up, Larry," Earl growled, his smirk sliding off his face. "We got work to do."

Larry shut his mouth and glared at the sheriff before opening the door for Earl and following him out into the street, leaving it hanging open for the sheriff to shut.

"We need to go get the rest of the gang," Earl said to Larry. "Looks like I shoulda brought 'em from the start." He shook his head, looking around the street in thought. "I underestimated the people in this town," he mused. "Apparently, they've forgotten the lesson I taught 'em in Narrow Bluff. Larry, I reckon they might need a little reminder of who's in charge."

Larry agreed with his boss quickly. "What should I do?" he asked, straightening his thin shoulders importantly.

"Go get the rest of the boys, and bring our horses from the farm. Bring 'em to me."

Larry nodded. "What are you gonna do, sir?"

Earl turned on him, and Larry instantly knew he'd made a mistake. "That's not for you to question! Do as you're told."

Larry apologized, backpedaling quickly. "I'll just go get the horses, then," he mumbled, and Earl ignored him. Seeing that he wouldn't get a response, Larry quickly hurried off down the dusty street to follow Earl's orders.

Earl headed for the saloon, stepping onto the shaded boardwalk. He deserved a break after the fiasco of the morning, and he wasn't about to let the townspeople think he was slinking off into hiding because of the shootout.

Some people in Widestone were trying to fight him, whipped up by that meddling Joe Chambers. He hadn't expected Joe to have any support, but that was a mistake he would not make again. Joe and any of his supporters would go the way of Joe's stupid sister, and all the others who had opposed him in Narrow Bluff.

Earl pushed open the swinging doors of the saloon, and walked in with his usual swagger. "Whiskey," he barked at the bartender, who jumped into action, much to Earl's private satisfaction. He took the glass the bartender handed him and knocked it back, swallowing the fiery liquor. He slammed the empty glass down, and tapped it in silent command. The bartender quickly refilled the glass.

Earl took the time to savor this one, enjoying the warmth spreading through his body, smoothing away some of the embarrassment from the morning's failure. "Keep 'em comin'," he told the bartender, heading over to a table where he could stretch out his legs and relax. He didn't bother to pay for the drinks, and the cowed bartender knew better than to protest or ask him to.

Earl was in charge, and it looked like some people had forgotten that. Well, he was going to make everyone in Widestone remember what it meant to move against Earl Gallagher.

20

"JOE...? Joe? Are you listening to me?"

Joe jumped a bit, and his eyes focused in on Nan's face. She was standing in front of him, a crease between her eyebrows and her hands on her slender hips.

He rubbed a hand over his face, trying to brush away the mental fog, and sighed. "Sorry, Nan. I haven't gotten much sleep lately. What were you saying?"

Nan's expression softened, and her hands slipped off her hips to gently touch his arm. "You're being worn to a thread," she said, her eyes warm and alive with concern.

For a moment, he covered her hand with his own, noticing how much smaller hers was than his own large, calloused hand. He squeezed it gently, then released it. Nan blushed a little, but she didn't comment on the touch.

"I was telling you that Archie made it back to my place safely. He'll be more comfortable in his room there, and it'll be easier to keep him taken care of."

Joe nodded appreciatively. "Glad to hear Louis was able to get him there last night. With Sheriff Pennington's lawmen patrolling the streets, it's gotten even more tricky to move around."

It was true. The situation in Widestone had gone from bad to worse when Sheriff Pennington had publicly announced a bounty on both him and Milton. Posters hung around town, offering a reward for their capture. If there had ever been a sliver of doubt that the sheriff was under the thumb of Earl Gallagher, that doubt had been thoroughly dispelled. He was no longer even trying to pretend to serve and protect the interests of the town; instead, he had his lawmen prowling the streets, keeping an eye out for Joe and Milton. Luckily, he didn't seem to know about any others in the group, which meant Earl and his gang didn't know any more specifics about who was on their side. That was the only thing Joe's team had going for them.

"Is there anything I can bring you or Milton, next time I bring food?" Nan asked, breaking into his thoughts once again.

Joe pondered the question for a moment, eating the last bite of the roast beef sandwich she had brought him when she'd first arrived, and washing it down with a gulp from the canteen of water that had accompanied it. "See if you can get word to Louis, Mack, Jeanette, and Nellie to meet here when it's dark. We need to come up with our next steps."

Nan nodded. "I can do that."

"And Nan? Don't always be the one to bring food and supplies here for Milton and me. It's too risky, and I don't want anyone getting suspicious about this barn. Bring whatever food and water you can spare when you come back tonight, and from here on out we'll have different people in the group take turns bringing supplies after dark. I don't want anyone to notice you leaving the boarding house so much."

"I'll see to it. Get some rest, Joe. We need you fresh to help us weather this storm." Nan's eyes were compassionate, but determined, as she spoke. "I've got to get back to take care of the lunch rush. I'll be back tonight with the others."

Joe watched her leave, her graceful figure slipping out of the back door of the barn. She was a strong woman, and Joe allowed himself a moment to appreciate and admire her. She was right, though—if he didn't catch up on some sleep, he would be useless moving forward.

Milton was out cold on a pile of hay in a darker corner, his hat pulled over his face to block any sunlight filtering into the barn. He'd been asleep all morning. Joe hated to wake him, but someone had to be on watch at all times. Joe woke him, and Milton shot up, scrabbling for his pistol.

"Easy, Milton," Joe calmed him. "It's just me. It's your turn for watch."

Milton scrubbed the sleep from his eyes with one hand, and shook his head wearily, pushing himself to his feet.

"Nan left you a sandwich and some water. It's in the bucket by the door."

Milton nodded wordlessly and shuffled to his post by the door, stretching as he went. By the time he got to the door, he was already regaining the usual alertness that marked him as an expert lawman.

Joe settled into the hay and, like Milton, pulled his hat over his eyes, welcoming the darkness. His whole body ached with weariness, and it felt as though someone had rubbed sandpaper across his eyes. With a quiet groan, he exhaled and forced himself to put aside thoughts of Earl and his gang. The most productive thing he could do right now was sleep.

~

"Joe, wake up."

Swimming through layers of sleep, the whispered direction and a touch on his shoulder pulled Joe back to the surface and to consciousness. Joe blinked and his eyes pulled Nan's face into focus. She was crouched over him once again, shaking him gently.

Joe sat up, biting back a yawn. He rubbed his eyes. "Is it nightfall already?"

Nan nodded, and then her eyes crinkled with a delighted smile, and a giggle escaped from her. Joe suddenly felt foolish.

"What is it? Is something funny?" he asked.

"Your hair is sticking up all over the place like Will's does in the morning." She bit back another laugh.

Joe couldn't help matching her smile as he reached up and tried to smooth his hair down into a semblance of order. Nan's smile faded and her eyes became serious.

"Everyone's here, they're all waiting on the other side of the barn," she said, rising out of her crouch and offering him a hand.

He took it, and clambered to his feet. "Lead the way."

They approached the group, huddled around the same small lamp as before. Louis was standing guard at the door, and he nodded at Joe as they passed, before turning his full attention back to keeping watch. Nellie, Mack and Jeanette, and Milton were talking among themselves as Joe and Nan approached, their faces serious. They looked up and grew silent, waiting for Joe to lead them.

"I guess we'll just get to it, then," he said, looking from face to face. "I suspect that Earl isn't in town anymore, or one of you would've seen him by now. It's not like the sheriff is hiding his allegiance, at this point. If Earl is gone, that means he's likely going to be back soon, but this time with reinforcements."

The gravity in his voice was reflected in the eyes of everyone watching him. He knew they understood the implication of what he'd just said, but he voiced it anyway.

"We can't risk facing his entire gang at once. Not after what happened at Todd's farm. There just aren't enough of us to take his whole posse down by ourselves. We've been cautious up until now, but that time has passed. We need to recruit more townspeople to our side, and we need to do it fast. Any ideas?"

Milton spoke up. "Like most of you, I've suspected Sheriff Pennington wasn't a straight shooter for a while now. I've been compiling evidence against him and holding on to it, just in case there would come a time when I could put it to good use. Looks like now's the time."

"That's brilliant, Milton," Nan said. "I'm not surprised, of course. My husband always spoke highly of you." She paused for a moment, thinking. "If we were able to spread that evidence around, get people to listen...it just might help us win the town over. Especially with the bounties on you and Joe. Folks around here know you're a good man, Milton. They're surely confused as to why Pennington posted it, especially since news about the shootout has spread."

"That should help tip the balance," Joe agreed. "Once people see that this isn't the first time the sheriff has aided the bandits, they might not want to back him anymore."

"I know some folks, like us, have already been seeing the similarities between what happened at Narrow Bluff and what's happening here," Mack chimed in. "There'll be more who want to take action against Earl when they see Milton's evidence against the sheriff."

"How are we going to spread the word, though?" Joe asked. "We can't just go out in the town square and shout it for all of Widestone. Pennington would squash that immediately."

"I think we can help you there," Jeanette said. She'd been listening quietly up until this point, but all eyes turned to her, now. "Mack and I have our rounds for bread deliveries, and we see people in our shop all the time. Folks trust us. We could start planting some rumors here and there, bringing up Narrow Bluff, too, and how it's starting to feel the same here in Widestone."

"I can do the same," Nan jumped in. "I have all of my lodgers, of course, but plenty of folks stop in for meals, as well. Gossip's traded all the time in my dining hall, and I can see to it that some useful gossip is spread around."

Joe frowned, wanting to argue. He didn't love the idea of the three potentially exposing themselves by trying to disseminate Milton's evidence in that way, but he had to admit that they were in the best position to do so without arousing suspicion.

"I say we don't just do that," Milton said, his voice hard

and determined. "I think we should also take the evidence to the mayor directly."

Everyone looked stunned at Milton's words. The idea was so bold, and very risky.

Milton forged on. "Even if he's already bought and paid for, there's nothing worse the bandits can do to this town than what they're likely already planning to do. If you think about it, Earl's removed our one reason for holding back and maintaining the status quo."

Joe nodded slowly. "I think you're onto something, Milton."

"The mayor and I are on good terms," Mack said. "I'll visit him in the morning."

"Are you sure, Mack?" Joe asked. "You and Jeanette have done so much already."

"I'm sure," Mack responded, and Jeanette nodded, as well, her shoulders straight and strong. "We meant it when we said we would do anything we could to help."

"We have a plan, then," Joe said, looking at the group in the dim lamplight. "Everyone, be careful getting home tonight. Nan, Mack, and Jeanette, be extra careful with how you plant that gossip."

The three of them nodded, and Joe noticed that Nellie was looking strained and uncomfortable. She hadn't spoken at all during the meeting, which was unusual for her. He wondered if she, like himself, felt frustrated at the lack of meaningful ways to help the cause, currently. He chafed against his forced inactivity, and he commiserated with her if she felt the same.

The group stood to leave, and Mack and Jeanette headed for the door, as the group would leave in staggered intervals.

Just then, Louis hissed at them to wait, one hand raised in warning. Everyone froze, tension snapping through the air. Louis's posture relaxed a moment later, and he wordlessly beckoned someone inside the barn.

To Joe's surprise, Reverend Jesse walked into the dimly lit barn and asked, "What can I do to help?"

21

BEFORE HE COULD STOP HIMSELF, a bark of derisive laughter escaped from Joe's mouth. It was a hard and contemptuous sound, and Reverend Jesse stiffened slightly at the response, but he didn't leave. Joe could feel himself flushing with anger—heat spread up and down the sides of his neck, leaving the skin blotchy and red.

"Since you can't go back in time and choose *not* to ruin the lives of everyone in Narrow Bluff, how about you just get your sorry hide out of here."

Joe was surprised to hear the venom in Mack's voice, and for a moment, it filtered through his own rage. Mack was glaring at the preacher with pure hatred, a far cry from his usual mild expression. His fists were clenched at his sides, and Jeanette was holding his arm fiercely, as if to hold him back. Her mouth was twisted and clamped shut, though, and Joe could easily tell she was holding back some anger of her own, as well.

Glancing at the others, Joe saw that all of them, except Nan and Milton, were having similar reactions of anger. The group was most certainly not happy to see Reverend Jesse. The preacher looked almost ill, and he swallowed hard, his Adam's apple bobbing violently.

"What is going on here?" Milton finally asked, breaking into the tension. "Can someone please explain why we don't want Reverend Jesse's help?"

"Where to start, where to start..." Nellie said sarcastically, tapping her chin with one finger. "How 'bout the part where this so-called *preacher*," this was said with dripping sarcasm, "is actually one of Earl's goons?"

At this, Louis rushed at the preacher, and for a moment it seemed like he was going to strike the man. Reverend Jesse flinched, lifting his arms to block the blow. It never came. Louis stared at the cowering man, his chest heaving, before turning on his heel and storming out of the barn. Joe understood Louis's anger, or at least, he thought he did. He wasn't sure, though, what had happened to Louis that would make it impossible for him to remain in the presence of the preacher.

Nan's face was white with shock, a hand to her throat. She stared at Reverend Jesse in disbelief, shaking her head over and over. "No," she finally whispered. "This can't be true. I can't believe it."

"There's a reason we don't go to church here in Widestone," Jeanette snapped. "We won't go listen to a fraud preach sermons." She had been speaking to Nan, but now she turned to the preacher and spoke directly to him. "I don't know how you find the nerve to pretend to know God after the things you've done. I'll never forget what you've done. Never." The last part was spoken with finality. Joe couldn't help but notice how strange it was to see the compassionate Jeanette so full of hatred.

Reverend Jesse lifted his hands, as if in supplication, before letting them drop limply to his sides. His eyes were hollow with pain, and he dropped his head sorrowfully. The group stared at him silently, waiting for him to take his leave, but the man stayed in his place. Finally, he looked up.

"I know I can never undo the past, but I'm a changed man. The things I saw—the things I *did*—in Narrow Bluff...it changed me. God changed me. I made a vow to serve God and His children for the rest of my life, to do all I could to right the wrongs I'd done." He paused here, looking from face to face. "I know you might never forgive me, and that's a penance I will have to live with for the rest of my life. I know I can't make you believe me, but it's all true. I have devoted my life to God, but the courage I've witnessed in the resistance of this group has shown me that my passive role is not enough."

Reverend Jesse began pacing now, no longer able to keep still, swept up in the conviction of what he was saying. "You inspired me—all of you—and I began praying and pondering about what I should do. God has shown me that I need to take a direct role in stopping Earl and his men. Jesus commands us to love our enemies, but even God strikes down the wicked." His voice was strong with passion and fervor, his eyes blazing with zeal as he continued. "I am still a God-fearing man, but that doesn't mean I won't follow God's pattern from the Old Testament to rid this town of evil. Even Jesus used violence, at times. For a greater good, it is sometimes God's way."

His words rang out in the silence of the barn and seemed

to echo for a moment over the tense group. Jeanette looked away from the preacher, shaking her head. Reverend Jesse's words had clearly not swayed her heart, but she didn't speak up again.

"What about the children you're taking care of?" Joe challenged him. "I thought you said they were the reason you couldn't be involved."

"They're safe," the Reverend assured him, taking a step toward Joe. He seemed to take the question as a sign of softening. "I had to know they would be away from the danger, so I placed them in the care of a trusted friend. He left with them this morning to go a town over until things pass and it's safe to return to Widestone."

Though that obstacle was removed, Joe was still loath to accept the preacher's help. He rubbed his chin in frustration. The image of Sophie's gentle face floated across his vision, and Joe had to force himself to stand still and not attack Reverend Jesse. The Reverend may not have killed his sister, but he'd stood, counting the killers as allies, and had done nothing to stop it. In Joe's eyes, that made him equally responsible. Breathing deeply through his nose, Joe closed his eyes and fought to clear his mind. If he truly wanted to avenge Sophie and help save Widestone, he needed to use whatever means were at his disposal—and that included trusting this man.

Reverend Jesse could be useful in helping to spread the information about Sheriff Pennington throughout the town. As the Reverend of the town's only church, his reach went far beyond what any of the others could manage. Joe opened his eyes, and saw that the group was watching intently for his decision. The Reverend, too, had his gaze locked on Joe, waiting for an answer. Slowly, Joe nodded, and the preacher's face lit up.

"We can't make this decision ourselves," Milton interjected here, his voice firm. "It's not for us to decide. He should be locked up for his crimes and stand trial in a court. A judge should decide his fate. It's the only way to do this right."

Joe shook his head. "Your commitment to justice is what makes you a good lawman, Milton, but the situation in Widestone is too dire for that. We need the preacher's help now." Joe continued on, seeing that Milton was starting to protest. Lifting a hand, he said, "I'm not saying he won't ever pay for his crimes. He will and he must, but that will have to wait until we've taken Earl and his bandits down."

At this, the preacher stepped forward. "Milton, I should have turned myself in long ago. I convinced myself that it was enough to preach God's word and try to atone for my sins alone, but I was wrong." He closed his eyes briefly, as if gathering strength. "I swear, in the Lord's name, that I will turn myself in once we've dealt with the bandits."

The solemnity of his voice sent a chill down Joe's spine, and Joe sensed that the rest of the group felt it, as well.

"What about the children in your care?" Milton asked, although his voice was less challenging now.

Reverend Jesse's eyes were sad. "Though they've become my own, they must see that I will do the right thing, even if it means leaving them. I will find a way to care for the children while I serve whatever sentence the judge sees fit to place upon me. I don't know how long it may be, but I never killed anyone in all my time with Earl, so please God and the judge, I will not be sentenced to hang."

Milton nodded slowly. Joe could see that it still rankled the straitlaced lawman to let a criminal walk free, even if the man had solemnly committed to turn himself in at the appropriate time. As much as he hated to admit it to himself, Joe believed the preacher. He felt the sincerity of Reverend Jesse's words, and knew that the man would not try to avoid his fate, come what consequences it would bring.

"Are there any other objections?" Joe asked, looking around the group. He saw the anger in many of their faces, but no one spoke up. It seemed that, putting aside their personal feelings, they saw the wisdom in utilizing the Reverend's resources. It was not an easy acceptance, though, Joe knew.

Joe turned back to face Reverend Jesse and gave one firm nod. "Here's what we know: after the shootout, Earl left town. We can only assume that he's gone to gather the rest of his gang, and that he'll be back soon. We don't have enough townspeople to stand against him, and we need to build resistance fast, or we'll have another Narrow Bluff."

"How can I help you build that resistance?" the preacher asked.

"Milton and I have to stay hidden, because of the bounties, but those with good trust and access to the town are going to spread the word about who the sheriff really is and what Earl is planning to do. Nan at her boarding house, Jeanette and Mack through their business. Mack is going directly to the mayor, as well. You can use your influence as the preacher to spread the word to your churchgoers."

Reverend Jesse nodded eagerly. "I'll spread the word to my flock at tomorrow morning's service."

"Good," Joe replied. "Unless anyone has questions about the plan for tomorrow, I think we'd better call it a night."

"Mack," Milton said, turning to the older man. "Stay around for a little while and I'll give you the information you'll need to convince the mayor about Sheriff Pennington. There's no doubt he knows about the bandits, but he might need some proof about his sheriff's involvement."

Mack nodded, turning to Jeanette, "I'll join you a little later, then, dear."

Solemnly, the group dispersed, leaving the barn separately and only after checking carefully that it was safe to go. The Reverend and Jeannette were last to go and, when she was done hugging her husband and saying her goodbyes to Milton and Joe, Jeannette paused to stare long and hard at the preacher, skewering him with her cold gaze.

22

Joe stretched out his legs, feeling the stiffness from sitting watch for hours. He chafed against the forced inactivity, especially since it had been more than a full day since the meeting where the group had decided to spread the truth about Sheriff Pennington around the town. He wanted to be able to do more than just wait, although he knew it would help no one if he was caught by the sheriff's men.

His stomach growled loudly, feeling like an empty cavern. He tried to ignore it, knowing that he would have to wait until at least nightfall for Nan or another member of the group to bring him and Milton more food and water. *At least Milton gets to sleep through the hunger*, Joe thought wryly to himself. He still had a few more hours of watch duty, and, with nothing to distract himself, the hunger was difficult to ignore.

Absentmindedly, he reached into his pocket and pulled out Sophie's silver necklace. He let the delicate chain slide through his fingers, and rubbed the small piece at the end of it. The necklace reminded him that a little hunger was a very small price to pay if it meant that he could continue in the task he'd undertaken to avenge her and save Widestone.

He was still running the chain through his fingers when he noticed, through the crack he'd been looking through, that someone was approaching the barn. Joe sat up, fully alert. He could tell from the blue homespun dress that it was a woman, but it wasn't until she got close enough for him to see beneath her shaded bonnet that he could tell it was Nan. She walked casually, not hurrying, and waving cheerfully to another passerby. She walked past the barn as if heading further down the road, then, when she was assured no one was watching, she doubled back and slipped around back and into the building.

"Nan, what are you doing here?" Joe asked, his voice gruff with surprise.

"Oh, hush," she replied, taking off her bonnet and smoothing her hair. "No one saw me. I was very careful, and I know you haven't eaten in a while—you must be starving. I brought some food."

Joe bit his tongue, realizing that arguing with the strong-willed woman was largely futile. Besides, he had to admit that the unexpected meal was sorely needed.

"Well, it might be that I'm a bit peckish," he said lightly. His stomach chose that moment to give an extended, and very loud, grumble. "Maybe more than peckish," he said with a rueful grin.

Nan laughed, and the sound eased some of the tension Joe didn't even know he was carrying in his shoulders. "Come on, then, let's get to it," she said, settling herself to the barn floor, spreading her skirt around her so that she could sit cross-legged but still covered. Joe admired the practicality of the gesture, and that she wasn't so ladylike that she insisted on sitting primly on a hay bale.

He joined her on the ground, biting back a small groan from the stiffness in his legs. He didn't need her thinking he was getting old and creaky. Nan lifted the cloth covering her wicker basket, revealing a large quantity of food. His eyes widened in spite of himself.

"You've been hefting that all over town? Your arm must be about ready to fall off," he laughed.

"I'm stronger than I look, thank you very much," Nan huffed.

Joe held up his hands in mock placation. "Whoa, there," he said. "I stand corrected. Blame my slip of the tongue on the lack of sleep, please."

Nan gave him a mock-ferocious glare. "Just so long as you don't make the mistake of underestimating me again," she growled, then laughed. "In all seriousness, though, there's no place for a weak woman out here in the West. I work from before dawn until after dusk, every day. I don't have any other option."

She didn't say this with any self-pity, she simply stated the truth without embarrassment or pride. "Now then, I have some leftover steak and potatoes from dinner last night. I packed smoked jerky, boiled eggs, fresh bread, pickles, cheese, and berries, too."

"Why, Nan, if I didn't know better, I might think you were trying to romance me," he joked, plucking a ripe strawberry from the basket and raising his eyebrows at her. "Strawberries, and a picnic together in the barn?"

Nan swatted at his arm playfully as Joe took a bite of the

strawberry. It was plump and sweet, the juice spurting from the berry and sliding down his chin. "Heavenly," he mumbled around his mouthful, taking the cloth handkerchief Nan handed to him for the berry juice. "Thanks for this," he said, wiping off his chin. "My manners have left me after all this time in the barn with only Milton for company." He sighed dramatically, and Nan laughed, her green eyes crinkling at the corners.

"Oh yes, it's well-known that Milton is used to sleeping in the sty with the pigs. He's just not fit for polite company." Nan rolled her eyes and shook her head, the sarcasm in her voice belying her words.

Joe dug into the tin plate heaped with steak and potatoes that Nan handed him. Even cold, the food was hearty and delicious, and he was too busy to reply for a moment. She had her own plate out, now, and Joe was glad to see that she was joining him for the meal. It got lonely eating alone, and she rarely had a break to sit and eat without boarders asking her for food or Will pestering her for a cookie.

They ate in comfortable silence for a couple of minutes, enjoying each other's company and the food. Joe was more relaxed than he had been since he had received Sophie's letter, and he knew that it was because of the woman sitting in front of him.

"Nan," he said, swallowing his bite of food. "I want to thank you for all you've done for me since I came to Widestone. You've been the one bright spot in everything that's happened." He spoke quietly, unused to saying such things, but wanting her to know his gratitude for her.

Nan blushed a little, but she didn't drop her gaze from his. "It's been my pleasure, Joe. Since my husband died, I—"

She started, looking away and swallowing before continuing. "Well...I'm just glad you're here. Will and I like having you around."

The sincerity of her simple words, and the sense he'd gotten that she had wanted to say more, sent a wave of warmth washing over him. He wanted to reach for her hand, slender and strong and holding her untouched forkful of potatoes. She was so lovely he felt a longing for her deep in his chest. He slowly set his own fork on his plate, trying to decide whether to take her hand or not. Would she be receptive to it?

He didn't have a chance to act on his impulse, though, because at that moment, Milton stretched and sat up, pushing his hat off of his face. He blinked in the brightness of the barn, then focused in on Nan and Joe.

"Nan?" he asked, still waking up.

"I brought some food, Milton," she said, smiling at him as he heaved himself to his feet and began walking over to them.

Nan dished him up a plate of the steak and potatoes, and Milton forked in a large mouthful after a hurried word of thanks.

"Nan, I should've asked when you first got here, but now that Milton is awake, it's worked out better this way—what's the situation like out in the town?" Joe asked her.

"I think things are changing already," Nan said, her voice serious, but her eyes sparking with a bit of excitement. "Word has spread through Widestone fast, and I hear people talking about it in my dining hall and on the streets. Sheriff Pennington's reputation has plummeted, and folks aren't happy with him."

"Good," Milton said sternly. "I'm glad they're listening.

Joe, if public opinion has shifted in our favor, we might be able to come out of hiding."

Joe looked to Nan for her opinion, but she was already shaking her head. "I don't think either of you should leave just yet," she said. "I still see the other lawmen patrolling the streets and asking if anyone has seen either of you. I know one of them is keeping a close eye on your house, Milton," she added, looking at him.

"Even if the town's view of the situation is changing, the lawmen still work for Sheriff Pennington," Joe mused. "I suppose it makes sense that they're still keeping a watch for us, although I wish they'd let up so we can get out and take action." He shook his head, frustration breaking through his usual calm a bit.

"I think in a few more days the opinion will have shifted completely," Nan said, encouragingly. "Narrow Bluff survivors already believe, of course, as do the business owners who have been affected most by Earl's gang. I don't think it'll be much longer. Maybe a few more days."

"I don't know that we even *have* a few more days," Joe said, worry creasing his forehead. "Earl will be back any day now, and the more time we have to prepare, the better."

He was just finishing his sentence when Mack slipped into the barn, checking over his shoulder and breathing hard. "Don't worry, no one saw me," he said between quick breaths. "I have news."

He took a moment to catch his breath, then continued. All eyes were on him, food completely forgotten. "I hurried over here straight from visiting the mayor about our movement."

"What did he say?" Joe asked eagerly, rising to his feet. Nan and Milton followed suit.

"He's nervous," Mack admitted. "I think he believes us, and I know he wants the town to stay safe, but he says he doesn't know how likely a victory is against Earl and his men. I think he's scared of having another Narrow Bluff. As if he'd know what that was like—he never lived through it like some of us did." He said the last part bitterly, and Joe could see that Mack was disappointed in his friend.

"Does that mean we have his support or not?" Joe asked, looking for a clearer answer from Mack.

"He didn't say no outright, but he didn't agree to support us. I expected more from him." Mack shook his head in frustration, his mouth a taut line of disgust. "Joe, he's asking to speak with you."

"Does he know there's a bounty on my head?" Joe asked, surprised.

"I'm not even sure that he knows you're the leader," Mack admitted. "I didn't get into specifics about who had started the resistance, just that one was building and that Earl and his men were coming back soon. And, of course, about Sheriff Pennington being in their pocket."

"And that wasn't enough for him?" Milton asked angrily. "He finds out his sheriff is crooked and that Earl and his bandits are trying to take over the town, and he's on the fence about fighting back?"

Mack nodded, as upset as Milton. "He says he needs to know more about the resistance movement and our leader. He wants to know he can trust you, Joe, and that the movement can actually succeed before he'll do anything definite."

Joe nodded slowly. "Then, there's no helping it. I'll pay him a visit later tonight."

23

THE SKY WAS FULLY DARK when Joe awoke from his fitful sleep. He'd had a difficult time calming his racing thoughts after Mack and Nan had left. It had taken a fair amount of tossing and turning while Milton stood watch for Joe to finally drift into a light and restless sleep. He awoke, hardly more refreshed than he'd felt earlier that afternoon.

Joe stood and brushed the hay off of his clothes, before unscrewing the metal canteen Nan had left with the basket of food. He swished a mouthful of water around his dry mouth, and decided he'd better take the time to brush his teeth with tooth powder before going to see the mayor. Better to do all he could to tip the scales in favor of the resistance, and he didn't know if the mayor was one who stood on niceties. Luckily, Nan had smuggled his saddlebags to the barn a few days before and he'd taken the chance to wash up a bit.

Milton glanced at Joe as Joe scrubbed his teeth with his wooden toothbrush. "Getting ready to go?" he asked.

Joe nodded wordlessly before spitting into the dirt of the

barn floor and rinsing his mouth with the canteen water again. He wiped his mouth on his sleeve before asking, "Is there anything I should know before I meet with the mayor?"

"I'm not on close terms with him," Milton replied. "Usually that's Sheriff Pennington's job. From the few times I've talked with him, he's a bit starched-up. He likes to do things the proper way, and he's not one that likes to ruffle feathers. He wants to be liked," Milton finished.

"Good thing I brushed my teeth," Joe muttered, wondering if he should've washed the rest of his body again before going to see the man. He pushed his hands into his pockets and leaned on a post in thought. "It sounds like he'd rather just keep the status quo than do anything drastic," he mused. "I'm going to have to convince him that this is a necessary battle."

Milton nodded. "I have a feeling it won't be easy. Do you know how to get to his house?"

Joe shook his head. "I've gathered it's probably near the courthouse, but I'm not certain."

"The mayor's offices are in the courthouse, but his house is a few blocks away." Milton picked up a small stick and used it to draw on the dirt floor, sketching his directions as he spoke. "Here's the courthouse," he tapped an x on the floor. "You'll want to go two blocks north and then one block west. He lives in a two-story frame house with black shutters. There's a carving of an eagle mounted above the door."

Joe memorized the directions, and put his hat on, readying to go out into the dark.

Milton peered out the door, then turned back to Joe. "It's been a pretty quiet night," he said. "I don't think you should have too much trouble. Be safe."

Joe nodded at him, and slipped out into the night. The desert air was brisk and cool on his face, and he relished the chance to be outside once again. He kept to the deepest shadows and watched keenly for any movement as he snuck away from the barn. It felt strange to be in the open after so many days indoors, and his senses were on high alert.

He avoided the main street, slipping through alleys between buildings instead, always stopping to scan his surroundings before moving from one patch of cover to the next. Music and laughter spilled out of the saloon as he passed on the opposite side of the road. It seemed like an eternity since he had sat in the saloon talking with Reverend Jesse, setting in motion a chain of events that had led to the current crisis—the imminent return of Earl with his reinforcements.

Joe was extra cautious as he slipped past the jailhouse. No lights were on inside the building, which likely meant that no one was being kept in the cells and therefore no deputies or lawmen were on duty. Still, he felt the tension in his chest lessen a bit once the main area of the town was behind him and he was on a street with cabins and frame homes. Crickets chirped and frogs croaked in the darkness, but otherwise the night was quiet and still.

Joe spotted a two-story home with dark shutters; he couldn't tell if the shutters were black in the darkness, but he squinted and thought he made out an oval hanging above the front door. That had to be the mayor's home. Joe snuck closer and could just make out the outline of a bird.

Scanning the area, Joe decided to loop around to the back of the house to see if there was a back entrance. He figured there was less of a chance of him being seen if he tried knocking at the back where he wouldn't be seen from the street. To his relief, he found a thick wooden door at the back of the house.

He rapped quietly on the door, hoping to be audible to those inside without alerting any passersby. He listened intently, but no one stirred inside the house. Joe knew he couldn't be too loud, but he had to find a way to rouse the mayor. Deciding to risk it, he knocked on the door again, this time louder. Within seconds he heard movement inside and it cracked open shortly after.

"Who's there?" a man's voice asked tensely. "I'll warn you, I've got a gun."

"It's Joe Chambers," Joe whispered back, fairly certain he was speaking to the mayor himself. "Mack told me you wanted to meet."

The door opened wider, revealing a surprised-looking older man in a nightshirt. "I guess you'd better come in," he said faintly.

Joe stepped past him into the dark room, and the mayor closed the door behind him. Joe heard the latch slide into place and then the sound of a match being struck. A small light flared from it, revealing the mayor's face as he lit a small lamp. He kept it burning very low, but it was enough for the two men to see each other.

"Have a seat," the mayor said, keeping his voice quiet so as not to awaken anyone else in the house. He settled himself into a chair at the table, and Joe did the same.

"Mack told me you'd spoken," Joe started, and the mayor nodded.

"He told me about the evidence that Milton Byers has been building against our sheriff," he said. "I'd known about

Earl, of course, but it makes me sick that our own sheriff has been working for those thugs." He shook his head in disgust. "I'll have him removed from office as soon as possible, rest assured."

"That's good," Joe replied, "but it's not enough. We need your support to take more direct action against the bandits."

"I have to do what's best for this town," the mayor said, frowning at Joe's words. "I don't see that trying to go to battle with a group of thugs is the best course of action. If we do something like that, it could make the situation a whole lot worse. Besides, I've got my family to think about. As mayor, they could be in a lot of danger if I do anything too drastic. I won't have them pay for my choices."

"I understand your fears," Joe said carefully. "I lost my sister to the bandits, so I know how real that threat is." He explained what'd happened with Sophie's letter to him and how that had brought him to Narrow Bluff and then on to Widestone.

The mayor looked sympathetic, but he still seemed unmoved. "I'm sorry about your sister, Mr. Chambers, but that just proves my point. If she and her husband hadn't tried to mount a resistance, then Narrow Bluff might still be standing."

Joe gritted his teeth, but forced himself to take a deep breath and keep his voice level. "Mayor, my sister was one of the very few that tried to fight. Most of the people in Narrow Bluff didn't fight back, and it didn't do them much good. The bandits took over their town and destroyed it. They've set their sights on Widestone, and you know it. They've got Sheriff Pennington under their control—"

"And I'm removing him—" the mayor cut in.

"Yes, but there's more," Joe continued. "As I'm sure Mack told you, the bandits are extorting some of the businesses to pay them a 'protection fee' already. Earl Gallagher and his thugs aren't going to be satisfied with that for very long. They're going to worm their way into even more businesses if they're allowed to continue. Eventually, they're going to take over the whole town."

The mayor tapped his fingers on the table nervously, deep in thought. He was biting the inside of his cheek, but he didn't speak, and Joe figured it was best to lay it all out on the table without sparing any punches.

"I know this isn't what you want to hear, but this is the truth. If the bandits are allowed to keep going, there will be no end to it. They'll just keep demanding more and more, and eventually the town won't be able to support it. Whether the gang was to destroy the town in one day like they did in Narrow Bluff, or leech away at its resources through extortion, the end result is the same. They *will* be the ruin of Widestone unless we stop them. Mayor, there's only a small group of us trying to stand against them. Sure, the opinions in the town are changing, but we need your help."

The mayor's face was drawn and grave as the enormity of the situation settled on his shoulders. Joe was afraid that the mayor would crumble beneath his own cowardice and refuse to step up, but the man took in a deep breath and squared his shoulders.

"Widestone is my town, and I have a duty to protect it."

Joe breathed in a sigh of relief as the mayor continued.

"Tomorrow morning I will have Sheriff Pennington removed from his position, and I'm going to appoint you as the Sheriff. Rumors of Big Joe Chambers' work as sheriff of

Shady Mesa have spread even this far and, even if you plan on leaving after the bandits are dealt with, you seem like the perfect man for the job."

Joe considered it for a moment before shaking his head. "Thank you for your trust, Mayor, but I think you need to consider Milton Byers for the position."

"The deputy?" The mayor rubbed his chin thoughtfully.

"When all of this is over and done with—and it will be— the town will need a stable and reliable man to help them rebuild. The townsfolk know and trust Milton. He's a good man with a strong sense of justice and honor. He's the man you want upholding and enforcing the law here in Widestone."

Joe said this kindly but firmly. Aside from his deep conviction that Milton was the sheriff Widestone desperately needed, he had to admit to himself that he didn't want to return to the work of a lawman after he'd dealt with Earl and his gang. His soul was, quite frankly, exhausted.

The mayor nodded slowly. "You're right. Milton Byers is just the man for the job. I'll see that this is taken care of in the morning. And, of course, the bounties on your heads will be lifted. You have my support, Joe. We're going to protect Widestone." His eyes, though serious, were clear as he looked at Joe.

The two men stood and shook hands firmly before the mayor unlatched the door and held it open for Joe. Joe nodded at him once, before slipping out into the darkness. For the first time in a while, he felt truly hopeful. These were more than just ideas and plans—real change was taking place, and it was starting to look like they just might have a shot at defeating the bandits.

163

ALONE IN THE BARN, Joe hurried to finish lathering the bar of soap on his body. He wasn't expecting anyone, but he still felt far too exposed as he hastily rinsed the suds off of his body with a washcloth and a bucket of water. Baths were not made for barns, he decided grimly, as he nearly fell onto the dirt floor while standing on one leg to dry his left foot with a towel. As he'd found out once before, it was nearly impossible to actually get clean with a bucket of water in a hay-filled and dusty barn.

This was the morning the mayor was going to announce Sheriff Pennington's removal and Milton Byers' instatement as the new town sheriff, which also meant that Joe would be free, once again, to move about the town freely. If it weren't for the public nature of this morning's events, he wouldn't have bothered trying to look presentable until he could get a proper cleaning at Nan's boarding house.

Joe pulled on his clothes, raked his fingers through his thick hair, and brushed his teeth with the last of his tooth powder. He smoothed his facial hair as best he could, now regretting that he hadn't taken the time to shave it while still living in the comfort of his room at Nan's. Well, he couldn't change the past now, but he was sure looking forward to a real bath and a clean shave when things settled down. It wasn't vanity, it was the fact that his clothes were so stiff from layers of dust and sweat that they could just about stand up on their own even if he hadn't been wearing them. And that wasn't even mentioning the fact that his beard itched him to distraction.

Well, he was as presentable as he was going to be under the circumstances, he decided. Cinching on his gun belt and settling his hat onto his head, Joe stepped out of the barn and into the morning sun. He paused for a moment to feel the sunshine on his face and the fact that he was standing out in the open in the light of day since the fateful gunfight.

As he walked toward the main street of town, Joe noticed many other townsfolk heading in the same direction. A few gave him lingering stares, likely because they recognized him from the bounty posters, but no one attempted to collar him, or even speak to him. A few looked angry to see him, but he noticed that more than one gave him a welcoming nod or smile. He figured those folks were the ones that had heard the truth spread by Nan, Mack and Jeanette, or at Sunday services.

As the square came into view, Joe saw a large crowd gathered in front of the courthouse. The mayor was standing on the raised boardwalk, a step or two higher than the crowd in the street. Sheriff Pennington stood beside him, thumbs in his belt loops, looking smug and fully at his ease as he lounged self-importantly in front of the crowd. His posture stiffened as he saw Joe, and he pointed right at him.

"Arrest that man! It's Joe Chambers!" the sheriff hollered at one of his deputies.

The deputy began to move toward Joe, the crowd parting to make way.

"Stop!"

The mayor's voice rang out, and the hubbub in the crowd stilled. Sheriff Pennington looked shocked at his direct command being interrupted, and he swung to face the mayor incredulously.

"Mayor, just what do you think you're—" he began angrily.

The mayor lifted a hand to silence him, then turned to face the crowd. "I've called for this gathering today to announce a change in our law enforcement." Sheriff Pennington's jaw dropped, but the mayor did not acknowledge him. "Sheriff Pennington, you are henceforth removed from your office."

Pennington's jaw worked in disbelief. He couldn't seem to grasp what the mayor was saying. Clearly, he had not expected the mayor to be anything but fully on his side. Joe took these moments of stunned silence to slip quietly next to Nan and Will in the crowd. They smiled at him, but their attention was quickly refocused on the scene unfolding before them. Before Pennington could gather his faculties to make a move, the mayor had continued speaking.

"I hereby appoint the new sheriff of Widestone—Milton Byers."

Milton stepped up next to the mayor, his posture ramrod straight and his face serious. He shook hands firmly with the mayor, utterly ignoring Pennington's stupefied face. Some cheers erupted from the crowd, Will's especially boisterous next to Joe.

"My first order of business is to arrest our former sheriff," Milton said clearly, turning to face the townsfolk. The mayor nodded in approval at his side. "Deputies, if you would escort Pennington to our jail..."

The deputies sprang into action, grabbing Pennington's arms as he struggled to free himself and shouted that he hadn't done anything wrong. The crowd was torn as cheers and angry shouts in support of Pennington erupted in a jumble of confusion.

"What do ya think you're doin'?" a whiskery older man hollered. "He's the only thing keepin' this town safe!"

"That's right!" a scowling woman shouted, cheered on by a few supporters. "Free Sheriff Pennington!"

"He's a snake!" another man shouted over the woman's cry. "It's high time he was jailed!"

The deputies had, by now, carted the struggling Pennington into the jailhouse and locked him in a cell, but the crowd was still torn about his removal, and the mayor was looking worried. His posture had wilted, and Joe sensed that he was losing a bit of his nerve. He was about to speak again when Milton clapped a hand on the mayor's shoulder, and gave him a look of strong resolve.

Milton lifted his hands for quiet, but the buzzing and shouting didn't settle. Milton pulled his pistol out of its holster and shot once into the air. The ear splitting gunshot shocked the crowd into silence as everyone froze. Gradually, the crowd settled and looked at Milton.

"I know this seems like a shock," he began, his voice resonating over the street, "but today is the day that justice returns to Widestone. Some of you already know the truth, but for those of you who don't, let me tell you what's been going on here in our town."

He paused, and scanned the mass of townsfolk, who stared back at him, waiting anxiously for him to continue. Nodding once, he said, "Pennington was put into power through the backdoor dealings of Earl Gallagher and his gang of bandits. They saw to it that Sheriff Riley was murdered—"

At these words, voices in the audience broke out, clearly stunned at the news. Will and Nan's faces were taut with emotion, but they didn't cringe away from the truth. In fact, Joe could see the relief and vindication in their faces as their suspicions had been proven correct.

"Yes, murdered," Milton spoke over the crowd, effectively quieting them once again. "They planned for him to lose that duel from the start, drugging him and tampering with his holster. I did not come to this conclusion lightly, I assure you. I interviewed countless eyewitnesses after the event, to be sure."

The crowd rumbled once again, though they were not nearly as loud as before.

"Earl's gang wanted a puppet they could control so that they could start taking over Widestone, and that's what they've been doing ever since. Some of your businesses have been harassed by his threats that he'd destroy them if you didn't pay up. You folks already know that he's going to tap this town dry and keep looking for more." A few heads nodded soberly in agreement, especially among the survivors of Narrow Bluff.

"Well, no more. No more." Milton's eyes blazed with

determination, and he raised his voice. "Gallagher's gang will no longer run this town!"

His words were met with some cheers, but then a voice shouted over the clapping.

"Even if Pennington was corrupt, he stood between us and Earl. Without him, Earl might destroy our town! Things are better staying as they are!"

A few heads nodded in agreement, and some rumblings spread through the group. Joe knew it was time for him to get involved. He pushed his way forward to the boardwalk and jumped up next to Milton and the mayor, turning to look out at the town.

"Listen," he said in a voice of steely strength. "I know you're afraid, and you have every right to be. Earl and his men are dangerous."

Those muttering worriedly and angrily in the crowd nodded at his statement and stopped talking to listen.

"My name is Joe Chambers," he continued. "Most of you probably recognize the name from Pennington's bounty posters, but here's the truth about me—my sister, Sophie Wells, was killed by Earl Gallagher in the town of Narrow Bluff. Most of you know what happened in that town, so you know that Earl won't hesitate to cut down anyone—man, woman, or child—that won't give him exactly what he wants. I came to this town with one mission: to avenge my sister and take down Earl and his gang. I won't let Widestone become another Narrow Bluff."

As he had been speaking, Reverend Jesse had made his way up to the boardwalk and now stood shoulder to shoulder with Milton and the mayor. He stepped forward as Joe finished.

"Joe's right," the preacher said, looking beseechingly at the crowd, his hands raised in supplication. "I have seen for myself what Earl is capable of. I know you're afraid of what he can do, but things will only get worse if we don't stand up to him. We will never be free unless we all come together to fight him now."

Silence settled over the people in the street. A breeze was the only movement as it pushed through the crowd, rustling women's skirts. Joe knew that this was the tipping point; this was the moment that would help clinch the resolve of those who were on the fence about which side to support. The truth was out now, but fear was a powerful force, and Joe knew that this was the moment to rally their spirits and stiffen their backbone to join the fight.

He stepped forward and lifted his chin, his voice strong and passionate. "We need to come together, and we need to do it now. Unless you're fine with living under Earl's boot, *now* is the time to resist." He paused, surveying the spellbound faces tilted up to his. He took his time, letting his words sink in. "People come out West because they want freedom," he continued. "Not because they want to live under the rule of thieves. That's why we're all here, and that's why—even if no one else will join me—I will fight these bandits to my last breath."

For a moment, his words rang out across the silent crowd, and then they erupted into cheers. Will was simultaneously holding on to his mother and trying to jump up and down with elation. Louis was pumping a fist in the air while Mack and Jeanette were clapping and shouting. Most of the townsfolk were repeating similar scenes throughout the crowd, but Joe noticed that a small portion were not joining in.

This minority was either standing stiff and quiet, or muttering angrily and breaking away from the crowd to leave the square. Their faces ranged from fearful to furious, and Joe's stomach sunk a bit. He was glad that it looked like most of the town was in full support of resisting the bandits, but he had the horrible apprehension that this pocket of dissenters might end up causing trouble. They needed every single hand lifted to fight Earl's gang, but it looked like they weren't going to get it.

25

"GATHER YOUR TEAM." The mayor clapped Joe on the shoulder where they stood on the boardwalk, watching the townsfolk dispersing. "Have everyone come to my home as soon as possible. We have much to discuss."

"I'll have everyone there within the hour," he promised. He looked to Milton and Reverend Jesse, who nodded, showing that they had heard the mayor's words and would be there. Joe and the two other men divided up the members of the group they needed to contact and then separated to go gather the team.

Joe walked with Nan to the boarding house to drop Will off and fill Archie in on the news. He, of course, would need to continue resting up in his room, but he deserved to know about the new developments.

"It's nice not having to sneak around," Nan commented, breaking their thoughtful silence as they approached the two-story frame house. "And not having to keep you hidden in that barn. That's nice, too, of course." She smiled a bit teasingly as she said this, and Joe smiled back.

"Joe! Nan!"

They looked up to see Jeanette holding the mayor's front door, beckoning them. "Everyone else is here," she called, and they hurried their steps. The visit to Archie had set them a little behind the rest of the group.

They walked into the front room where Nellie was sitting in a rocking chair, and Louis was helping Mack to bring in chairs from the dining room. Mack and Jeanette settled onto the sofa, Jeanette patting the cushion next to her for Nan, who sat down beside her. The mayor's wife slipped in carrying a tray with a pitcher of lemonade and glasses, which she set down on a side table, and hurried back out of the room, shutting the door behind her softly.

The mayor, Louis, and Milton took their seats, leaving an empty chair for Joe by the fireplace where he could easily see everyone. Joe took his place, completing the circle.

"Mayor, thank you for letting us use your home," Joe began, tipping his head at the man, who nodded graciously. He turned to look at everyone in the group. "We all know that we don't have much time before Earl comes back with his men. We need to know how many he's got with him, at the very least, a rough guess. We've got to be able to prepare."

Everyone turned to look at Reverend Jesse. He was the only one who had firsthand experience with the inner workings of Earl's gang.

"I would guess he's got at least thirty-five men in his forces. Maybe more, if he pulls in men from jobs he had them working in nearby towns," the preacher said. "That could have changed since I left, but we had at least that many when I was still part of his gang."

A weight of worry, almost palpable, settled on the group.

"That's more fighting men than we have," Milton said quietly.

"We have far more people in town than that," Nan spoke up in protest.

"We don't know how many in the town are both willing *and* able to fight," Joe pointed out. "And we won't let this become a slaughterhouse. No one will be engaging in any battle that can't shoot a gun, and anyone who fights will do so of their own accord."

Nellie leaned forward in her rocking chair to chime in. "Joe 'n Milton are right—we don't have enough folks to fight here in town, but why don't we send out a call for reinforcements to the next town over?"

Reverend Jesse was already shaking his head. "If we had more time, that would be the right move, but we don't have that luxury. When Earl swoops in, he comes in fast and strikes hard. He'll be here soon. Very soon. We can't spare anyone to ride over looking for help."

Milton nodded. "Every last able-bodied fighter is going to count."

Nellie sat back, looking discouraged, but she didn't protest their logic.

"And we saw at the town meeting this morning that there are some in town who are not on our side," the mayor said wearily. "I think we have the support of most folks, but how many of those in support will actually fight when the time comes? Todd Osborne led a group of men out of town just a few hours ago and I don't doubt that more will follow. We know that every one of Earl's men is willing to fight and they've done it many times before."

"We have to do what we can," Joe said firmly. He was not

going to let discouragement stop them from the work they had ahead. They needed to focus on the preparations they could make instead of all the ways their force was lacking. "Preacher, what can you tell us about the structure of Earl's troops? Does he have leaders or lieutenants? I can't see that he could control a group as large as that by himself."

Reverend Jesse nodded. "He's got two lieutenants. Well, it's more like three groups that merged, with Earl as the main leader." Seeing the confusion on everyone's faces, the preacher hurried to elaborate. "There are two lieutenants that each led their own crew of bandits before Earl convinced them to join up with him and unite, making himself the head of the entire gang."

"I can't see how any gang leader would want to give up control to work under someone else," Milton commented.

"Earl's a powerful man," Reverend Jesse said simply. "He can be very persuasive when he wants to be. There's a reason so many of us were willing to join him and do what he said. He promised us that we'd be rich and powerful beyond belief if we'd listen to him. I'm willing to bet he told the two other crew leaders that they'd be able to get more if they worked together rather than alone."

"What can you tell us about his lieutenants?" Joe asked. "They're going to be key pieces in the fight, and it might be that we could leverage them against each other."

"One of the lieutenants goes by the name Friendly Nick," the preacher began, but he stopped by a sudden shattering of glass.

Everyone jumped, and turned to see Louis standing, his glass of lemonade shattered on the wooden floor, a small trickle of lemonade spreading slowly around his boots. He stood, his face a mask of hard anger, heedless of the mess at his feet. Jeanette jumped up and left the room to gather rags and a broom.

"Louis?" Nan asked softly. "What's the matter?"

"He killed my wife," Louis choked out.

The group sat stunned. None of them had known about the tragedy, and for a moment, no one spoke. Jeanette knelt by his feet and quietly mopped up the mess, pausing only to gently touch Louis's hand in silent comfort and apology. Nan rose and quietly led Louis to take her seat at the sofa. She didn't speak, but all knew that she understood the pain of a spouse taken by Earl's evil men.

"Friendly Nick," Reverend Jesse said quietly, "is a man of incredible cruelty, like Earl, himself."

"Is there anything else you can tell us about him?" Joe asked.

"He's not a tall man, but the men are afraid of him, so he'll stand out. He's got black hair, and there's something off about his eyes," the preacher replied. "He's clever and sly, so don't underestimate him."

Louis nodded, his eyes wide and his lips a thin line. Joe could almost feel the fiery rage flowing out of him as he spoke. "That one's mine."

"What about the other lieutenant?" Milton asked after a moment's silence.

"They call him Edwin the Giant. He's not bright, by any means, but he's a *very* large man. Trust me, you'll recognize him when you see him. He's one of the biggest men I've ever seen, and it's all muscle. His men respect him because of his size. And his fighting ability. He's one of the best shots in the West, and he never runs from a fight."

"Which of the two do you know more about?" Milton asked.

"Edwin," Reverend Jesse said, looking down. "I used to be one of his men."

The group digested this information. They all knew of his past, but somehow knowing more specifics felt shocking.

"He actually caught me when I was about to run away from the bandit camp," the preacher said quietly, still looking down at his hands. "I thought he was going to kill me on the spot, and he and I knew he could snap me like a twig. I had no chance of outlasting him in a fight, guns or otherwise."

"Why didn't he kill you?" the mayor asked, curiosity getting the best of him.

Reverend Jesse finally looked up, meeting the stares of everyone in the circle. "I told him I couldn't keep hurting innocent people. Especially after I saw what happened to Sophie Wells..." His voice caught, and he swallowed. Joe felt his stomach tighten. "Earl and Friendly Nick don't care who they kill, and they won't spare women and children. It was senseless and evil. I couldn't stay any longer."

"So, Edwin just let you go because he's such a good person?" Joe couldn't keep the sarcasm and disbelief out of his voice.

The preacher shook his head. "Edwin isn't a good person, by any means, but he doesn't like hurting women and children. He doesn't agree with Earl about it, but Earl always convinces him to stay. He understood why I wanted to get out. I think if it had been for any other reason, if he hadn't witnessed the horror of what happened to Sophie, he would never have let me go."

177

Nellie leaned forward during this explanation, her eyes glued to Reverend Jesse, but she didn't speak up.

"If we don't have enough men to take them in a battle, what can we do to prepare?" Mack spoke into the silence. "It's good to know this information about the enemy, but we've got to be able to do something. I don't just want us to be sitting ducks."

"What if we fortified some areas?" Joe said, his mind racing to come up with options. "If we can have a place for those folks who can't fight to hunker down, we'll have a smaller area to guard."

"There's a cellar below the church," the preacher spoke up. "I don't think the gang knows about it and I think it's big enough to hide a good amount of people, and they'll be safer down there."

Milton was nodding. "If we set up a system of keeping watch, we'll know ahead of time when the bandits are coming. That could give us enough time to get as many of the vulnerable hidden as possible before they're upon us."

"We'll need more than one person on watch," Joe said, "but I'm in agreement with you. If we can be on the alert and notified before the gang gets here, that gives us an advantage. Having a smaller area to defend may help us with the difference in numbers. Especially if those of us fighting can find good spots of cover to take the bandits out while they're in the open."

"I still think we should send out messengers to the towns closest to us, in addition to that," the mayor now chimed in.

"Mayor, they won't be able to get back to us in time, even if they find help," Milton responded.

"I know," the mayor said, looking bleak. "But we need to

give ourselves every lifeline we can. If this ends up lasting longer than we expect, it could be a lot of help to us. We'll send someone who can't use a gun, so it won't reduce our fighting force."

The group looked at each other, the full weight of the impending storm clear in each of their minds. Things were going to come to a head soon, one way or another.

26

"WILL, go help Joe carry wood to the front of the house," Nan called to her son from the kitchen. Steam from the pot of boiling potatoes was curling her hair as she stirred.

Joe poked his head into the kitchen and watched her for a moment, before mentally shaking his head and reminding himself to focus on the task at hand. It was ridiculous that he was distracted by her at a time of such danger, but it seemed as though the danger was adding to the sense of urgency in his growing feelings for her.

"Nan? Keep Will moving the boards for me. I need to direct the volunteers in storing and distributing ammunition."

She looked up at him and nodded, and he ducked back out of the kitchen and returned to the dining hall. Louis, Milton, and Archie were standing with a group of men who had declared themselves ready to fight.

"As you may already know," Joe said to the group, "Nan has offered her boarding house as a headquarters for the resistance in the coming fight. We'll be gathering as much ammunition as we can find in the town and divvying it up here. I need all of you to go out and round up all the resources you can. I know some of the other men are preparing other buildings as fighting points, so we'll leave them to that. We don't have much, but we'll use whatever we can—bags of feed, boards, wagons tipped on their sides— whatever we can find to help make access to our safe spots more difficult."

The men listened closely, their faces set in hard lines of determination.

"Nan is preparing as much food as possible for the volunteers who will be sleeping here, as well as coordinating the storage of food for the women and children who will be hiding in the church cellar. Does anyone have any questions?"

Joe scanned the faces, but no one raised a hand or voiced any concerns. "All right, then. Let's get to it."

The group dispersed quickly, moving with purpose to accomplish their tasks. Everyone felt the unspoken urge to prepare with careful haste; they all knew it was only a matter of time before Earl was upon them, and the uncertainty spurred their preparations.

Joe went outside to the front porch, where Will was setting another board against the front of the large building.

"Is this enough, Joe?" he asked, his little voice pitched a bit higher with excitement. "Do I get to help you put them up?"

"Yep, we're going to board up the windows on the ground floor," Joe responded. "We'll keep the upper windows free so we can keep watch, but we want to make the ground floor harder to break into."

He grabbed a board and handed it to Will. "Hold this for

181

me right here against the bottom of the window—yes, that's right—and keep it real steady for me while I nail in the sides."

Will was quick to comply, his face screwed up in determined concentration, trying with all his might to keep the board level and unmoving. Joe bit back a smile at the boy's grave efforts as he hammered the board into place.

"Joe, I'm going to fight those bad men right beside you!" Will said with gusto, as he reached for a second board. "They won't even know what hit 'em! They're gonna wish they never came to Widestone!"

Joe hammered in the second board as Will continued to chatter excitedly, giving himself a moment to form his words with care. "Son, the most important thing you can do for me is take care of your mother when the fighting comes."

Will's face darkened. "But I want to help you and fight with the men! I'm a man, just like my pa!"

"You're becoming a man, Will, that's true," Joe said, as he handed Will another board, silently reminding him that they needed to keep working. "But your mother shouldn't have to lose both her husband and her son. Your pa would want you to care for your mother more than anything. That's how you'll make him proud."

Will quieted at this, turning Joe's words over in his mind, and they finished the window and moved to the next before he spoke again. "If it's what my pa would want," he finally said, "I guess I better protect my ma..."

Joe smiled down at him as they continued working. "I knew I could count on you, son."

Will's little chest puffed a bit with pride at Joe's simple praise, and he worked with eagerness as they finished boarding up the front windows. Joe stepped back to examine their work and looked down at the boy.

"Well, do you think that'll pass muster?"

Will smiled up at him, his small eyes crinkling at the corners. "Yes, sir! We better go check on Ma to see if she's got any more chores that need a man's touch," he said, his boisterousness back and at the ready.

Joe followed Will back into the kitchen, where Nan was now mashing the massive pot of potatoes, both arms straining with the effort. She looked up at them as they entered, and smiled.

"Will, could you give me a hand with these potatoes?" she asked, and his face fell a bit. Guessing correctly that her son likely wanted to feel important, she added, "There's so much food to make sure all of our fighters are well-fed, and my arms are so tired they might fall off. You're strong enough to finish mashing them, I think."

Will nodded eagerly, and he hurried over to his mother. "You take a rest, Ma, I'll get these potatoes mashed real good," he said, his voice serious with the importance of his task.

Nan bit back a smile as she kissed him on the head, then gestured to Joe to help her at the table on the other side of the kitchen where several bowls were covered with cloth. She uncovered them to reveal large rolls of resting dough.

"These should be about finished rising," she commented, pushing up the sleeves of her dress to the elbows. "One more good knead and rise and then they should be ready for baking."

Joe was content to watch her work, but she speared him with a mock severe look. "And don't think you're going to lounge about like a king," she sniffed at him. "Wash those hands and help me get these finished."

"Yes, ma'am," he said with a smile, going to the sink and scrubbing his calloused hands with a bar of lye soap. "Do you need to inspect my hands, now? Check under my fingernails?" he joked as he dried his hands.

Nan sighed dramatically. "Let's see them," she said, and he stretched out his hands for her scrutiny. She took them and looked at them closely, turning them over to check both sides.

Her hands held his with great care, and she traced a line in his palm gently with the tip of her finger, her head bent down and her cheeks burning at her own forwardness. Joe captured her hands with his, so that hers were cradled within his own large ones. They felt so slender and tiny inside of his own, and for a moment he forgot about the bandits and the looming battle. All that existed was this moment with Nan.

"Nan..." He began to speak, but found he had no words to express to her what she had come to mean to him over his time in Widestone. Words seemed painfully inadequate to tell her how deeply he admired her strength and tenacity, her courage in taking on so much responsibility alone, her commitment to doing what was right, and her unbending determination to keep moving forward, no matter the situation. She was, quite simply, the most beautiful woman he had ever known—inside and out.

Nan was watching him, waiting expectantly for him to finish his sentence, her cheeks still tinged with a rosy blush. He cleared his throat and tried again. "Nan, I'm not much for words, but you have become very dear to me." He stopped again, mustering his courage.

He had faced Earl in a shootout only days before and he was having a hard time speaking to Nan? He mentally smacked himself and gathered his resolve.

"Nan, I'd like to take you to dinner." The words rushed out of him.

Nan's eyes widened, and then she broke into a soft smile. "I'd like that very much, Joe. But...the bandits...?"

Joe chuckled. "After this is all done, of course."

"Of course." She smiled, raising a teasing eyebrow. Then, the laughter left her eyes and she became solemn. "Joe, do you think we're going to make it out alive?"

He squeezed her hands tighter. "I don't know, Nan," he said softly. "We can only hope, and meet what comes. I began this fight for my sister, and I still fight for her. But now, I'm fighting for you, too. For everyone here who deserves a life free from Earl's gang."

Nan's eyes shone with rising tears, but not a single one fell. She straightened her back. "My husband died because of them, and he would've been on the front lines if he was still alive today. I think he'd be proud of us using this boarding house, his dream, to help in the fight. I'm proud to fight back, and... I'm so grateful you're here to do it with us, Joe."

They stood there for a few moments in silence, hands intertwined. Joe pulled her a little closer, but he didn't wrap his arms around her. He just looked down into her green eyes, swimming in them so deeply he never wanted to return to the real world. Joe took in a deep breath, squeezed her hands once more, and then reluctantly released them. She blinked as he took a step back, as if she, too, were coming back to reality.

Joe turned to the table and began kneading a ball of

dough, or at least making the attempt to do so. Nan couldn't help but laugh as she joined him.

"Maybe I better have May help me with this dough," she said. "She's gathering eggs from the chickens so that we can boil them and have them on hand for the men, and she'll be back any minute. You might be doing more harm than good." The last part was said kindly, and Joe stepped back with a rueful smile.

"I think Will and I had better go string up some barbed wire along your gate. I saw some in your shed when I was gathering boards. It'll help keep the bandits from trying to jump it or have their horses go over it. Just one more ring of protection."

Nan nodded, her face serious, now. "That would be good. Thank you, Joe."

Joe stepped away and turned to Will, who was still mashing the potatoes vigorously.

"Come on, Will," he called, and Will looked up. "I need your help, and I think you've just about wrung the life out of those potatoes."

Will's face broke into a grin. "Ma, these potatoes are mashed real good."

"Thank you, love," she called back, smiling at him, and he hopped off the stool he was standing on to reach into the pot, trotting after Joe out the back door.

"Let's go find some gloves," Joe said to him as they walked outside. "This is going to be a nasty job, and we'll need some protection. Have you ever strung barbed wire?"

Will shook his head, skipping along beside Joe.

"Today's a good day to learn, son," he said, foraging in the shed and finding a couple of pairs of leather gloves. He realized as he spoke that Will could one day be his own son, and the knowledge sent a wave of gratitude over him.

He turned and ruffled the boy's hair. "Let's get to work."

27

"They're coming! They're coming!"

Joe shot out of bed at the shouted words, racing to the window and pushing it up. Outside, one of the men who had been on guard duty sat astride his horse in the dusty street, shouting his warning to Nan's boarding house.

"How many? How far away?" he called back.

"At least forty!" the man yelled. "They're only a few miles out!"

Joe cursed, his mind racing on to the next steps.

"Are the women and children being sent to the church cellar?" he shouted back.

The man nodded, his horse dancing nervously beneath him, clearly itching to run. "Another sentry rode to the church first thing when we saw 'em. We're riding through the rest of town to warn the stragglers to get to the cellar or to their fighting posts."

"Good, I'll ready the men here!" Joe shouted back, and the man raced off.

Joe slammed the window down quickly, the panes

rattling at the force. He rushed toward the door, shouting for the house to wake up and ready themselves as he did so. He paused only to stuff his feet into his boots and grab his gun belt. His rifle was waiting for him in the corner, and he slung it over his back. He heard shouts and feet thudding in the hallways as the other fighting volunteers in the house ran for their weapons, some thundering down to the dining hall where more ammunition was laying out on tables.

Joe ran down the hall to Archie's room, which faced the western edge of town, which was where they expected the bandits to ride in. He banged on the door, not waiting for Archie to respond before pushing the door open.

"Archie, I need to use your spyglass," he cried, breathless.

Archie was still in bed recovering, but he struggled to rise at Joe's urgency. "It's already there by the window," he gasped out, and Joe was to it in a few steps.

Joe squeezed one eye shut and pressed the other to the spyglass, scanning the horizon slowly. It didn't take long for him to spot the mass headed toward the town. He couldn't get a clear read on numbers since they were still a few miles away, but he saw a great many horses and men, and even wagons. Earl was coming in fully prepared and stocked with supplies. He cursed again. There were too many of them. He needed to go find Milton and the other members of the group and get everyone ready.

Joe turned on his heel. "Archie, get yourself as ready as you can! I'll have someone take you to the church cellar to wait out the fight." Archie tried to protest, arguing that he was ready to fight and he could try and shoot a pistol with his left hand, but Joe overrode him. "I don't have time to argue. You're in no position to fight, and the best thing you can do for us is watch over the women and children. It'll add more worry if we're trying to protect you, too."

His words came out more harshly than he intended, but he had no time to spare the man's feelings. He turned and ran down the hall, other men joining him as they hurried to the dining hall. Milton was already inside, as were most of the other fighters who hadn't already raced to their hidden posts throughout the town. They were milling about, clearly unsure of what to do, talking worriedly to each other.

Adrenaline pumped through Joe's veins, and he forced himself to take a deep breath and clear the panic to prevent it from clouding his judgment. "Milton, we need to get everyone ready. We've got less than an hour before they're on us."

Milton nodded gravely, and quieted the group. "Listen up, Joe's got information!" The chatter died down immediately as everyone turned to face Joe and Milton.

"Men, there's at least forty men headed our way with Earl. They've got wagons of supplies, and more men than we expected." Joe looked at the men gravely, some of whom were clutching their weapons tightly, but no one spoke. "We don't know if he's planning a full-on shootout or if he's going to try to negotiate, first. We do know that it's unlikely that he'll just give up even when he sees that we've prepared for his arrival."

His words settled heavily on the solemn group. "We've done what we could the last few days, fortifying the town and gathering supplies. You all know your posts, you have your ammunition, and we've gathered the women and children and hidden them away. We're as ready as we're going to be.

There's far more of them than there are of us, and we can't change that."

It was true. The town had only been able to scrounge up twenty-five or so men who were willing and able to face the bandits. It had already been a small number, but with Earl's band even larger than they'd been anticipating, the sobering fact that they were quite likely to die in the coming battle could not be ignored.

"Thank you for your willingness to fight for our town," Joe said quietly. This was his town, now, too. "We may not have as many men as Earl, but we're fighting for a noble cause, and I'm proud to go into battle with you." He stopped speaking, his throat choking up with emotion.

Reverend Jesse stepped forward at this moment, pushing his way through the men so that he stood before Joe. Joe noted with surprise that the man wore a pistol on his belt.

"Reverend?" he asked, shocked. "I thought you were watching over the women and children in the cellar?"

Reverend Jesse shook his head, his eyes locked on Joe's. "I left Jeanette in charge. They're in good hands. I can't sit idly by and watch evil men kill good ones for a second time. I may be a man of God, but that doesn't give me the right to step away from this battle. I'm ready to fight for this town." His voice was firm and steely with resolve.

Joe stepped forward to shake his hand, surprising even himself.

"We're grateful to have you," he said simply. "We need every able-bodied man we can get."

The hatred and distrust he had nourished since he found out about Reverend Jesse's past was gone, he realized. The man had been involved in atrocities in the past, but he had truly changed, and his willingness to fight alongside the men of the town and risk death was proof of his transformation. Louis stepped up beside the preacher, and clapped him on the shoulder. He didn't speak, but he looked Reverend Jesse in the eye and nodded once, showing that he, too, accepted the man.

The preacher looked shocked. "Louis?" he asked, his voice barely a whisper, and his eyes suddenly swimming with tears.

Louis's mouth tightened with emotion, and Joe sensed this was a conversation that needed to happen, but not under the watchful eyes of the rest of the group.

"Men," he called loudly. "You know your posts, and you know the risks. Godspeed, and God bless. Let's move out."

The men nodded, gathering their weapons and ammunition, and dispersed, most leaving the boarding house. Soon, only Joe, Louis, and the preacher remained.

"I know there's something that needs to be said here," Joe said to the two of them. "So we need to say it. We don't have much time, and we may not have another chance."

"Louis," Reverend Jesse said again. "From the depths of my soul, I'm so sorry about your wife. May God forgive me."

"I don't know about forgiveness," Louis said tightly, his face hard and impassive. "But I will say I'm thankful you're fighting with us today. That's all I can give for now." He spun on his heel and left the boarding house, hurrying down the street toward his post on the second floor of the dry goods store.

"Preacher?" Joe asked, looking at the man who was now quickly wiping away a silent tear. "We don't have time. I need to know what's going on, especially if it could compromise us during the fight."

Reverend Jesse took a deep breath and squared his shoulders. "When I joined the group, I recognized Louis's name, so I looked at the list of those who died in Narrow Bluff. Louis's wife, Lara, was on the list. It didn't take me long to remember what had happened to her, though I had tried to block it from my memory."

Joe waited impatiently for the preacher to finish, but the man seemed to be stopped by grief. "Reverend, what happened to her?"

"Friendly Nick," the preacher whispered, his voice strangled. He cleared his throat and continued, "I told you he's just as cruel as Earl, if not more so. He didn't just kill Lara, he tortured her. He made her death excruciating and slow, and he forced Louis to watch. He killed Lara as a punishment for something Louis did—to teach him a lesson."

Joe took a step back, horrified. No wonder Louis couldn't bear to be near Reverend Jesse; knowing his past allegiance with the bandits, one of whom had murdered his own wife in front of his eyes, it was a miracle he had even thanked the preacher for joining their side now. It explained so much about Louis's hard and largely silent demeanor. What had he been like before that? Without that anger and hate. Once this was all over, Joe hoped to find out.

Joe hoped that Louis would be able to fight with a clear head in the coming battle, although, surely, visions of his wife would haunt him as he faced, once again, the very man who had forced him to watch her cruel death. The upcoming fight had far more at stake than just saving the town from becoming another Narrow Bluff—this was personal for Louis, for Joe, and for every single person who had lost something to Earl and his evil gang.

Looking at Reverend Jesse, he knew the time for any more digging into the past was now long gone.

"Get Archie to the cellar with the women and children," he ordered. "Then come back here to help me in the fight."

The man nodded, a determined look in his eyes. "Time to atone for all I did wrong."

2 8

MILTON AND JOE were stationed together in the second floor of the boarding house, and they had assigned most of the fighters to hole up together in twos and threes so that it wouldn't be as difficult to get messages spread to one another once the action began. They waited in tense silence, checking the spyglass from time to time as the minutes ticked by. It had been almost half an hour since the meeting with the recruits had ended, and they both knew that Earl and his gang would be near at any minute.

"Look, they're within sight now," Milton said softly, and Joe followed his outstretched finger.

Earl's gang was rolling toward the town, and they no longer needed the spyglass to see the mass of men, horses, and wagons. Joe was on high alert, although there was still nothing that could be done; it wasn't like the small town of Widestone had cannons or other military-grade weapons that could take the thugs out before they even reached the town. They would have to wait until they were within rifle range.

Time seemed to warp, crawling in slow motion at the

same time as it seemed to be speeding like a train. In this strange sensation, Earl and his band eventually reached the edge of town, and halted in some confusion before fully entering. It seemed as though the entire town was holding its breath.

"I don't think they were expecting a ghost town," Milton muttered softly. "The only thing that gives us the upper hand right now is that they're in the open and we're hidden. Once they get a little closer, we should start shooting..."

He had barely finished his sentence when a shot exploded through the air and a man in the front of Earl's group crumpled to the ground, bleeding. A war cry that sent chills down Joe's spine split the previously silent air, and the scene instantly broke into pandemonium. Earl's men whipped out their guns, but they were shooting largely at nothing, as they couldn't see an enemy to aim for. Meanwhile, Joe's men tried to take precise shots without giving away their hiding places. So far, neither side was having much success.

Using anything they could for cover, the bandits inched toward the town as shots from both sides continued to ring out. To Joe's horror, one of the townsfolk lifted out of a crouch from the roof of the saloon for a better shot and was torn down immediately as multiple bullets from different bandits rained down on him. He jerked around like a rag doll before tipping over the edge of the roof and plummeting to the dusty street.

By now, Earl's men had gathered that most of the buildings were empty, and they stormed a few at the very edge of town, taking shelter inside of them and using them as cover to shoot back. It now became a battle of locating where the shots were coming from on each side. Joe used this opportunity to swing his rifle off of his back and aimed at what he thought might be movement behind one of the windows in a home at the edge of town. It was a long distance, even for his rifle, but he chafed against sitting idly by. He squeezed off a round, shattering the glass of the window he aimed for, not knowing if his bullet had found a human target.

"This is a waste of ammunition," he bit out to Milton, reloading his rifle. "There's got to be a better way to do this."

Seeing an unlucky bandit scrambling for cover, Joe took aim and loosed another bullet, this time with more success. The man slammed into the wall of the home he had been running for, leaving a bloody trail as he slid to the ground and lay in a heap. Joe lowered his gun, scanning for any last stragglers, but everyone seemed to have found a hiding place.

"We need a new plan," Milton agreed. He had only fired off a couple of shots himself, and Joe could tell that he, too, saw the futility in trying to engage in a shootout where none of the combatants could see each other. The horses and wagons had been hidden right behind the houses where the bandits were staked out, and Joe wasn't about to rain fire on defenseless animals.

Shots continued to ring out from both sides, although they were slowing down. Neither side seemed willing to fully let up their guard to regroup, and no one was willing to come out into the open for a fair fight. It looked like the town itself was taking the brunt of the shooting—bullet holes checkered many walls and shattered glass lay strewn in the street.

"We need to find a way to meet with some of the other fighters," Joe agreed with Milton. "Get some messages out.

Earl and his men aren't coming out of those cabins any time soon, and they'll be having their own strategy session by now."

"They're well-guarded where they are," Milton agreed. "We need to funnel messages to the church and to the key fighting spots throughout town. The men know this is the headquarters, so they should know to meet back here when they can do so safely."

The two men settled in to wait, and an eerie hush settled over the town. The fighting had begun and ended within half an hour, but Joe knew it wasn't over just yet. The only reason Earl and his men hadn't stormed the streets openly was that they knew most of their men would be picked off one by one from Joe's men in hiding. The situation had become a sticky impasse, as both sides considered how to gain the advantage.

Joe stiffened as he heard soft footsteps coming from the floor below them. He motioned to Milton, who nodded, showing that he heard them, too. Cautiously, Joe pulled his pistol from his gun belt and edged to the bedroom door, peering down the long hallway. If one of Earl's men had somehow snuck as far into town as Nan's boarding house, Joe would maintain an edge if he let them come to the hallway and into his line of fire.

He cocked his pistol and waited, barely breathing. The treads of the stairs were creaking under the weight of the unknown intruder; he was getting closer. Joe lifted his pistol to the crack of the ajar door, ready to take them down should they be a threat. Louis's head came into view, and Joe let out a huge sigh of relief, lowering his pistol. Louis was followed by two other men from town.

"Joe? Milton?" Louis called softly.

"We're over here, Louis," Joe called back, opening the door.

Louis and the two men came into the room, and Joe began peppering them with questions. Had any of their assigned group been hit? Had they managed to take anyone down? Had they been seen on the way over?

"We hit maybe one or two men," Louis responded. "No more than that. There wasn't time before most of them were hiding in the cabins. And no, we weren't seen."

One of the volunteers with him swore bitterly. "We didn't think they'd hunker down like that," he spat. "Not when they have so many men."

Joe nodded, wishing he'd done more to stop them from doing so. Perhaps they could've laid traps in that part of town or-- Well, no use thinking about it now. The situation was what it was and they'd have to deal with it.

"I say we push toward them," Louis growled, his fists clenched. "We can't just sit by and wait for them to kill us off. We need to bring the fight to them and end this once and for all." The men standing behind him were nodding vigorously in full agreement.

Joe was already shaking his head before he finished his sentence. "Not yet. We need to come together with the other recruits and make a plan. They know to come here or go to the church. We'll be sitting ducks if we try and fight without everyone knowing what's going on."

"Joe, these men are murderers. I don't care if I die, as long as I get to see the life drain out of Friendly Nick," Louis was nearly shouting, his chest now heaving. "There's no time to wait around for them to come up with more plans!"

"Louis, I need you to calm down," Joe said, his own voice

raised. "They've taken so much from all of us—you don't get to sacrifice yourself for revenge. We need you. We can't afford to lose a single man." His tone was harsh, but he needed Louis to understand what was at stake.

Louis looked mutinous, and Joe knew he needed to defuse the situation before it blew up. There just wasn't time for this crisis. He tried another tactic.

"You'll get your chance to take out Friendly Nick, Louis. I promise. But if you're really serious about taking down these bandits, we need to keep a cool head and be smart about it." Joe stared him hard in the eyes, and Louis finally nodded his head slightly, the barest movement.

"Good. More men should be here soon so that we can discuss what to do. At least we know that the folks at the church should be safe. They're on the other end of town, and none of Earl's men made it past the cabins. Clark, you stand watch in this room while the rest of us go down to the dining hall to wait for more recruits."

The volunteer took his station by the window, and the rest of them trooped down to the dining hall. Within the hour, ten more of the recruits had made their way back to the boarding house. Two were wounded, one having been shot in the leg. Two other men had carried him to the boarding house, having been able to make it by sneaking through alleys and taking a longer route to the boarding house that kept them under cover. Joe figured the rest of the fighters either didn't think it best to come to Nan's or had gone to the church to check out the situation there. Either way, it was time to talk to those present.

"Men," his voice carried over the tense conversations taking place throughout the dining hall, and they stopped talking to listen. "It looks like we've only lost one man—that we know of—and only a few have fallen on Earl's side. We need to make a new plan. I know that some of you are in favor of trying to storm their cabins and force the fight once and for all." He didn't look at Louis as he said this, but he knew there were likely a few more who felt the same way. "I know things look bad right now, but this is actually a good situation."

"How do you figure?" one of the volunteers called out. "Our town is gettin' torn to pieces and nothin' is gettin' done! We might as well get it over with!"

"Not a chance! We should retreat to the next town over," another man called. "There's no winnin' this situation!"

Arguing broke out among the recruits. It worried Joe that morale was already slipping, and the battle had barely begun. They couldn't afford to be discouraged or divided, not if they wanted to have any chance of winning.

"Listen up!" he shouted, but the men paid no heed. He hated to break Nan's property, but he needed their attention, and he didn't have time to waste. He grabbed a glass from the sideboard and shattered it against the wall. The men froze, staring at him.

"That's better," he said with a forced calm. "We're only hurting ourselves if we start fighting each other. I know we're in a rough situation, but this is actually a good thing— hear me out. Remember that we sent messengers to the nearest town, but we thought there would be no hope of any help coming to us in time. The longer this battle is prolonged, the more likely it is that help will be able to join us and strengthen our numbers. A prolonged fight favors us, not Earl and his gang. We've got them surprised and unnerved by being ready for a fight and having the advantage of cover in the town, and we're going to keep that advantage."

A few of the men still looked angry, and Joe noticed that a few still looked discouraged and beaten, but most of the men were nodding at Joe's words. A bit of the tightness in Joe's chest loosened. As long as he and Milton could keep the men's spirits up, they would still have a chance.

"Men, we've got someone keeping watch upstairs, and we'll set up a watch duty so that the rest of you can eat and get some rest while we wait for help and for Earl's men to make a move. Clean your weapons, gather any supplies you're low on, and rest up."

The men began talking amongst themselves as they settled at tables in the dining hall, while some trickled upstairs to rest.

"We're going to need to speak with the men often," Milton said quietly to Joe. "There might be insurrection or chaos if we don't keep everyone on the same page. Especially the weaker ones."

Joe nodded. "My thoughts exactly. This is going to be a different kettle of fish than either of us was expecting." The volunteers had been ready for a short, heated battle over the town, but even the most determined man's fire would fade with time. The feeling of being packed together so tightly, too, would create a breeding ground for discontent.

"I'll keep watch over here," Milton said. "It'd be good if you went to the church to check on things there and spread the message to any of the men that headed that way."

"I'll see what help I can get for the wounded men, too," Joe said, preparing to leave. "I'll be back before nightfall, if I can."

Certain that things were under control in the boarding house, Joe slipped out of the back and headed toward the church, sticking close to the buildings and using every alley and bit of cover he could. He grew more confident as he got further from the bandits' edge of town. He figured they were pretty locked in where they were, but he didn't let his guard down.

Joe slipped into the church through the back door, using Reverend Jesse's home as an entrance. He was surprised to hear talking in the chapel—he had expected everyone to still be hunkered down in the cellar. Peeking into the chapel, he saw Jeanette and a small group of townsfolk, including Nan and the mayor, huddled together and talking. They looked up as they saw him.

"Joe!" Nan's voice was heavy with relief as she hurried to him. "I'm so glad you're alright," she whispered as she reached him, her eyes searching his.

He reached for her hand and squeezed it, but he knew they didn't have time for any close conversations right then. "What's going on up here?" he asked, leading her back to the group.

"Some of the people are beginning to waver," the Mayor whispered. "We had to hold a few back from going to surrender to the bandits when the shooting started."

Joe clenched his jaw. "I'm sure that didn't help morale for everyone else."

Nan shook her head. "They're terrified, Joe, and they need someone to look to. We need you to come and talk to them about the day's battle."

"In a moment. Jeanette, we have a couple of wounded men back at the boarding house, and I'm sure there will be more before this is all over. I saw what you did with Archie. I need you and anyone else with any medical knowledge to go there and help. Can you do that? I'll take you back myself when I've spoken with everyone below."

"I can do that," she responded. "I know there's another woman here that some folks go to when they need stitching up or poultices."

"Good, get her and grab anything you have here or in the Reverend's home that would be of help."

"There are some supplies at my place, too," Nan added, much to Joe's relief.

The group made their way down into the cellar, which was lit with a couple of lanterns. Women and children, as well as older and sickly men, were huddled on the floor. Many were clutching each other, and one mother was singing quietly to a young girl on her lap who was trembling violently. Archie was leaned against a wall, a fresh bandage around his shoulder wound, and Nellie stood just behind him, her arms crossed. They all looked up as Joe entered.

"Joe has news from the front," the mayor said, and ushered Joe in front of him.

"I'll cut right to the point," Joe said, looking around at them. "The bandits are holed up in a few cabins on the very edge of town. There was some shooting, but we only lost one man on our side, and only a few on theirs."

"Do you know who we lost?" a woman called, her eyes anxious.

Joe shook his head, cursing himself internally for not checking that, first. "I don't know yet, ma'am. I'm sorry. Right now, we need everyone to stay here and stay safe. Jeanette is going to Nan's boarding house to lead the medical effort, and the mayor will stay here to lead you."

"Aren't you staying, Joe?" another woman asked, and many others were nodding.

Joe shook his head, yet again, realizing with dismay that the people now recognized him, and not the mayor, as the real leader in the town. His ever-growing list of responsibilities had expanded, yet again, but it couldn't be helped. He would just have to keep pushing on.

"I need to go back to the boarding house, as well, so that I can help direct the fighters. Right now, our plan is to wait the bandits out. We've got the advantage since we still control the town and they can't leave their cabins without being seen and shot. The longer we wait, the better. We've got a watch duty set up, and we'll be ready around the clock to fight at any moment, but time is on our side. We're hopeful that the messengers that were sent to other towns will come back with help."

He stopped speaking, and felt weariness wash over him. He didn't let his posture sag; the townspeople couldn't know how exhausted and worn he felt. They needed him to be a pillar of strength, and to see any weakness in him would only promote more terror on their part. They needed a task to keep them occupied.

"Since we don't know how long this is going to last, we need to divvy up some tasks over here. Mayor, you'll need to direct a rotation of watch duty." The mayor nodded, and Joe continued. "You can leave the cellar and go up into the church, as long as you're able to get back into the cellar immediately should the watch see any danger coming. Do you understand?"

The group nodded mutely.

"For the time being, you should have enough food and water for a few days—" seeing a few of the adults start to protest, he lifted a hand and continued, "although the fight won't necessarily last that long. But, you have what you need. I need the adults to entertain the children. Everyone will be safest if we just stay calm. We're all counting on you."

Joe scanned the room, and nodded to himself, assured that they would obey his orders for the time being. He turned to Nan, Jeanette, and the mayor and waved for them to follow him back upstairs.

"We'll have a meeting in a few hours' time once we've gotten Jeanette to the boarding house. Mayor, you and Nan can make your way over when everything is settled here," he said once they arrived at the main floor. "Archie and Nellie, too, assuming that Archie is able. Don't take his word for it, either, he's a stubborn one. Mayor, if you'll set up the watch rotation here, Milton and I will expand our watch with the volunteers at the boarding house."

The mayor agreed, and Joe turned to leave with Jeanette and the woman who was coming to help her. He paused and gave Nan a long look, trying to convey without words all that he felt for her.

"We'll see you soon. I promise."

29

Joe, Jeanette, and the woman she'd chosen returned to the boarding house to find that more of the fighters had gathered, and two more were wounded. Joe was discouraged to hear from these survivors that two of the other fighters had been fatally shot, increasing the death toll among the small band of volunteers.

Jeanette and the townswoman who had come with her immediately set to work on the wounded men, commandeering two of the bedrooms as their makeshift hospital. Joe and some of the fighters carried the wounded to them, leaving them in their care.

The time flew by with the work, and Joe was surprised to see the sun beginning to set. He was just checking in with the volunteer on watch duty when Milton came up to him, telling him that the original resistance team was gathered down in the kitchen.

Joe entered the kitchen to find Nan, the mayor, Mack, Louis, and even Archie sitting at the table. Jeanette, though busy with her post, had left the other woman in charge so she could slip downstairs for the meeting.

"Where's Nellie?" Joe asked, and a few of those present shook their heads.

"We haven't seen her in some time," Nan said, a worried look on her face.

"She was at the church earlier..." Joe said thoughtfully.

"I was with her not much more than an hour ago," Archie said, "but she went upstairs and never came back down."

"Maybe she's defected," Louis piped up. "They said some of the people were thinking about it, right?"

"There's no way Nellie did that," Joe said. "I don't believe it for a second. There's a good reason she's gone, so everyone keep an eye out for her and tell me if you see her. Ask people when they come back from watch, too."

Louis looked unconvinced, but he held his peace for the time being. Joe thought it best to shift topics and forge ahead with the meeting.

"Jeanette, why don't you fill everyone in on the medical situation," he suggested, sitting and giving her the floor.

Jeanette wiped her hands briskly on her apron, her face showing none of the exhaustion she must surely be feeling. "The recruits have told me that at least three men have died," she began, and the group winced at the sobering news. "I have a few men who've been wounded, although most will be fine—gashes from bullets that didn't fully enter them and the like. I've got them bandaged and resting. One of the recruits was shot in the leg, and his situation is pretty serious. We cleaned his wound to avoid infection, and we've bound it, but there's no way he can put weight on it for days, at the very least. He won't be able to continue fighting."

"It's not good," Mack commented, "but it's not as bad as I thought it might be. There's that to be thankful for."

Louis looked like he wanted to chip in sarcastically, but Joe speared the man with a look and he stayed quiet.

"Milton, what can you tell us about enemy casualties?" Joe asked.

"I've talked with every fighter that's made it back here," Milton said, shaking his head. "Earl hasn't lost many men, that we know of. Maybe five, six at the most. We're still outnumbered by a long shot."

Joe sighed. "That's what we expected, but I'd hoped for better news. So far, they're staying put in their hideouts, though, which gives us some time to make plans. Nan, how much longer do you think we can last on the supplies we have?"

"We've got a good amount of time left," she replied. "We have plenty of food stockpiled at the church, and you know my cellar and kitchen are full of food for the fighters quartered here. I don't think you need to be worried on that front, Joe."

"Good. Let's move to our battle plans, then," Joe said, folding his hands and leaning on the table. "Given how things have panned out, I think that our basic plan should be to wait for reinforcements from other towns, should they be willing to help, and not to make a forward move on the bandits in the meantime. We'll be ready and waiting to pick them off if they try to push further into town."

"We've been moving around town fairly well, though," the mayor pointed out hesitantly. "What's to stop them from doing the same? They might be able to take over more parts of the town that we don't have occupied."

"Mayor's right," Louis spoke up, his eyes alight with emotion. "I bet they're sneaking through the town right now. We need to do something about it!"

"And we will, Louis," Joe assured him. "But we need to be smart about it."

"They burned a lot of Narrow Bluff to the ground," Mack said quietly. "There's nothing to say they won't do the same, here, aside from sneaking some of their men further into town. What can we do to stop them from destroying Widestone?"

The group mulled these words over silently, deep in thought about the precarious situation in town.

"Maybe there's a way we could carefully bring the fight to them." Joe spoke slowly, turning various ideas over in his head. Louis snapped to attention, but Joe didn't look at him, yet. "We are already expanding the watch here, and I know the mayor set up a watch at the church. Mayor, are any of the folks at the church willing to assist with watch duty in other parts of town?"

The mayor sighed. "A few volunteered, but not many." He looked worried, but he didn't offer any further guidance.

Joe forged ahead. "We could send some of our volunteers to sneak closer to the bandits' strongholds on the edge of town to set some traps and cause some havoc for them."

"What do you have in mind?" Milton asked. "It's not like we can burn buildings."

"Freeing their horses, destroying supplies...What if we tried to pick off members of their watch?" Joe suggested. "That could help us to gain an advantage. And we could try to set up ambushes for key members of their gang—Earl, Friendly Nick, and Edwin."

"I can lead that," Louis jumped in eagerly, even as Archie shook his head.

"Too dangerous," Archie bit out. "We're just puttin' ourselves in harm's way if we do that. I say we wait for help."

"No one's making you fight," Louis turned on him angrily, and Nan laid a hand on his arm to calm him down.

"Easy, Louis," Milton said quietly, and Louis lowered himself back into his chair.

"Without their leaders in place, they might turn tail and run," Louis argued. "I say we set ambushes for them. I can get some volunteers to go with me."

Joe didn't like the dangerous gleam in Louis's eye, but he knew that taking out the bandit leaders would do a lot to tip the advantage to their side. "Louis, you have to promise you won't do anything too rash. We can't lose you and your men, so, if it comes down to it, you need to get yourself and your men back here to safety."

"I swear it, Joe," Louis said gravely, although, the unholy gleam was not fully gone from his eyes, and Joe's worry did not abate. "Milton, can you help me pick out a few men who will be best for this mission? You know the townsfolk better than I do."

Milton nodded silently.

Joe caught his eye, silently urging him to be cautious, but he said only, "Louis, you and Milton go find recruits for your mission, but check in with me before you set out. We need to talk more about your plans."

Louis agreed hastily, rushing out of the kitchen, followed by Milton. Joe sighed worriedly, but turned his attention back to the rest of the group. They were watching him tensely, and Archie still looked upset over his brush with Louis's rage.

"We need to talk about morale," Joe said quietly. "I've seen it here with the troops, and at the church with the other townsfolk. The deaths, the uncertainty...it's having a bad impact on everyone, and we can't afford to lose strength now. We need everyone ready to fight and protect, and we can't have mutinies breaking out, and we *definitely* can't afford to lose anyone to those bandits or they'll be able to use them against us."

He rubbed a hand wearily across his eyes, and for a moment, his posture sagged in his chair, but he forced himself to sit straight once more. He looked from person to person. "Any ideas? I'm just about out of 'em myself."

"I have a few," the mayor spoke up timidly, and Joe was a bit surprised. He turned to face the man more fully, and the mayor cleared his throat a bit self-consciously. "I know that, at least over at the church, what the folks need most is distraction and comfort. I was thinking of organizing a singing—having everyone down in the cellar singing hymns and campfire songs to help pass the time and build unity."

Joe nodded appreciatively. "That's a fine idea, mayor."

The mayor's shoulders straightened a bit. "A good meal wouldn't go amiss, either. We have food, but I think most people haven't eaten—we've been trying to save rations because we don't know how long we'll be down there."

Nan jumped in, at this point. "We have more than enough supplies, for now, and folks will stay calmer if they aren't fighting hunger. It turns everyone into animals, and a full belly will help the little ones settle in to sleep. I can organize a big meal for everyone, although, I'll need help."

"We could call it a victory celebration," the mayor added. "We may not have won yet, but it might comfort everyone and strengthen resolve if we frame it as something that is going to happen."

Nan nodded appreciatively, her green eyes sparkling in her weary face. "That would be just the thing, especially for the little ones who are so afraid right now. I'll start the meal here, if you can have some recruits finish it, Joe?" When he nodded, she continued, "And those of us going back to the church can help me carry a few supplies I need to take there. I'll get some of the women to help me cook in the Reverend's kitchen. It's not big, but it'll do for now. We may not all be able to eat the meal together, but the victory meal will help connect us, I think."

The mayor smiled, clearly happy to hear that his ideas had been helpful. Joe was relieved to have some of his burdens lifted by these good people so willing to help out. He was, in particular, happy to see the mayor gaining confidence.

Milton stepped back into the kitchen. "Louis is talking with a couple of men that will be going with him," he told Joe. "He'll be in to speak with you before he leaves. Is there anything else we need to discuss before splitting up?"

"Just working out the expanded watch duty," Joe said, nodding a farewell to Jeanette, who was quietly slipping out of the kitchen to return to her patients. "We should post some guards in more places than just here at the boarding house. We need guards on all sides from now on."

Milton nodded. "I was thinking the same thing. We need to make sure the bandits aren't sneaking through town. I'm gathering a group of the volunteers to set up a watch schedule, and we'll stake out some key locations to keep watch. We'll need some of the townsfolk from the church,

Mayor. We'll place them in safer spots, but we need more bodies than we've got among the recruits."

The mayor bit his lip in thought, then straightened his shoulders. "I'll talk with the group when I get back to the church. These are good people, and I'm confident that I can find some willing to help with the watch. I know these folks. We'll work it out."

Joe nodded approvingly at the man, glad to see the change from the man from earlier who had been cringing into the background back at the church. Looking with weary gratitude at the rest of the faces around the table, Joe rose and pushed in his chair. The others followed suit, and Joe opened his mouth to thank them for their efforts, but he found he had no words. They seemed to understand, though, as each shook his hand or tipped their heads to him as they slipped out of the room one by one.

30

———————

Joe was just finishing his shift on watch duty at the boarding house a tense day later. So far, the bandits hadn't pushed into town, but there was also no word from any messengers or help from nearby towns, and he could feel his nerves fraying, along with everyone else waiting in the town.

He tried to scrub the tiredness from his eyes as he nodded to the recruit taking his place and headed down the stairs to the dining hall. He would check in with everyone down there to make sure there was no news, before climbing into bed for some much-needed rest. Turning the corner at the foot of the stairs, he was surprised to see Louis emerging from the kitchen. He looked even more exhausted than Joe felt, if that was possible.

"Louis!" Joe called to him. "Let's talk in Nan's office. I want to hear what's going on with your mission."

Louis followed Joe into the small room wearily, settling himself into a chair with a sigh. Joe closed the door for privacy, before turning to Louis. He didn't bother with any niceties.

"What news do you have?"

"I lost one of my three men," Louis said, his mouth tight with worry. "We've managed to pick off a few of Earl's watchmen, but we haven't gotten eyes on any of the leaders."

Joe nodded, biting back a curse. They couldn't afford to lose any of their small number, but at least Louis and his men had managed to take out a few of the bandits. "Have you had anything to eat? Any rest?"

Louis shook his head. "I haven't slept in more than twenty-four hours, but I can't rest right now. There's too much to do and I wouldn't sleep anyway. I grabbed a bite to eat in the kitchen before you came downstairs. I just wanted to report to you before heading back out."

Joe knew that arguing with Louis would be of no use—the man had too much fire for his mission to obliterate the bandits to listen to reason and get some rest. He would let Louis sort that out for himself.

"Be careful, Louis. I don't want to lose you, too," he said, and Louis merely nodded, not bothering to respond.

They rose and left the office, Louis heading for the door. The morning quiet was splintered by sudden gunshots and shouting in the distance. Joe and Louis, on high alert, looked at each other. They didn't have to speak; they knew what to do. Each grabbed extra ammunition off a table in the dining hall.

"Louis, round up some men and have them get ready to meet the bandits. It sounds like the fighting is on the main street."

Louis nodded, rushing off to obey Joe's directions. Joe could hear Milton shouting from upstairs, gathering fighters. Anyone that was able to fight in the boarding house was ready to go, and footsteps thundered down the stairs as men toting their weapons rushed for the front door. Joe was among them.

"Stay as covered as you can!" he shouted. "Head to the town square!"

Joe's sole comfort was that the fighting was still far away from those hiding out at the church. Hopefully, he and his men could keep the violence from spreading past the town square. It looked like the bandits were not going to hide out any longer, which was bad news for the resistors. They had had the advantage of their defensive position and the waiting gave them an edge, but now the bandits were pushing in for a fight. Joe hoped they could find good cover to help make up for the disparity in skill and numbers. It was all he could hope for, because he acknowledged grimly to himself that Earl wouldn't be sending his bandits out on a death mission. If they were going into battle, they clearly expected to finish the problem once and for all.

Joe and the other men were approaching the town square carefully, staying low and covered. He knew they were in for a tough fight—Earl and his leaders had certainly had time to prepare, and it was likely they had a few tricks up their sleeve. It was going to be a bloodbath. He could only hope that the obstacles and cover his men had set up in the time before the bandits had returned to Widestone would give them enough of an advantage.

The gunshots began coming more and more frequently as Joe found a hiding spot behind some barrels at the edge of an alley that fed into the square. A deputy and Milton were crouched near him in the alley, and Joe could see Louis and the preacher hidden across the way under their own cover.

The bandits were employing the same strategy of keeping under as much cover as possible, and it was clear they were taking things slowly, advancing in from the west side of the square. Joe couldn't tell how many there were, as the only clue as to their location was the flashes before a gunshot and heads popping into view every now and then as they assessed the situation in the square.

"There's at least two hiding behind the western wall of the dry goods store," Milton said quietly, raising his gun and watching the spot intently. "Come on...come out into the open..." His gun exploded with a shot and a scream of pain sounded immediately after. His bullet had found the shoulder of one of the bandits that had emerged from hiding just a little too far.

Joe fired off a shot near the livery, where he had seen flashes of gunfire, then quickly ducked back down as returning fire rained down. He had been correct about some bandits hiding out there. Cocking his gun, he waited a breath, then rose just high enough to squeeze off another round at the stable. This time, his aim was true—a bandit sprawled out into the dirt, no longer moving.

Joe didn't get his hopes up, but he was grimly satisfied that at least none of his men had been taken down in this fight just yet. He glanced over to see how Louis and the preacher were faring. They were still huddled, but Louis was looking murderous and it seemed as though Reverend Jesse was trying to restrain him. What on earth were they wasting time for?

Joe's question was answered in the next moment. He peeked out from behind the barrels to squeeze off another shot, and he saw what had riled Louis up. A short man with black hair, who could only be Friendly Nick, was just visible at the edge of the square. He was clearly leading the fight, and he had taken control of one of the obstacles the resistance had created. He and a few men were stationed behind an overturned wagon surrounded by bags of feed. The bags would stop bullets, and the tipped wagon provided cover.

Joe gritted his teeth, trying to get a clear shot of the bandit leader. The man kept bobbing in and out of view. No wonder Reverend Jesse was having to keep Louis from running across the square and strangling Friendly Nick with his bare hands. It would be a suicide mission, but it was galling to see the villain so close and not be able to land a good shot on him.

Joe squeezed off a shot at the wagon, but his bullet landed in a bag of feed, burying itself deep and sending some grain flying. Instantly, shots from the bandits behind the wagon sailed toward Joe's barrels, smacking into the walls behind him. Beside him, Milton shot back fiercely, but he didn't manage to hit anyone, either.

The square was a mass of noise and confusion with the incessant shooting and the smoke from the shots, but there was also a strange yelling and whooping from the bandits. They weren't saying any discernible words to Joe's ears, and he wasn't sure whether the yipping and hollering was a system of command or a tactic to further confuse and overwhelm his men with the added chaos.

Joe fought to maintain his focus despite the pandemonium. He needed to make his shots count. Peeking through a new hole forged by a bullet in one of the barrels, he was able to make out a bandit in the wagon enclosure that was just a little too far to the side. In trying to hide from

Louis's side of the gunfire, he had inadvertently exposed himself to fire from the opposite direction.

Joe carefully lined up the shot and eased up to let it fly. His rifle kicked back against his shoulder with the blast, and he slammed himself back into the ground immediately after shooting.

"You got him," Milton shouted, who was lining up his own shot. "Nice shot, Joe."

Joe didn't have time to be pleased that another of the bandits had fallen. A bad feeling was creeping over him. Something was off about the situation. He reloaded his rifle, trying to sift through the endless barrage of information coming in from his senses. He knew to trust his gut, and his gut was telling him there was a problem bigger than just the shootout occurring.

Carefully, he fired off another shot, although this bullet didn't bury itself in the enemy. Then, it hit him—though it was difficult to tell in the chaotic situation, it felt like there had been more bandits present when they had rolled into the edge of town a few days earlier. He knew they had killed some in the initial gunfight, Louis and his men had taken out some of their watch, and a few had died today, but the number still didn't match his sense of the shootout that was currently happening.

On top of that, he hadn't seen Earl anywhere nearby. Was Earl hiding back at the cabins? Was he just a coward? That didn't make any sense to Joe. Earl had been ready enough to fight at their first shootout, and, from what he'd heard of the man, he was a killer shot who didn't like to run from a fight. If Earl wasn't at the square right now, there was a good reason. Joe needed to figure out what it was, and his gut was telling him that the matter was urgent. He needed to find Earl, and he needed to do it now.

"Milton, you're in command here," he said urgently to the lawman.

Milton squeezed off another shot and ducked. "Where are you going?" he gasped out.

"I have a hunch Earl is up to something. He's not here. I'm going to pull back with a couple of men and head to the boarding house in case he's making a move there."

"Got it," Milton said, his attention fully on the fighting at the square.

Joe grabbed a couple of deputies and they hurried back down the alley, away from the town square shootout. Keeping under cover, they started making their way back to Nan's boarding house. As they got further away from the fighting, Joe lifted a hand and they halted.

Before, they had only been able to hear the hollering of Friendly Nick's men and the incessant gunfire, but with some distance, Joe could now hear something even more terrible. His stomach dropped in horror.

Gunshots were coming from the direction of the church —right where the most vulnerable of the town were hidden together.

31

JOE JUMPED INTO ACTION. There was no time to wait.

"Clark, go back to the square and round up some more men. Meet us at the church!"

The man took off back toward the fighting, while Joe and the other deputy charged toward the church. No one seemed to be coming to alert the others that the church was in danger, which could only mean that any of those on watch at the church had been picked off by the bandits. Joe's heart was in his throat as he ran, and he had to rely on his years of experience as a lawman to remember to move carefully and keep to cover.

The church came into view. Joe didn't see the bandits immediately at the church or pouring into it. It looked like they were still some distance away, but they were firing at someone or something he couldn't see yet. Joe and the deputy with him ducked into the barn across from the church that the original resistance group had used for meetings and as a hideout. He took his familiar place at the crack in the door where he could see out into the street, taking a moment to catch his breath and assess the situation with as much cold calculation as he could muster.

There were maybe eight or so bandits, definitely no more than ten. His inner hackles rose as he recognized one of the men as none other than Earl Gallagher, himself. The bandits were being held back from getting closer by someone Joe couldn't see, and Joe intended to keep it that way.

Taking careful aim, he leveled a shot straight for Earl's head. The shot blasted off, but hit the dirt behind the bandits —Earl had dropped to a knee to reload his rifle at the exact moment Joe had sent a shot his way. Joe cursed bitterly at the wasted opportunity. Earl's head snapped around as the bullet lodged in the dirt near him, and Joe could see the exact moment he realized that he was dealing with more than just the unseen fighter at the church.

Earl shouted for his men to take cover, and they dove behind barrels, walls, and anything else they could use. Then, at another order from Earl, bullets began whizzing toward the barn. A bullet slammed into the wood by Joe's head, splintering a hole into the wall where he had been standing just seconds before. Instinctively, he ducked and rolled onto the ground, putting some distance between himself and the door.

The deputy with him was doing the same, frantically scrambling further into the barn.

"The hayloft," Joe bit out. "We can see more from up there. Go!"

The deputy didn't need to be told twice. Scrabbling to get to his feet, he tore up the ladder on the wall that led to the hayloft with Joe hot on his heels. Bullets continued hitting the outer wall of the barn, but, luckily, no one was shooting for the second floor yet. Joe scurried to the wall and peered out of the cracks to the street below.

"They don't have enough rifles to go around," Joe muttered to the deputy, squinting at the action. "It looks like some of them are just using pistols. We can use that to our advantage. Let's get some shots off from up here, and then we're going to have to find new cover so that we don't get trapped up here. We just need to hold them off until we get some backup."

The deputy nodded silently, already arranging his gun into a space between the slats. Joe did the same. Joe aimed for one of the bandits holding a rifle, just rising out of a crouch to shoot at the church. Taking less than a second to take in a deep breath, Joe focused hard on the man and pulled the trigger. The bullet slammed hard into his target's chest, sending him backwards into the dirt.

The deputy didn't waste a moment. He fired at another bandit who had just fired at the church, and cut him down with a shot to the face. The bandit's hat was blown off, along with the upper half of his head. The grisly sight wasn't enough to slow the bandits for long, though, as the few with rifles swung to shoot at the barn again.

"Come on!" Joe hissed to the deputy. "We need to get out of the barn! You go ahead, I'll try and take one more out before I join you!"

The deputy ran toward the ladder, pausing behind a beam to reload his rifle before descending the ladder so quickly it was more of a half-slide and half-climb back to the ground floor. Joe took those moments to reload as quickly as possible and fire once more into the group of bandits. Earl was fully covered, to his angry annoyance, but he clipped another bandit in the knee, effectively disabling the man's ability to run. Joe knew it was a risk to spend even one more moment in the hayloft, but he wasn't going to leave when he had a chance to finish this bandit off.

Pulling his pistol from his gun belt, he aimed at the fallen bandit who was trying to drag himself to cover. Joe aimed for the man's exposed back and landed an impressive shot right on target. At that range, his pistol was far less likely to be accurate, but he hadn't wanted to waste the time to reload his rifle. His instincts proved correct in this case—the bandit lay sprawled face down in the earth, crimson blood staining his shirt from a large hole in his back.

Three down, at least six or seven to go, including their leader. Joe swung down the ladder, first following the deputy's example to reload his rifle before rejoining the action. Joe slipped out of the back of the barn and made his way around the edge, creeping toward the street. He was more exposed by being outside, but hiding out in the barn wasn't looking like much of an option anymore.

As he approached the front edge of the barn, Joe heard Archie's distinctly gruff voice swearing like a sailor, his voice a raspy yell interspersed with gunshots. Joe realized, with relief, that Archie was the unseen shooter who had been holding the bandits off from overrunning the church. He was grateful for the man's bravery in protecting the church, especially since Joe had never anticipated that the wounded man would be among the fighting number.

He needed to help the man before he gave out completely. Joe peered around the edge of the barn carefully, just far enough to pick out his next target. He whipped back behind the barn wall, cocked his gun, and took a deep breath, preparing himself to take the shot. Lining up his shot carefully, Joe's next bullet buried itself in the throat of a bandit just raising his rifle to shoot where Archie must have been hiding behind the church.

Blood sprayed from the man's obliterated throat, and Joe could hear the sickening gurgle as the man gasped for a breath he would never again take. Before he even hit the ground, however, Joe's mind was already on securing his next target.

Suddenly, a bullet buried itself in the wall beside Joe, only a few inches from his head, and he dropped to a crouch, whipping his gun to his right, squeezing off a shot on pure reflex. His aim was lucky, as he didn't have time to fully aim. It tore through the bandit that had snuck around the back of the barn to creep up on Joe unawares. Adrenaline coursed through Joe as he realized that several previously unseen bandits were rounding the corner of the barn, only a few feet behind their fallen compatriot.

Joe hurled himself around the front of the barn, as he and the deputy burst out of their hiding spots to race across the open street to the church. Bullets rang through the air around them, just barely missing the two men. One bullet cut so close to him that he felt his shirt tear. Less than an inch closer and it would have struck his side.

Joe collapsed behind the church, taking what cover he could, the deputy doing the same. Both of them were gasping for breath, even as they struggled to reload their weapons and regain their bearings.

"They must've snuck some of the men to this end of town for an ambush," Joe said, between panting breaths. "They were planning this all along." He didn't have time for more, not even to swear, because the gunshots and footfalls were coming closer. The situation was becoming dire.

Joe peered around the edge of the church and shot at a bandit that was just diving for cover, his bullet glancing off the wooden wall behind the bandit, having missed them entirely. Simultaneously, another shot rang out and slammed into the head of the deputy right beside Joe. Within a second, the brave lawman had become a lifeless corpse, eyes glassy and staring up at the sky.

Joe whipped out his pistol and took down the bandit that was coming around the edge of the church, who'd just killed his deputy. The bandit was jolted by the force of the shot, and he collapsed in a heap, slamming into the church wall as he fell. Joe edged around the back of the church. He needed to get back to the front end to protect the doors of the church, where the remaining bandits would surely try to breach the entrance any moment now.

Archie staggered around the church wall, and Joe only barely stopped his reflexive instinct to shoot on sight. Archie was clutching his shoulder and gasping. His face was a sickly gray, and the wound in his shoulder was once again bleeding freely. Joe felt a hopeless panic settling in on him, even as he struggled to reload his rifle, knowing he would fight until the bitter end.

"Joe!" Archie managed to grate through his cracked lips. "Milton's comin'!"

Archie was right, he saw. Milton and a small group of men were making their way toward the church, bobbing in and out of sight as they maintained their cover while simultaneously trying to help Joe and Archie by taking shots at the bandits, although most of their shots were going wild because of the range. It was slowing the bandits down, but not by much.

Things were going from bad to worse—if the bandits made it inside the church, it would be over. The noncombatants hiding in the cellar were sitting ducks, and Joe wouldn't stand for a massacre. Joe met Archie's eyes, and made a split-second decision. No matter the cost, he had to slow down the bandits who were even now breaching the front doors. Images of Nan and Will floated before him, almost as if in slow motion, strengthening his resolve for the moments before he did what he knew would result in near-certain death.

Keeping his back to the corner, he lifted his rifle, ready to blast at the group of bandits that would be literally feet from him. Carefully, he whipped around the corner, firing off a shot, but his bullet zoomed through empty air, lodging in the street beyond. He stopped, stunned.

Where there should have been a group of bandits, there were, instead, only three corpses. His jaw dropped, and he looked around wildly, shock stunting his senses. Milton wasn't on this end, so who could have mowed down the intruders?

He turned in the direction the firing had to have come from, and was stunned to see Nellie standing next to a hulking figure. The enormous man was looking down the sights of a rifle, and, in the next moment, he had fired off another shot, leveling a bandit who had just emerged from a hiding spot.

Joe couldn't seem to make his brain accept the scene before him. He could only stand and stare in disbelief as Nellie raised a hand to wave at him. She was standing with his rescuer, who was none other than the bandit lieutenant, Edwin the Giant.

32

JOE WAS STARTLED out of his momentary shock as gunshots erupted once again. Instinctively, he hurled himself back behind the wall of the church, chest heaving. His mind was racing, struggling to catch up with the bizarre chain of events that was unfolding. He didn't have time to ponder on the fact that it appeared that Edwin the Giant had turned on his own gang and was now assisting the town. He needed to figure out what was happening with the new round of gunfire.

It sounded as though the gunshots were coming from down the road, closer to the town square, where he had seen Milton emerging a minute before with more of their men. Carefully, he peered around the corner of the church to take stock of the action. He had to bob back and forth, never keeping his eyes in the open for too long, but he was able to piece together what was occurring.

Milton and his men were scrambling for cover as Earl's bandits were moving in on them. That meant that they'd broken past the barricading and cover his men had tried to set up in the town square, and the battle was now fully advanced to the church—the last place in town they wanted the gang anywhere near.

The fighting was a wild mass of chaos and disorganization. It was clear that no one was quite sure what to do, and the shooting was at random. Joe cursed to himself. He needed to bring back some order and rally the men for this fight. The bandits would soon be on the church, and they couldn't afford to endanger their most vulnerable townspeople.

"Cover the church!" he bellowed, fighting to be heard above the noise. "Milton! Louis! Tell your men to take cover! Don't let them get to the church!"

With rising panic, Joe ripped open a new canister of ammunition for his rifle, scattering some of the bullets on the ground in his hurry. He dropped to one knee, scrabbling for a bullet in the dust, eyes on the scene before him. He didn't have time for any distractions like this. His fingers closed around metal and he jammed the bullet into his rifle, loading the gun with reflexive habit, his eyes already searching for his next target.

In the nick of time, he saw a bandit sneaking around the edge of a building closer to the main street, his gun lifted and poised to take a shot at one of the town's fighters. Joe set his sights on the man and launched a shot, but not before the bandit had discharged his own weapon, felling one of Joe's recruits. The bandit screamed as Joe's bullet lodged in his stomach, his hands flying to staunch the waterfall of blood gushing ceaselessly around his fingers. He wouldn't last more than a couple of minutes longer.

Joe reloaded and discharged his rifle with an almost mechanical precision, and within the next few minutes he had felled two more of Earl's men. Rather than buoying his confidence, he was holding on with a grim panic—the scene was becoming a bloodbath. The dusty street was strewn with men from both sides, blood seeping from the various corpses and fatally wounded men, staining the ground a rusty brown and forming tiny rivulets in the hard packed dirt of the street.

Despite the large losses on both sides, Joe knew they needed to do something to turn the tide in their favor if they could. Plenty of Earl's men had been killed, but they still outnumbered Joe's men, and he could see far too many of his own lying motionless and bleeding in the scene before him. Joe reloaded his rifle yet again, simultaneously trying to conjure up a fresh plan to protect the church and those that were still alive.

Archie was still nearby, slumped behind a fence, but still managing to heave himself up on his elbows to take more shots at the bandits. Milton was too far away for Joe to get to, but Joe thought he might be able to get to Archie and a few of the other recruits. They needed to shore up the protection directly around the church. If nothing else, they had to stop the bandits from advancing inside the building and making their way to the cellar.

Joe took careful aim, taking down a bandit about to catch Reverend Jesse unawares. It was a killer shot, straight through the man's forehead, and he dropped without even the chance to scream.

"Preacher, take cover behind the church!" Joe screamed. "Bring anyone you can!"

He didn't wait to see if the Reverend had followed his directions. Joe whirled away and ran down the side of the church, heading to the back to loop around and yell for

Archie. The back of the church was still the safest and most protected part of the building, and he hoped the Reverend and Archie, plus a few other fighters, would be able to make it to him so that they could formulate a plan.

"Archie!" he hollered around the edge of the church. "Archie! Get over here if you can! Bring any men who can hear you! Hurry!"

Joe prepared to cover Archie, as the older man struggled to do Joe's bidding. Joe picked off a bandit that was in a position to take Archie down, and Archie scrambled to meet Joe while the coast was clear for those precious few seconds.

"I didn't have time to get anyone else," he gasped, clutching his shoulder as he slammed himself against the back of the church.

Joe didn't answer, already setting his sights on another bandit. He pulled the trigger, but his bullet went wide and buried itself harmlessly in the wood of the abandoned barn. Joe swore and threw himself back behind the church next to Archie, reloading his weapon. Reverend Jesse, Louis, and two other recruits turned the corner behind the church at a dead run, terror and mingled relief on their faces as they saw Joe.

"What's the plan?" the preacher asked hoarsely, trying to catch his breath.

"We need to make a firm barrier at the head of the church," Joe said. "We have to stop the bandits from getting inside. We can go through your quarters and shoot through the front doors at anyone trying to get in through the main entrance. That's the direction they're coming from. We'll leave one man back here to guard the back. Understood?"

The men nodded, and immediately jumped into action, funneling into the church to get to their positions at the front.

Joe left one of the recruits at the back entrance, and chased after the other men heading through the chapel. They could still hear the violence raging outside in the streets, and the eerie quiet from the storm of bullets as they hurried to the front doors felt strange.

They didn't have much time to enjoy the reprieve, as they took their places at the front windows, with Joe at the front door, opening it a crack so he could see and take shots. There were still a few of Joe's recruits alive out in the street, but most were in defensive and covered positions. Joe hoped it would be enough to stop Earl's men, who were more spread out. In the distance, Edwin was still taking shots at the bandits, and Joe wondered if he had convinced any of his own men to join him. Joe took heart for a moment at the thought—maybe they would be able to beat Earl and the bandits. So far, they still had the church, and those men on his side that were still alive were closer to the church than most of the bandits. That, plus the help from Edwin, might be enough to stop the battle from advancing any further.

He was jerked out of this hopeful moment as one of his recruits was shot from the side by a bandit. The bullet ripped through the man's neck, nearly severing his head, and sending blood spraying. The recruit slumped over the barrel he had been using as cover. At this close range, Joe could just make out the bandit, and he slid his revolver out of his gun belt, planting a bullet in the man's shoulder. Not a fatal shot, but hopefully enough to slow the man down.

Joe felt a rising sense of urgency like bile in his throat. He needed to find Earl Gallagher. If he could take the man down, he might be able to end the fighting without further loss of lives among his recruits. He scanned the area, looking hard, but he couldn't see the man anywhere. For that matter, Friendly Nick, who had been in the square earlier, was also nowhere to be seen. Had the leaders used their own men as a distraction so they could turn tail and run? Did they have other nefarious plans?

Joe lifted his rifle, hunting for another target in the chaos. He thought he saw a bandit bobbing in and out of the doors of the old barn across from the church. He had been there himself earlier in the fighting, and he had a pretty good idea of where the man was probably keeping himself covered. Finger poised on the trigger, Joe waited for the bandit to appear for a moment in the doorway of the barn. It was only a sliver of a second, but it was enough time for Joe's bullet to find its home. He heard screams, and knew that he'd hit the bandit. He couldn't see where the shot had landed, whether it was fatal or just a wound, but it was better than nothing.

He reached for another bullet to reload his rifle, when he heard screaming from far behind him. He whipped around, trying to make sense of what he was hearing. The screaming was coming from inside the church, which could only mean the cellar. Panic tore through his body like fire, clouding his brain.

"Come quick," he shouted, not bothering to look back to see who followed. Dropping his rifle, he pulled his revolver from its holster and took off down the chapel, racing between the pews. Gunshots continued to blast outside the church, the ongoing gunfight was no longer important—he had to get to that cellar.

He slammed open the door leading out of the back of the chapel and into the Reverend's private quarters, where he simultaneously registered two things: the dead body of the recruit left to guard the back entrance of the church splayed face down in the dirt, and the cellar doors flung open. Throwing caution to the wind, Joe raced down the cellar stairs. At the bottom, he skidded to a halt, the other men with him only narrowly avoiding slamming into his back at his sudden stop. Joe's heart stopped beating for a moment, arrested by the sickening sight before him.

Earl Gallagher, dressed in the bloodstained outfit of a sheriff's deputy, stood before him. There was no doubt that he'd taken it from the corpse of a fallen deputy. He'd clearly used the uniform, including the hat and the badge, to confuse Joe's recruits and edge toward the church without being picked off by the men of Widestone.

It wasn't the sight of Earl in the cellar that had stopped Joe's breathing, though. It wasn't the uniform of the dead deputy, or the wicked leer that contorted Earl's features, either. It was who he was holding in front of himself as a human shield.

Nan.

Earl licked his lips lasciviously, maintaining eye contact with Joe. He clutched Nan to his chest a little more tightly, his dirt-encrusted fingernails standing out against her clean homespun dress. Gently, with relish, Earl brushed her thin throat with an enormous jagged knife, his wicked grin widening with pleasure.

"Hello, Joe," he said silkily. "So good of you to join us."

33

His FROZEN THOUGHT processes began to awaken, and Joe instinctively moved toward Nan, his fingers reaching for his revolver.

"Not another step," Earl bit out, his voice no longer silky. "You make another move, and I'll slit her pretty little throat."

Joe froze once again, terrified. In one easy motion, Earl could end Nan's life. Earl's knife hovered so close to Nan's neck that Joe was sure she could feel its cold metal edge whispering on her skin, promising to draw blood at the slightest provocation. Joe's mind raced, trying to come up with a plan to rescue her, but he knew it was futile. Anything he attempted in that moment would surely end with Nan bleeding out on the floor. Joe eased backward slightly, wordlessly conveying to Earl that he would not attempt anything rash. Seeing Joe's obedience, Earl's good humor returned, and he tsked gently.

"That's better, Joe. I knew you'd start to see things my way."

Joe's entire body ached with the force it was taking not to rush at Earl and tear the slimy man limb from limb, and it galled him that Earl knew his powerlessness. Earl was, no doubt, reveling in his control of the situation, in the terrified attention of everyone in the cellar.

"She's beautiful, isn't she?" Earl drawled lazily, as if he had all the time in the world. He bent his head toward Nan's neck, inhaling deeply, his eyes never once dropping from Joe's. "Smells good, too. Makes me want a little taste..." His tongue emerged from his dry and cracked lips, and slowly he licked the length of Nan's neck. Her body was stiff with revulsion and fear, but she didn't make a sound.

Will suddenly shot out of the shadows, hurling himself at Earl's leg and pounding the man with his little fists. "Get off my ma!" he screamed, his words echoing off the cold cellar walls. "I'll kill you! I'll kill you!"

Earl's mouth twisted with annoyance. He kicked out at Will viciously, and his boot landed squarely in the boy's stomach, knocking the air out of him. Will was bent double, arms around his belly, fighting for breath.

"Will, get back!" Nan cried out, straining for a moment in her desire to save her child.

"Shut up!" Earl snarled, his villainous grin replaced by the fury contorting his face from the little boy's interruption and Nan's cry. He jerked Nan hard, gripping her hair and yanking so that tears rose in her eyes.

"Someone hold on to Will," Joe called, trying to keep his voice soft and even, although he could hear the panic breaking through. "He's going to get himself hurt."

Joe heard shuffles as someone enfolded Will in their arms

238

and pulled him further back into the cellar. The boy's wild sobbing rang out as his breath returned, his hysteria to save his mother emerging loudly. The woman who had grabbed him clamped a hand over his mouth, trying to stifle the screams so as not to incur more of Earl's wrath. She shushed the boy gently, whispering urgently in his ear, and Will eventually quieted.

Earl ignored the scene behind him as if it fully bored him, rolling his head and cracking his neck loudly, as if mentally shaking off the past few moments. "Joe, why don't you and your boys head on back upstairs."

Joe didn't move. He wouldn't leave Nan alone with the man, even if it meant his own sure death. To disobey Earl was not wise, but to obey the man was even more unthinkable.

Earl sighed paternally. "Worried about your lady, huh? Go on, get on up those steps. She and I will be right behind ya." He jerked his head once more toward the stairs. "Don't make me ask again. I might not ask so nicely, hear?"

Joe's jaw was clenched so tightly he thought his teeth might crack under the immense pressure, but he forced himself not to speak. He couldn't risk any move that might send that knife across Nan's throat into action. Carefully, he slid his revolver back into its holster and turned to go back up the stairs, nodding at his men that they should follow Earl's instructions, as well.

Joe climbed the stairs, keenly aware of Earl forcing Nan up the stairs behind him. He could hear Earl's loud breathing as he shoved the stumbling Nan ahead of him. Joe's thoughts raced through various scenarios, trying to land on a plan that would enable him to rescue Nan and reverse the deadly situation. Within the span of a few seconds, he had thought of, and rejected, half a dozen plans. None of them would work, and all would end in the same unthinkable outcome—Nan's death.

"Keep walkin'," Earl said once they reached the top of the stairs. "Into the chapel."

Joe and his men edged into the chapel, moving cautiously.

"Prop the doors open," Earl commanded, jerking his head at Louis. Louis gritted his teeth, but followed Earl's bidding. "Now then," Earl continued, once Louis had obeyed, "all of you can take a seat. It's time for our negotiations."

Joe and his men lowered themselves slowly to the front pews, their postures tense and ramrod straight. Joe was perched on the edge of the bench, barely sitting. Earl noticed, and let out a sharp laugh.

"Why so nervous, Joe?" Earl mocked, lounging against the pulpit and hauling Nan up against him more firmly, his free arm trailing languidly to brush her breasts.

Joe nearly shot off the bench, but he restrained himself. Earl laughed, the sound grating harshly in the stillness.

"Might be you'll feel more calm without your guns, so this feels more like a nice conversation." Earl pretended to think hard for a moment, then broke into a grin. "Let's do that. You and your men drop your guns on the floor, nice and easy—don't try anything stupid, or my hand might slip. This knife is mighty heavy..."

Joe and his men slowly lowered their weapons to the church floor, never breaking eye contact with the vile man standing before them. They were powerless to do anything but obey.

Earl crowed heartily, enjoying his victory over the men, nearly preening. "It's downright adorable the way you all thought you could stand up to me. Too sentimental about this good-for-nothin' town. And look what it cost, why don't you? You went and made me hurt you." He shook his head in mock sadness. "We could've all gotten along, but I guess you folks couldn't stand that. Well, it's alright now. We're gonna put things back to the way they should've been."

Joe felt himself twitch as he strove to keep himself from lunging at Earl. He was trying to get a rise out of them, and it was working. Joe's fingers itched to retrieve his gun, and Earl seemed to sense it. The man's laughing manner disappeared instantly, and his voice was sharp and focused when he spoke again.

"All of you, kick your guns across the floor toward me."

Joe cursed himself mentally for betraying, even in the smallest way, what his thoughts were. He and his men began to obey Earl grudgingly, and Joe felt the chances of his ability to right the situation slipping even further away than before. He was just about to follow suit and kick his revolver toward Earl when he heard a clatter at the church entrance.

All of them whipped around to see a group of four bandits filing into the chapel. They entered easily, as if they owned the room. With Joe, Archie, Louis, and the Reverend captive to Earl's whims, there was no one guarding the church to block the progress of the bandits.

"I expected you all sooner," Earl called to them. "Next time, don't be so slow about following orders, got it?"

The implication of Earl's words was not lost on Joe. It was clear that the bandit leader had planned this ambush on the church, and possibly even the hostage situation, beforehand with some of his men. The first three bandits spread themselves out, making room for the fourth bandit to enter the room. When the fourth man walked in, Louis's face turned scarlet—the fourth bandit was none other than Friendly Nick.

When his eyes settled on Louis, Friendly Nick's yellowed eyes narrowed with glee, and his lips curved into a huge grin, revealing his rotting teeth. As quickly as they could, Joe and Archie reached for Louis, trying to hold him back in case he tried to do anything, but they were too late.

Louis leapt off the pew, lunging to the ground for his pistol and twisting mid-motion to train his pistol on the bandit leader leering at him from the church entrance. He moved so quickly he was nearly a blur, and in that moment two things happened almost simultaneously.

With incredible speed and deadly accuracy, Earl whipped his own pistol from his waistband with his free hand, discharging a bullet at Louis. In the split second before Earl's bullet lodged in the back of Louis's head, Louis pulled the trigger on his own pistol. Louis's dying aim was true, and his own bullet plowed through Friendly Nick's face.

Joe barely had time to register what'd just happened before his very eyes. As Friendly Nick's lifeless body fell toward the church floor, mirroring Louis's own falling body by the front pew, Joe lunged for his own pistol. He knew that this was likely the only shred of an opportunity he would get to save Nan and take Earl down.

Joe's fingers closed around his revolver just as Nan struggled away from Earl. It was only a few inches, but it was plenty for Joe. In the space of a breath, Joe trained his gun on Earl and took the shot, even as Earl whipped his own pistol toward Joe. Before he could pull his own trigger, Joe's bullet had buried itself into his chest, sending him backward.

Acting on instinct, Joe whipped around, dispatching two of the three bandits at the door with deadly precision and speed. The men crumpled, their attempts to pull their own weapons futile before Joe's shooting. Joe pointed his revolver at the final bandit and pulled the trigger.

Nothing happened. He stared down in horror, realizing he was out of bullets. Before he could scramble for another of the weapons on the floor, he heard a crack, and a millisecond later felt a sudden warmth in the right side of his chest. The impact threw him backward and pain exploded through his body like lightning, searing through every nerve of his body.

His head slammed into the church floor as he fell. He instinctively tried to reach for his bleeding chest, but found that he was unable to move. Shots rang out above him, but they seemed to be coming from a great distance. A roaring filled his ears, and his vision began to tunnel, the edges turning black. He struggled to breathe, trying to remain conscious, but it was nearly impossible through the blinding pain and the vast amounts of blood he knew had to be seeping from his chest.

He wanted to call out for help, but his throat and tongue wouldn't cooperate. He couldn't seem to form words or even sounds. He knew in that moment that he was dying, and there was nothing he could do to stop the darkness from taking him.

The blackness in the corners of his vision lengthened, taking over what little sight he had left. The last thing he saw before the darkness utterly consumed him was Nan's pale and frightened face, bending over him. Her mouth was moving, but he couldn't hear what she was saying to him. He longed to reach for her, to assure her that it would be alright, to tell her that he loved her, but he was trapped in his motionless body.

One last look at Nan's face, and then he slipped into the blackness.

3 4

Joe felt as though he were swimming up from a great depth as he began to awaken. He could feel soft sunlight on his face, and he knew that all he had to do was open his eyes to greet it. Still, it seemed to take a herculean effort to lift his eyelids; it was as though they were weighed down by boulders. He tried to speak, but all that emerged from his lips was a soft gurgle.

"Joe?"

He recognized the quiet voice, strong and sweet. He exerted himself with all of his might to pry his eyes open, and by focusing all of his energy, he was able to slowly lift his lids. He blinked a little as his vision cleared and Nan's face came into focus. She seemed to be surrounded by a halo, at first, nearly glowing in the sunshine pouring in from the bedroom window.

Her face split into a relieved smile, crinkling her eyes happily. She leaned over from the chair by his bed and grasped his hand, squeezing it as gently as she could in her joy. "Oh, Joe," she whispered, her eyes roving eagerly over his face.

"I have to go send a messenger to tell Milton you're awake," she said, suddenly sitting up straighter. "I'll be right back."

"Nan," he managed to croak out, his voice hoarse with disuse.

She turned back immediately.

"Water...please..."

"Of course, I'll be back in two shakes, Joe. Rest easy, and don't try to move until I get back." She speared him with a lovingly firm stare, before rushing off to take care of her errands.

Joe lay alone in the bedroom, staring at the ceiling. He was too exhausted to disobey Nan, even if he had wanted to. He became aware of a dull throbbing coming from the right side of his chest, and memories of the fateful battle in the church resurfaced slowly. He had killed Earl, saving Nan, but he had been shot when his revolver had run out of bullets. When he thought of how close he had come to losing Nan... It was unbearable to consider.

Nan returned to the room as he was turning the last thought over in his mind, and just seeing her alive and well filled him with a deep sense of peace. She reached beneath his neck to gently prop his head up while holding a glass of cool water to his lips. He swallowed eagerly, his parched throat grateful. He dribbled a little, but Nan wiped his chin tenderly, teasing him only a little. When his thirst had been quenched for the time being, Nan lowered his head again and settled herself on the bed beside him, reaching again for his hand.

"What happened...after...?" The water had helped, and it was a bit easier to speak, but he was still so tired. Fortunately, Nan understood him perfectly.

"Reverend Jesse shot the last bandit—the one who shot you, Joe," she paused, shuddering at the memory, then swallowed and continued softly, "he dragged Earl and Friendly Nick's bodies outside the church for all the bandits to see. There was still a gunfight going on outside, but he didn't take a weapon. He could've been killed, but he didn't care."

She stroked Joe's hand for a moment, reliving the scene in her mind as she related it to Joe. "He stood there alone, just silent for a minute. He seemed like a new man, Joe. I don't know how else to explain it... Anyway, he started shouting for all the bandits to hear, telling them to look and see how their leaders were gone and the battle was over. Archie came to stand beside him, then, and eventually, the shooting stopped. Everyone, on both sides, listened to them, and I think it was then that the bandits still alive realized there was no point in trying to fight anymore. Not without Earl to push them along."

They sat in silence for a moment as Joe took in what Nan had told him. She let him think without interruption, quietly rubbing his hand. She reached over once to smooth his hair from his forehead, and he closed his eyes as he savored her gentle touch.

"And Louis?" Joe asked eventually, breaking the silence.

Nan's face dropped, sadness seeping into her green eyes. Joe knew what she would say before she spoke. "Louis didn't make it," she said softly.

Joe turned his face away to stare out the window, his

chest aching from more than the gunshot wound he had endured. Louis had known that his rash decision to try and kill Friendly Nick would result in his own death, yet he had still done it. Surely, there could have been another way if Louis had just held on.

Joe felt a swell of unexpected anger rising within him as he realized that Louis had endangered Nan's life in his blind rage to murder Friendly Nick. True, it had ended with Joe able to act quickly enough to take out Earl and save Nan, but that could so easily have failed. It would have been so easy for Earl to have slit her throat before taking the shot at Louis, and it made Joe almost physically ill to think of how Louis had risked Nan in his own quest for revenge.

Revenge. Joe understood the depth of Louis's desire to avenge his wife and all that he had lost to the bandits. He, himself, had been spurred to action against Gallagher's gang of bandits by the steely promise within his soul that he would not rest until he had seen justice served for Sophie's horrific death. In the beginning, it had consumed him. It had been the only reason he had risked everything to stay in Widestone and fight. But then, things had changed.

What had made his journey different than Louis's, he realized, was the relationships he had formed with Nan and Will. As he had become closer to them, he had wanted more than just vengeance—he had wanted to ensure that they, and everyone like them, would be kept safe. He had wanted to rebuild a better Widestone, one that was free from the tyranny of a mob of thugs and their greed. He had wanted to see justice for her late husband, and to help Nan continue fulfilling her dreams of running a successful boarding house.

And where before, he had not cared whether he died in his pursuit of vengeance, meeting Nan had made him realize that he cared very much about whether or not he survived.

Joe turned his face back to look at Nan, who had been sitting quietly and letting him process all that had happened. He squeezed her hand gently, staring up into her green eyes, grateful to simply be in her calming presence. He wanted to reach up to brush her cheek, but when he tried, his chest sent a shock of pain through his body, and he gasped involuntarily.

"Easy, Joe," she said, caressing his forehead. "You've had some good rest, and the care of a surgeon, but you need more time to heal before you'll be ready to move about."

"Surgeon? How long have I been out?" he asked, realizing that he truly had no idea how long his unconscious state had lasted.

"Doc Brown came with the reinforcements from the next town over. They got our message and came to help us, but they didn't arrive until all the fighting was done. You were in pretty bad shape, Joe." She paused and bit her lip, remembering the deep worry of that first day. "I wasn't sure you would make it—your wound was deep, and it needed more care than Jeanette or anyone else could give you. When Doc Brown arrived... I promise you, Joe, I had never been so grateful to see anyone in my life. He came and stitched you up, and he gave you a lot of medicine for your pain. It kept you in a deep sleep, which your body needed desperately. You've been asleep for nearly three days."

"Three days?" he asked, shocked.

Nan nodded, smiling now. "I was starting to get worried,

but it turns out, you were just having a nice long nap and letting the rest of us do all the work, Mr. Lazybones," she teased him, and he grinned back.

It felt as though a huge weight had lifted off of his shoulders. Ever since he had received the letter from Sophie, he had been on high alert, racing against the clock to get to Narrow Bluff, and then to help save Widestone. So many had depended on him to be their leader, despite being relatively unknown. He had carried the weight of his sister's murder, the worry of Nan and Will being hurt in the fighting, and the trust and hope of all in Widestone to save them. Now, it felt as though he could finally take a breath. The town, though damaged from the fighting, and having lost many good men, would still need a lot of work. But for right now, things were safe, and he was here with Nan. And things with Nan just felt right. She was the first woman who had ever made him want to settle down.

"Nan, I'm so grateful you're alright," he began quietly, wanting to tell her how he felt. "When I thought I might lose you..."

She squeezed his hand gently, her eyes meeting his. Joe was about to continue, when someone knocked on the door and then pushed it open without waiting. Milton and the mayor stepped into the room, Milton holding his hat against his chest respectfully.

"Well, if it isn't the hero of Widestone, Big Joe Chambers, alive and well," the mayor said with a grin, and Milton nodded, as well. "We can't thank you enough for what you've done for the town."

"We lost a lot of good men," Milton said, "but it would have been far, far worse if you hadn't been there, Joe. You taking Earl down once and for all saved this town, not to mention your leadership before the battle."

Joe was uncomfortable at their praise and wanted to shift the conversation away from his part in the battle. "I'd like to stay here in Widestone," he told them. The mayor broke into a smile at Joe's words. "Nan, could I stay here until I recover? I'd be glad to take on the task of running the boarding house with you, after. You've been doing a two-person job alone for too long."

Nan nodded enthusiastically, tears springing into her eyes. "I'd love that," she whispered, her words a little muffled by her unshed tears. Her tight grip on his hand served as a second witness to her words. Joe squeezed her hand, then turned his attention back to Milton and the mayor.

"What happened with Reverend Jesse?" he asked.

"He left town to turn himself in to a judge because of his involvement at Narrow Bluff," Milton admitted, his face showing a hint of embarrassment. He shook his head. "After seeing what he did to fight the bandits here, I sort of softened toward him. He was a hero at the end of the battle, and he put his life on the line to bring an end to the fighting. To be honest, I was ready to pretend he was never involved, but he insisted that he needed to serve his time anyway."

Joe gazed at Milton, impressed at the preacher's staunch commitment to integrity, and a little surprised at Milton's willingness to bend from his rigid adherence to the letter of the law. It seemed that the events in Widestone had changed them all in more ways than one. Joe studied Milton's face as he pondered these changes, and he became aware of how haggard and exhausted the new sheriff looked.

"Milton, how are you doing?" he asked perceptively.

Milton sighed, and ran a weary hand across his bloodshot eyes. "I'll admit, me and my deputies have had our work cut out for us. We've been processing the bandits who surrendered and getting them jailed and getting ready to put them on trial. A few of the surviving bandits escaped instead of surrendering, but we've been putting together a list of their names by interviewing the arrested ones. We'll put a bounty out on them and send it to all the nearby towns."

"That, and we're all working to repair the damage done to the town," the mayor chimed in. "Milton's been helping us with those efforts, too. I don't know that he's gotten more than a couple of hours of sleep in the last three days." He clapped Milton on the shoulder as he said this, and Joe could see that the two men were truly working together to lead the town back to normalcy.

"And Archie?"

"He's a room over," Milton said. "It's gonna take time to recover from that shoulder injury of his but he should be fine."

Joe nodded, opening his mouth to say more, but was interrupted by the opening of the door. A tall man Joe didn't recognize stepped into the room. "Glad to see you're awake, Joe," he said, studying Joe's face. "I'm Doc Brown," he continued, answering Joe's unspoken question, and then turning to look at those surrounding Joe's bed. "Everyone, Joe still needs his rest. You can come back and visit him later, but for now..." He lifted his hand, gesturing them to the door.

Milton and the mayor said their goodbyes and departed, Nan leaving after kissing his cheek softly. Doc Brown checked Joe's bandages and, assured that all was in order, took his leave, as well. Though he hadn't been awake long, Joe felt his weariness return in full measure, and he sank into his pillows, his eyes closing into a deep sleep.

ONE MONTH Later

Hands clasped loosely, Nan and Joe walked down the street side by side. Joe held a small bouquet of wildflowers in one hand that Will had gathered for him earlier that morning. Will skipped along beside them, holding Nan's free hand. The afternoon sun glinted off the boy's hair and highlighted his freckles. The events a month prior had not dimmed the boy's natural buoyant spirits—although he had been sober and frightened for the first few days, once he had fully grasped that the town was safe and, most importantly, that his mother was free from harm's way, his good humor and mischievous attitude had returned in full force.

Joe was glad to see it. His affection for Will had only grown stronger over the past month, especially now that Nan had agreed to be his wife. Will was more than an energetic ball of high spirits; he was Joe's future son. And his lovely Nan was so much happier these days. Now that he was splitting the tasks of running a successful boarding house, Joe had no idea how she had shouldered it all alone for so long. She was certainly less tired now that she wasn't being worn to the bone day in and day out. It was incredible to Joe that he was building his own family, and that it felt so natural. Two months ago, such a thought would have seemed strange, but Nan and Will had changed everything for him.

"Are you gonna teach me how to shoot your rifle, Joe?" Will was asking excitedly, tugging on Nan's hand as he hopped from foot to foot.

Joe and Nan exchanged a laughing look, and Nan shrugged as she raised a questioning eyebrow at her intended.

"Shooting a gun is a serious responsibility, son," Joe responded, "but it's a skill every man needs to learn. We can go shoot some cans out behind the house for practice later this afternoon as a start. What do you say?"

Will nodded enthusiastically, his expression clearly pleased beyond words at Joe's implication that he was a man and therefore ready to learn such a serious skill.

"When I get really good at shooting, I can bring home food for the boarding house," Will said, his chest puffed.

Nan smiled down at him, tenderness shining from her eyes even as she laughed. "My little provider! You'll be a wonderful shot, Will, and I know you'll keep my kitchen well-stocked."

"You bet!" Will nodded again, his attention already wandering as he caught sight of a prairie dog popping its head out of a hole a few yards away. He dropped his mother's hand to try and sneak up on it, and Joe and Nan stopped to watch contentedly as he played, a little boy safe in his town.

"You're going to be a wonderful father to him," Nan said softly, nestling into Joe's side. "I never imagined he would have another man in his life to help guide him. I'm so glad it's you."

Joe squeezed her closer, enjoying the feel of her soft strength beneath his arm. "The honor is mine," he said simply. The words sounded too formal for everyday conversation, and he felt as exposed as if he had begun spouting off poetry or singing a love song in the middle of the street. Nan, uncharacteristically, didn't tease Joe, and he was grateful for that.

"You know," he said, steering the conversation back to lighter waters, "we still haven't decided where we're going for our honeymoon once you become Mrs. Chambers."

"Mrs. Chambers...I do like the sound of that," Nan said, smiling up at him.

"I hear there are some hot springs closer to Denver that we could visit. You could do some shopping and we could have the fanciest meal we can find."

"Having someone else cook meals for me is the height of luxury," Nan said, sighing dreamily in an exaggerated manner.

Joe grinned mischievously at her, "Of course, the most important thing about wherever we go will be the hotel... I have a feeling we'll be spending quite a lot of our time in bed." He enjoyed watching her blush a deep scarlet at his teasing, and he couldn't pretend that he wasn't also looking forward very much to their union as man and wife, and all that would bring with it.

Sensing that he'd better ease off with his teasing, Joe wrapped her in a quick embrace and squeezed her gently. "All in good time," he whispered in her ear, before planting a soft kiss on her forehead.

"I love you, Joseph Chambers," she whispered back. Her eyes had been closed in quiet contentment while he had kissed her forehead, but she opened them to look into his eyes, now. "Shall we keep going to the church?"

Joe nodded, releasing her from his embrace and calling for Will to rejoin them. The boy ran back to them, kicking up dust in the street and a smile splitting his cheeks. Nan took his hand again, and the three of them resumed their leisurely progress down the street.

They were largely quiet now as they walked, each lost in their own thoughts. Joe reflected about how much Widestone had changed since he had arrived. The town was being repaired and rebuilt by those who had survived the fighting. They still had a long way to go, but the town was getting back on its feet.

It helped that there was a new sense of safety in the town, thanks to Milton's hard work as the new sheriff. The former sheriff, Pennington, had been sentenced to some hard time because of Milton's evidence against his corruption, and thanks to that evidence, everyone in town now recognized that Nan's late husband had been murdered by the bandits that Pennington had allowed to run rampant.

Thinking about Pennington's jail time reminded Joe of Reverend Jesse, and he couldn't think about the man without a touch of sadness. The preacher had been sentenced to half a year in jail, which he had willingly subjected himself to when he had turned himself in. Some cousins a few towns over were taking care of his adopted children while he was gone.

Everyone in town recognized that Reverend Jesse was a truly changed man and there weren't many who would have

257

opposed him staying out of jail, but he had insisted that he serve his due time. Joe respected him for his integrity—which was something he never could have imagined when he first learned of the preacher's former life as one of Earl's bandits.

Joe, Nan, and Will approached the church, which looked far better than it had at the end of the fighting. The bullet holes in the walls had been patched and the outside had been repainted, a fresh start for the church that symbolized a fresh start for the town. Just beside the church stood the monument that Reverend Jesse had been putting together for those who had died in Narrow Bluff. He had painstakingly inscribed all of their names into the stone.

Joe stopped before the stone, and the three of them stared quietly at the long list of names. The mayor had added to the preacher's work, with his blessing, by adding the names of those who had died in the battle to save Widestone. Close beside the monument was a smaller stone monument just for Louis, who the town now regarded as a hero and a pivotal reason for their success over the bandits. As Joe looked at the monuments, he felt an ache of pain in his chest. So many needless deaths, all due to the greed and avarice of Earl Gallagher and his men.

Footsteps approached, and Joe looked up to see Nellie approaching the monuments, hands clasped in front of her. She nodded at Joe and Nan, coming to stand beside them silently, the three of them paying quiet homage to those they had lost.

Joe glanced at Nellie's profile, and he reflected on the fact that, although Louis had been martyred for their cause, Nellie had made a contribution that had helped to make their success possible, as well. She had helped to save the day by convincing Edwin the Giant to switch sides and add some of his number to Joe's small band of ragtag fighters. Joe didn't know much about how Nellie had managed this incredible feat, but she had commented that she'd convinced him when he saw that Earl and Friendly Nick weren't above attacking the women and children at the church. With a bit of seduction and charm on her end, honed from years working at a brothel, the simple man had finally decided to take a stand. Much to Milton's chagrin, however, he'd disappeared before he could be arrested for his past crimes, which, though not as bad as Earl's, were still quite heinous.

"I hope he's found peace, now," Nellie said quietly, gazing at Louis's stone. "I like to think that he and his wife are together, now, and that they're happy."

Nellie bent to touch Louis's monument, resting her hand there for a moment with her eyes closed, before standing straight again and nodding a final goodbye to Nan and Joe. She said a quiet goodbye to Joe and Nan before turning and walking back toward the town square.

"I'll just be a minute," Joe said to Nan, and she nodded in understanding before taking Will a few steps away to give him some privacy.

Joe lowered himself to kneel before the monuments, and his eyes found his sister's name carved into the stone, as well as that of her husband's. A lingering sadness curled around his heart, as it always did when he thought of Sophie. He missed her so deeply, and he wished he could see her just one more time to say a proper goodbye.

He reached out to trace her name with the tips of his fingers. Even in his sadness, there was a measure of peace that he couldn't have imagined a month ago. Knowing that the bandits wouldn't be able to hurt anyone again and that he had avenged her death helped to bring a sense of closure to the still-healing wound.

Joe gently laid the bundle of wildflowers he had carried at the base of the monument, resting it with the various other bouquets left by other townspeople. Many visited to pay their respects and mourn for those they had lost. After settling the flowers, Joe reached into his pocket and pulled out Sophie's silver necklace. He closed it in his fist and held it against his chest for a moment, sending a silent prayer upwards on her behalf.

"I'll bring you more flowers next week, Sophie," he whispered, laying Sophie's necklace among the flowers. He gazed at the stone for another quiet moment, allowing the healing grief and closure to wash over him. Through all of the grief and pain, he had also found new life with Nan and Will.

Joe rose to his feet and turned to his future wife and son, reaching for Nan and closing her in his arms. He bent his head and kissed her deeply, her hand raising to rest on the back of his neck as she kissed him back.

"Ugh," Will groaned, disgusted by their kiss.

Joe and Nan broke apart and looked down to laugh at his look of extreme disgust, comical in its intensity.

"Come on, son," Joe said, reaching for the boy's hand, but still holding on to Nan's with his other. "What do you say we go get a bite for lunch?"

Want more classic westerns? Check out Showdown at Rusty Gorge, coming March 16th!

. . .

Wade Skinner is a wanted man…

After barely escaping the hangman's noose, he finds himself down river of his troubles in a new town called Rusty Gorge. Only problem is, Wade never did learn the good Lord's lesson to turn the other cheek. And now, his troubles have followed him to his new hometown. With a posse on his trail, and an angry mayor who won't stop until he's had his revenge, Wade will have to figure out how to protect himself and the people of Rusty Gorge, who he's come to care for.

Can Wade find redemption, or has his very presence put his neighbors and pretty schoolteacher Addie Perkins in mortal danger that not even he can save them from?

Chapter One

The moon cut a bright white figure through the pine trees as John Russell paused, taking a long drink from his canteen. It was almost empty. He tucked the canteen back into his pants next to his holster and his gun, and took a deep breath and looked up at the moon.

"Please God," he said. "If you just let me survive this, I promise I'll be good and faithful till my dying day."

The only answer was the howl of a faraway dog. At first, it was just one dog. But then, more began barking. The hairs on the back of his neck stood straight up, and he suddenly knew with certainty—those weren't just any dogs. They were Sheriff Hansen's dogs, and they had his scent.

He began running further through the dark woods, his path only illuminated by the full moon cutting frightening shapes on the dirt floor. The yips and barks and squeals behind him grew louder, and he heard the thundering of hooves.

This could be it, he realized as he ran. He was a fast runner under regular circumstances, and now he was running for his life.

Suddenly, John came upon a cliff, with an eight foot drop into a deep rushing river. He stood at the edge of the cliff, and looked across. In the half-light of the moon, he had no idea quite where he was, but he suspected it was perhaps a tributary of the Arkansas, considering he'd been running south. The river was high, but it wasn't too wide. He could probably cross it, he thought to himself. It wouldn't be easy, but even if he died, it'd be better than being torn apart by a pack of wild dogs.

He knew the dogs could get across if he could, but it was his only choice. And besides, if he made it across, he'd have less of a scent, and maybe a chance of losing them. The dogs were coming closer, their barks now echoing across the walls of the canyon.

He leapt into the abyss.

The water was ice cold, and the current was faster than he expected. He tried to swim as hard as he could across the river, but he was quickly swept through the rapids. He tried to grasp onto a big boulder, but it was futile—it slipped through his fingers. He turned and looked down the river. The yapping of the dogs was loud now, almost as thunderous as the river itself. He looked up and saw them, standing at the edge of the cliff he'd jumped off. They weren't stupid enough to jump into this river, he thought. He should have known by how steep the mountainside was that this wouldn't be an easy crossing. It's easier to cross a wide and shallow river, than it is to cross narrow rapids.

He looked back at where he was headed, just in time to avoid a huge stick from poking him in the eye. The river was moving faster now, and it was getting out of control. Over the rushing of the water, he could hear the shouts of the men above. "He's down there in the river!"

"Shoot 'im! I swear to God, I'll kill him! I want that bounty!" one of the men squealed.

God damn you, Hansen, he thought just before he realized that the river was racing down towards a steep gorge. Just then, a bullet raced by his head, hitting a boulder inches above him. He opened his eyes, and just as he wound around a bend he looked up and saw two men on horseback standing with a pack of dogs.

"Never mind, Jim. Don't waste your bullets," he heard the calm, steady voice of Sheriff Hansen, his smooth as molasses voice belying the man's evil nature. "He's as good as dead. Trust me. There ain't no way a man could survive this river."

John struggled to keep his head above water, thrashing and spluttering. But then he remembered something his Dad had taught him: if you ever get in a river, just try to float with your feet downstream. That way, if you hit anything, you'll at least not hit your head.

He surrendered to the river, lying on his back. If he died, he died. As if to confirm his thoughts, he heard the shouts of men above him, the sheriff's deputies and probably some brown-nosing town-folk arriving on the scene. "Turn back," said Sheriff Hansen. "Give up. He's as good as gone, anyway."

Good as gone.

He was still fighting with the mighty current as it moved faster and faster. As his head slipped beneath the frothy rapids, he realized that there was a very good chance he was on his way to meet his maker.

JohnWade said a silent prayer that God knew his heart. He'd done wrong, but he'd done it for the right reasons.

Might not count for much, but maybe it counted for something...

CHAPTER TWO

"Pa," said a boy's voice, "There's a dead guy in the water."

John groaned and tried to open his eyes. They felt glued shut. His head throbbed, and he could hardly see for the blinding light that shone on his face, and framed by that like a halo, the head of a little boy. A cherub?

For a moment, he thought, he must have met his maker. But no, that didn't make sense. Why would an angel be calling God Pa, and him a dead guy? No. He wasn't at the pearly gates, he realized, as he felt the rough caress of river rocks on his back and the gentle flow of river water over the bottom half of his body. He'd survived, somehow. But he was definitely in hell. *Definitely* in hell. His right shoulder was throbbing and burning.

When the kid saw the rough, grizzled man open his eyes, he jumped back and screamed. "Pa, come quick!" he shouted. "He's alive!"

John came to, and slowly the pines looming above him stopped spinning. The world settled into place and he felt the cool mountain air on his skin. He was at a bend in the river. Somewhere below the rapids, it must have gone gentle, and he'd washed up to shore somehow. His body was in the shallow creek water, freezing cold and soaking wet. But his shoulder throbbed, and when he finally mustered the strength to lift his head, he saw that his entire torso was covered in blood. No wonder the kid was terrified. He'd been shot, he realized, probably by an angry bounty hunter after he'd passed out, hoping to retrieve his body later. Besides the throbbing bullet wound, his entire body was numb, freezing cold.

Buck Bowman was standing a few feet away in the river in his waterproofed waders, leaning over looking at his pan, which he'd just filled with gravel and was slowly rotating to look for those signature sparkly specks. He heard his son yelling, and he stood up. "What is it, Pete?"

Pete began hopping into the river after his father, jumping over river rocks in his bare feet. No matter how much Buck tried, he could never get the kid to keep his damn shoes on. Ever since Bonnie had died, he'd done the best he could to raise him. But he could hear Bonnie rolling in her grave at the sight of her son wading through river water in his bare feet. Buck began to wade out of the water and put his hand on the kid's shoulder.

"There's a dead guy! But he opened his eyes!"

Buck looked down at his son. It wasn't the first time, nor would it be the last, that his son would see a half dead man washed up on the river while they were panning. In these parts, it was par for the course.

"Well, let's go see who it is."

The two of them walked over to where he lay, groaning. "And who might you be?" asked Buck, watching the pale, soaking wet young man worming his way further onto the riverbank. Probably an outlaw, considering the way he was covered in blood.

John looked up at the man, opening his mouth to say his real name but thinking better of it. "Wade. Wade Skinner," he said, barely getting the words out. He realized suddenly that his teeth were chattering so badly, and he was shivering so badly, that he could barely move or speak.

Noticing that the trembling man who lay on the riverbed was unarmed, which was a plus, Buck knelt down, suddenly feeling a bit more caring than he was defensive. "I'm Buck Bowman, and this is my son Pete." Wade looked between them, and Pete smiled.

He nodded, trying to be polite, but every movement sent searing pains from his shoulder across his chest, neck and arms.

"I can't imagine you're feeling too good, now, Wade."

"No sir," he groaned.

Buck stroked his three-day scruff, evaluating the man. "Now, if we clean you up, are we gonn' regret it?"

"No, sir," said Wade, and he meant it.

"All right then. Good nuff. I always try to demonstrate kindness towards strangers," said Buck. "Within reason," he added, gesturing to the gun on his holster.

He nodded, understanding. Buck turned to his son. "Now, would you go get Millie and help me haul this poor gentleman up on to her? And get your damn shoes on!"

Pete nodded and scampered away, returning a few moments later with a braying donkey. Buck put his arms underneath him, who was bigger than he'd looked all crumpled up in the river. He grunted under the man's weight and threw him across the donkey's back, roughly. Wade closed his eyes, grateful for the donkey's support. A few seconds later, a horse blanket was thrown over him. It smelled like hay and other unmentionables, but he was grateful for it, and in a few moments, he was asleep.

He woke up again only minutes later as the donkey began moving. Each jostle sent searing pain through his shoulder. Vague thoughts of wanting to know quite where he was interspersed with the only thing he could think of, his pain, weakness, and confusion. He opened his eyes occasionally and stars mixed with the scenic mountain views of snow-capped peaks. He was completely dizzy, and he couldn't tell if he was dreaming or drunk. He was shivering uncontrollably, and eventually, his body took control. He was lulled to sleep by the freezing cold.

He woke up wrapped in more blankets, to the sound of a blazing fire. He opened his eyes and looked around him. He was in a dimly lit room with a dirt floor and log walls, small but homey. He was lying on a cot in front of the fire.

He heard a sound behind him and turned to see a man. He recognized him somehow as the man from the river who'd saved him, but he couldn't remember his name. He was tall and broad-shouldered, with blue eyes that sparkled in the firelight and silver hair but a young, warm, tanned face.

"You're awake, then," Buck said, surprised. "Well, then I oughta give this stew to you," he said, holding it out.

Wade attempted to reach for it and thank him, but found he could barely move.

Buck nodded, awkwardly, realizing that the man was still too weak to even feed himself. He grabbed a stool and pulled it up next to him, resting the bowl on it. Awkwardly, he began to spoon the soup into his mouth.

He accepted the soup gratefully, and then waved it away. It was too much effort, he felt, to eat right now.

"Sent Petey to the doctor," said Buck, throwing another log on the fire. The man had a somewhat nervous manner, but harmless, and caring. "Takes him a while to get places. But should be back soon, I reckon."

"Thank you," whispered Wade.

"Your clothes are dryin'," said Buck, somewhat embarrassed. "I'd lend you some 'a mine, but I reckon you're bigger'n me. Sorry 'bout that."

He realized gradually that he was naked underneath the layers of scratchy wool blankets, and even a bearskin.

"Thank you," he said again.

"Well," said Buck. "I've got some wood to chop. You're alive, that's good. I'll let ya eat and get your bearins. Sawbones'll be here soon."

Wade slowly drank the soup that Buck gave him, regaining strength. Soon enough he heard Buck puttering around in the other room, and then come in and dump another heap of logs in front of the fire. He threw some onto it and soon it was raging again, and Wade closed his eyes at the warmth, feeling relaxed for what felt like the first time in weeks.

"You were rambling pretty incoherently back there," said Buck, coming in and handing him a steaming cup of hot coffee. "I can't imagine that ride down the river felt quite good, now did it?"

"No, it did not. I don't even remember how I got there. I just remember tryn'a cross it, and then eventually the river was navigating me, not the other way around. I don't even remember how I got this bullet in me."

Buck raised his eyebrows, but he knew that there was more to the story than that. But if Wade didn't want to share it, he wasn't going to press it.

That was sometimes just the way of the West. A man's past was a man's past, and what mattered now was his present.

"Well, look. You got a home?"

"Ain't got no home right now. Been on the road, lately," said Wade, looking down and sipping his coffee. It was good, strong, and warm.

"Well, I reckon if you got nowhere to go, and if that wound don't kill ya, then I wonder if you'd want to help around the saloon and keep that kid entertained and outa my hair. I'd give ya three squares and a cot, as well as a few dollars a week, for your trouble."

Wade thought for a minute. It was true, he had nowhere to go. But he still didn't know where he was. "Where are we, if I might ask?"

"Rusty Gorge."

A two day ride from Longdale, thought Wade.

Just then, they heard noises outside. "That must be the sawbones," said Buck. "You think it over, all right?"

Buck got up and went to get the doctor.

He considered his options. He certainly couldn't get any further now, what with his injury. And if he declined Buck's offer, who's to say he would be willing to nurse him back to health? He had to repay the man somehow. And maybe he could shave his face, cut his hair or something and he wouldn't get recognized. It was a long shot, but it was better than being back out in the cold and in the woods with a wound that could kill him. Besides, those men thought he was dead. At least for now they did.

It was passing strange. Yesterday, he'd wanted nothing less but to just die by the river. And now, he thought, there might be a glimmer of hope that he just make it out of the mess alive. Maybe he'd get lucky and they wouldn't come looking for him down in Rusty Gorge at all.

But then again, he thought, nobody ever accused John Russell of being lucky. He could only hope that Wade Skinner would be a different story.

Pre-order Showdown at Rusty Gorge, now, or sign up for Wyatt's email list to get a notification whenever he has a new release!

Other books by Wyatt Shepard:
  Showdown at Rusty Gorge
  Bounty
  The Sheriff (A Western Classics Novel)